THE LAST CITY

A ZOMBIE NOVEL

MICHAEL J. TOTTEN

Copyright © 2019 by Michael J. Totten

All rights reserved. No part of this publication may be reproduced in any form or by any means without the prior written permission of Michael J. Totten.

First American edition published in 2019 by Belmont Estate Books

Cover design by Kathleen Lynch
Edited by Sara Kelly

Totten, Michael J.
The Last City

BOOKS BY MICHAEL J. TOTTEN

Resurrection

Into the Wasteland

The Last City

Taken

The Road to Fatima Gate

In the Wake of the Surge

Where the West Ends

Tower of the Sun

Dispatches

PART I

THE UNIVERSE IS COMMITTING SUICIDE

1

Annie thought she'd never see skyscrapers again. Yet there they were, a handful of modest ones in the center of Omaha, Nebraska, rising from the prairie as if announcing to visitors coming in from the wasteland that human beings still lived in this part of the country.

At least human beings used to. Annie saw no signs of them now. Just stopped cars, frozen in time and ice, heading away from downtown across all lanes of traffic, the blanketing snow printed only with deer tracks. Wintry trees reached toward the skies like the claws of dead insects. Here and there on the side of the road were soft snow-covered mounds that Annie assumed were dead bodies—or whatever was left of the bodies after the hordes of infected had their terrible way with them.

She was in the back seat of the Chevy Suburban with Hughes at the wheel, Kyle beside her in back, and Parker up front in the passenger seat. They were heading south on a four-lane bisected with a median strip toward the derelict urban core. The road itself was jammed up with cars, so Hughes had to drive on the grassy strip next to the pavement.

That strip was a barely passable obstacle course of ditched vehicles, lamp posts, telephone poles, leafless deciduous trees, and abandoned suitcases. Progress was slow. The Suburban's tires emitted a muffled sound as they made fresh tracks in the snow.

Kyle squinted at the map he'd grabbed at a vacant gas station. "Missouri River's just a few hundred feet to the left. Looks like there's a riverfront park up ahead. Miller's Landing."

If all went well, they wouldn't have to drive very much farther. Plan was to find a marina, unmoor a sailboat, make their way down the Missouri River to the Mississippi River, then float past the states of Missouri, Arkansas, and Louisiana to the Gulf of Mexico. From there they could sail east until they reached the Florida Gulf Coast, then hotwire a car and drive north to Atlanta. If the Centers for Disease Control was still up and running, the doctors there might be able to study Annie's natural immunity and develop a cure.

The Missouri River was just far enough away to the east that they couldn't see it, nor could they drive to it when they found the exit to Miller's Landing. The four-lane was too clogged with cars. It could only be crossed on foot. They'd have to get out and walk.

Hughes killed the engine, and a hush that sounded eternal settled over the world. Everyone just sat there for a moment, taking it in.

Annie didn't know how many people used to live in the Omaha area. By the looks of the place, probably not much more than a million. Omaha wasn't any kind of major metropolis. Just a medium-sized Midwestern city with a clutch of midrise towers in the center of low-density sprawl, but after no-rise Wyoming and the barrenness that made up the rest of Nebraska, Omaha, to Annie's eyes, could have been Chicago.

But it was as dead as Seattle and Portland, where the plague started—in North America anyway—after spreading by plane from the Russian Arctic and Moscow. Annie had hoped that distant cities thousands of miles away might have barricaded themselves in a kind of reverse quarantine once they knew what coming from the Pacific Northwest, but there she was, almost two thousand miles away and halfway across the continent, and Omaha hadn't fared any better.

She'd grown up and spent most of her life in South Carolina, and she'd still have no idea how sparsely populated the western half of the United States was if she hadn't just driven through it. Much of it resembled the surface of the moon, and even most of Nebraska was staggeringly blank, devoid of topography, its desolate expanses almost entirely treeless. Driving across it in winter felt like spending two days on a snow-covered ocean.

And yet the virus that turned once-decent people into predators had spread from Seattle across that vastness to Omaha as if it hadn't encountered so much as a speed bump.

"What are we doing?" Annie said.

"Looking for a boat," Kyle said.

"No, I mean what are we *doing*?" Annie said.

"Not this again," Hughes said.

"Look at this place," Annie said.

"I see it," Hughes said, averting his eyes from the bleakness surrounding them.

"You really think Atlanta looks any different?"

"It might, Annie," Parker said.

She doubted it. "Okay. Let's say, by some miracle, Atlanta is perfectly fine."

"Doesn't need to be perfectly fine," Hughes said.

"Well, let's say the CDC is perfectly fine," Annie said. "Doctors put my blood under a microscope and *voilà*. They find a cure. Then what?"

Nobody said anything.

"They going to show up here in Omaha in a government helicopter?" Annie said. "Hop out with a case full of vials and say, *great news, everybody, come and get yourself vaccinated?*"

A light wind whispered through the wreckage, the city otherwise silent as a cemetery.

"They going to vaccinate the deer and the rabbits?" Annie said.

Hughes opened the driver's side door and stepped out. Cold air washed into the truck. "Out," he said.

Annie shivered.

"Out," Hughes said again.

Annie, Parker, and Kyle got out and closed their doors. Hughes pressed the key fob in his hand and *thunked* the four doors into the lock position even though there was nobody left to steal anything.

Nobody spoke as they made their way across the four-lane between stopped cars to a short road through open parkland that, according to Kyle's map, led to Miller's Landing on the edge of the Missouri River. No cars blocked their path any longer. No point fleeing downtown only to stop along the riverside less than a mile out.

They soon came to two covered picnic areas next to a frozen artificial lake. Beyond it, Annie saw the Missouri. It hadn't iced over and was smaller and narrower than she had expected. She'd imagined the Missouri as a grand river like the Columbia or the Mississippi, but it was just a few hundred feet wide at the most. There were no boats.

"Maybe there's a marina downtown," Kyle said.

"Maybe," Hughes said, sounding doubtful to Annie's ears.

Annie shivered and hugged herself. Before seeing the river, she'd pictured marinas on the waterfront, the kind she was used to in Seattle, but the Missouri was a middling river at best, and Omaha wasn't a coastal city.

"Going to be dark soon," Parker said.

Colder too, Annie thought, though the January sun had precious little warming power anyway.

They headed back to the Suburban, silent and mopey, and continued the slow drive along on the grassy strip next to the crammed four-lane, barely making two hundred feet of progress before the strip that made progress possible ended abruptly at an overpass ferrying cars above an enormous railyard below. The overpass was too jammed to drive on, and the railyard was blocked by a train that stretched for at least a half mile in each direction. Proceeding on foot wouldn't be any kind of a problem, but continuing in the Suburban was impossible.

"Wonderful," Kyle said.

They'd have to backtrack, and they'd have to backtrack for miles. They were not going to find a marina in Omaha. Certainly not today.

They'd have to spend an entire day picking their way through the suburbs, and no other route would take them anywhere near the banks of the Missouri. Better to just back up, skirt the city entirely in a wide orbit, and pick up the river's edge farther south in the countryside.

Kyle checked his watch. "We should go back and camp at that park."

Hughes and Parker nodded. Annie said nothing.

They sulked on the way back to the park—Parker, Hughes, and Kyle because they weren't going to spend the night in beds on a boat, but Annie for another reason entirely. She'd spent the past two days hating herself since their escape from Lander, Wyoming. The others didn't know it because she hadn't said anything, but she'd lost confidence in herself.

When she and her friends had encountered that warlord of a mayor, Joseph Steele, on the road in the small town of Belt, she had wanted to kill him. Wanted to kill him for taking her prisoner, kill him for milking her blood like she was a farm animal, kill him for throwing Parker into the county lockup for no good reason at all, kill him for ruling over the only intact town she'd seen anywhere in the ruins of America, and for bringing the whole thing crashing down on everyone's heads. She wanted to kill him, out there on the road with none of his men around to protect him, but her friends wouldn't let her.

Something stopped normal people from pulling the trigger when pointing a gun in somebody's face, but nothing would have stopped Annie if she'd been alone.

What was wrong with her? When the world had circled the drain, it took her civilized morality with it. That's what was wrong with her. And not just her, either. She doubted Lander's mayor was a monster before the infected showed up and threatened his town. She doubted the pre-apocalypse Parker would have attempted to murder Kyle on the San Juan Islands. And she was certain that the pre-apocalypse version of herself wouldn't have wanted to kill anyone for any reason.

Annie was not the same person she used to be. And if that was true of her, it was true of everybody.

Parker hated "camping" in the Suburban. It wasn't at all like proper camping in a tent during the summer where he could recline next to a crackling fire until his eyelids grew heavy at midnight, then zip up and retire horizontally in a sleeping bag. No. Camping in the Suburban during winter meant sitting there in the cold and the dark for six hours before finally feeling exhausted enough to sleep half-assedly upright. It was only slightly less awful than trying to sleep on a plane.

He wished they'd found a sailboat. Sailboats had beds. Sailboats didn't have fireplaces, but then, neither did the Suburban. And no one thought it wise to build a fire in the ruins of a city and attract a band of barbaric survivors—or, worse, a pack of those *things*—that could see the glow for miles around. So he just sat there in his seat in the dark with his own thoughts in a half daze, willing himself to get tired, with two cups of dehydrated and reconstituted chicken tetrazzini in his belly.

Stewing in his own thoughts didn't bother him as much as it had on the road from Seattle to Lander, when he'd convinced himself that he could snap at any moment and sink his teeth into somebody's neck. Annie had recovered from her bout with the infection a whole lot better than he had. Even so, he was surer now that the virus was gone from his body and mind, that it hadn't actually turned him into a psychopath. Betty the therapist, whom he'd met shortly before her death in Lander's prison, had more or less cured him by convincing him that he was merely suffering from a whopping case of anxiety, some kind of post-traumatic stress response after spending three days strapped to a chair while the virus turned his mind into a buzz saw.

So, sure, he felt better, but he wasn't ready to use the word *recovered* quite yet. He still felt on edge, like he might plunge into a panic state again just by thinking about it. Better to have something to do and something else to think about.

"I need to go find a tree," he said and opened the passenger door, grateful that his bladder would rescue him from his own jagged thoughts for a couple of moments. "Back in a minute."

He stepped into the cold and the dark and produced a small LED flashlight from his pocket.

They'd parked a hundred or so feet from the river. He had half a mind to walk down there and pee in it. He knew he shouldn't, but he wasn't sure why now that he thought about it. Fish peed in the river. Deer most likely did too. So why shouldn't he? He headed toward a line of skeletal trees and did his business there instead.

Someone else stepped out of the Suburban and closed the door as he zipped up.

"Hey." Annie's voice.

"Don't pee in the river," Parker said.

She laughed. "Wasn't planning on it. I just wanted to talk. And I had to get out of that truck."

"I hear you," he said and stretched his neck by craning his head to each side.

She didn't bother with a flashlight. Didn't really need it with the ambient starlight reflecting off snow. He flicked off his own LED light. He could see her well enough, though he could not read her face.

"Let's walk," Annie said. "Maybe down to the river so we don't keep the others up."

"Sure," Parker said, though the others weren't sleeping yet anyway. The sun had been down for hours, but he doubted it was even 9:00 p.m. yet.

Their boots scrunched in the snow as they made their way to the riverbank.

"Are you and Kyle okay?" Annie said.

Parker knew what she meant. He and Kyle hadn't exactly gotten along famously since they met in Washington state. At first, they had just bitched and sniped at each other, but later they went at it like two rats in a sack until Parker finally snapped and tried to kick Kyle over a cliff. That's when Annie told the others her secret—and when Annie, Kyle, and Hughes made the momentous decision to tie Parker to that chair, inject him with Annie's blood, then infect him on purpose to see if her immunity could be transferred. It was either that or execute him for attempted murder.

"Kyle and I are okay now," Parker said.

Kyle was the absolute last person on God's earth that Parker had expected to save him in Wyoming. Kyle had risked his life and damn near gotten himself killed, and he did it alone.

"I'm tired of fighting all the time," Parker said. "Tired of being mad all the time. Tired of everything all the time."

"Interesting," Annie said.

"Why's that?" Parker said.

"Because recently you were scared all the time."

"I haven't had any more panic attacks."

"You haven't. I'd know."

Parker chuckled. Indeed she would. There was no such thing as a silent, secret panic attack. Not for him, anyway.

"I'm learning to trust myself," he said. "It's not easy, but I'm working on it. I don't want to say this in front of Kyle and Hughes, but I'll tell you."

"Tell me what?" Annie said.

"I'm trying to be better, Annie," he said. "The world isn't making it easy, but I promised myself that I would, and now I'm promising you."

He couldn't read Annie's face in the dark.

Annie felt groggy from oversleeping as they set out again in silence at first light the next day, back the way they had come along the grassy strip next to the four-lane, away from the center of Omaha toward the outskirts to the north, dodging and weaving past abandoned cars, the ruined urban environment as familiar now as it was dismal.

They made a wide counterclockwise circle around the Omaha metro area, with stalled traffic finally thinning near the small town of Blair, and they eventually ended up in Nebraska City—just a small town, really—also along the Missouri River, roughly fifty miles south of their starting point. The journey took them four hours, and they had five hours of daylight left at the most.

"Half the day and hardly any progress at all," Kyle said.

"We always knew this was going to be the hard part," Hughes said.

Having grown up on the East Coast, Annie understood that more instinctively than the others. Hughes, Parker, and Kyle had spent their entire lives in the western United States, with its mind-boggling distances between places. The hinterlands east of Seattle were so vast that Minneapolis was the next big city over, almost two-thirds of the way across the country.

Their free ride, so to speak, was always going to end when they reached the more densely populated eastern half of the country, and the eastern half of the country effectively began and ended at Omaha. Satellite photos of the country at night revealed the stark difference, with the eastern side lit up like a circuit board and the West consisting mostly of darkness mottled by far-flung islands of light limited almost entirely to the coast. Even supposedly rural states like Iowa were as crowded as Manhattan compared with Idaho, Wyoming, and most of Nebraska. Annie expected from the very beginning that they'd encounter more survivors, more infected, more stalled cars, and more obstacles in general once they reached Omaha—hence the need for a boat.

The only real surprise was the fact that they hadn't seen a single sign of life, infected or otherwise, since reaching the continental midpoint.

There was no marina along the Missouri River in Nebraska City. Just some grain elevators, a chemical plant, an electrical station, and a storage facility. Central Avenue, the traditional main street, ran at a ninety-degree angle away from the river instead of alongside it. The people who built this town seemed to have had no real interest in the

Missouri, thinking of it strictly as the state line between Nebraska and Iowa rather than as a place for recreation and transport.

Just south of downtown, such as it was, a bridge headed over the river into Iowa. There were no cars on it.

Kyle scrutinized the map. "I think we should cross."

"Into Iowa?" Hughes said. "Why?"

"Couple of reasons," Kyle said. "We might have to cross at some point, and for all we know, this is the only clear bridge."

Parker groaned.

"And the route looks better. Highway 29 in Iowa follows the river south in a more or less straight line. No road traces the river here on the Nebraska side."

"Let me see that," Hughes said.

Kyle passed the map to Hughes in the driver's seat.

Hughes slowed down as he scanned it but didn't stop. "Mmm," he said. "Goes as far as Kansas City. And if we don't find a boat by the time we get there, we'll have to cross the state and look for one on the Mississippi River."

Annie stared at her hands. Parker turned his head and looked out the passenger window. Hughes seemed to take their silence as an assent and made a left onto the bridge and over the state line.

A sign greeted them on the other side: THE PEOPLE OF IOWA WELCOME YOU. FIELDS OF OPPORTUNITIES.

But there were no people, of course, in Iowa anymore. And at first, the beginning of Iowa looked exactly the same as the end of Nebraska. Wide and flat, corn and wheat fields gone fallow and covered with snow, trees devoid of their leaves, the winter landscape as stark as a black and white photograph. Annie saw a rise of hills off to the left, though, perhaps a half mile away, that looked like the foothills of a modest mountain range.

The highway was clear, but Hughes kept the speed to a respectable forty miles an hour.

Annie chewed her thumbnail and replayed that final scene in Wyoming in her mind, when they had come upon the mayor of Lander in the small town of Belt.

"What would you all have done if I had killed Steele?"

"What do you mean?" Hughes said.

"Back there in Wyoming," Annie said. "If I shot him. Or bashed in his head with a crowbar. What would you have done?"

At first, nobody said anything.

Then Hughes shrugged. "Probably nothing."

Annie had thought not. It's what she would have said if she were one of the others.

A person could commit a homicide right there on the street in the middle of the day in front of witnesses, and nobody would do anything. That was the world she lived in. Murder was allowable now. Frowned on, perhaps, but allowable.

"Something up ahead," Parker said. "Blocking the road."

The road was straight and flat to the horizon, so Annie could just barely see it, but there it was in the far distance, a dark horizontal barrier stretching across the asphalt and into the adjacent fields. It looked like it might be a train.

Hughes slowed from forty to thirty miles an hour, then to twenty as they got closer.

It was a wall, not a train. Built with sheets of corrugated metal most likely attached to some kind of fencing. At first, Annie figured it was built to keep the infected out, but no. Someone had written a message on it in white paint, which became legible as the Suburban got closer: NOT WELCOME IN HAMBURG. FOREIGNERS WILL BE SHOT.

Hughes stopped the truck and leaned forward at the wheel a couple of hundred feet out.

"Foreigners?" Kyle said.

Not outsiders, Annie thought. *Foreigners*. She knew, though, that whoever painted that sign wasn't referring to Mexicans or Canadians. They were warning people from the next town over.

"What the hell's Hamburg?" Parker said.

Kyle squinted at the map. "Small town in Iowa," he said, "just on this side of the Missouri border."

"Turning around," Hughes said and made a U-turn in the median strip.

Annie had been wondering why she hadn't seen any cars anywhere, not a single one even on the side of the road, but now she understood. Nobody who knew the area would go anywhere near Hamburg.

"Get back on Route 2," Kyle said, looking at the map. "Where the bridge into Nebraska is. Just turn right when we get there instead of left."

The turn was only five minutes away. No big deal. Annie noted, though, that it was the second detour they'd made in less than twenty-four hours.

Hughes made a right onto Route 2, and minutes later they arrived in Iowa's hill country. The state looked strikingly different now from Nebraska. Annie had always assumed the Midwest was as flat as a board, but it wasn't, at least not in this part of Iowa. The ground rose up in steep rippling waves high enough that it would take thirty minutes or more to hike to the top. They could drive to the top, she thought, and survey the surrounding plains from a high point with binoculars, but she doubted they'd see much in the emptiness. Aside from the wall around Hamburg, she'd seen no evidence that anyone was still alive in any direction. And now that she thought about it, she'd seen no evidence that anyone in Hamburg was still alive either. They could have built that wall months earlier and all died in the meantime, their fortress now a graveyard picked clean by crows.

"Kyle," Hughes said. "Where do we turn south again?"

Kyle studied his map.

"Keep going through Riverton up ahead," Kyle said, "then hang a right on 59. That'll take us well past Hamburg and into Missouri. If you want to be cautious, keep going a little farther and turn right on Hackleberry Avenue instead."

"Hackleberry Avenue?" Hughes said. "Is that in a town?"

"Not really," Kyle said. "But there are towns everywhere. Every town in the state is within walking distance of the next one. We're not in Wyoming anymore."

Hughes continued through tiny and empty Riverton, barely a thousand feet from one end to the other. The place was just a village, really, with hardly even much of a Main Street. Annie noticed, after reaching the other side, a sign indicating that the route they were on was called 250th Street. The state of Iowa seemed to be laid out on a grid like a blown-up version of a modern American city, minus the city.

Not ten minutes later, the road plunged into a small river. A bridge had collapsed—or had been destroyed. Hughes pumped the brakes, and the Suburban slid on the snow and ice to a stop.

"Should we get out and check?" Parker said.

"For what?" Hughes said. "Someone blew the bridge. We'll just go around."

Annie felt heavy in the chest.

"There's another road," Kyle said. "Just a half mile south of here crossing the same river."

"Over a bridge?" Hughes said.

"Well, yeah," Kyle said. "It's just a creek, actually. Middle Takio Creek."

If this bridge really had been blown on purpose, Annie thought—and it certainly hadn't fallen down in an earthquake—there could be only one reason for it. Whoever lived on the other side wanted to keep cars out. It wouldn't stop anything else. Anyone not in a wheelchair could cross the creek on foot without too much trouble. The infected certainly could and would if they saw prey on the other side.

Hughes turned the Suburban around, backtracked, made a left on C Avenue, then another left on 260th Street. It was a rural road, though, not any kind of street in an urban sense. Annie wondered where 1st Street was.

Almost immediately after turning left on 260th, they came across another collapsed bridge.

Hughes braked to a stop and killed the engine.

"What are we doing?" Kyle said.

"I have no idea," Hughes said.

"Why'd you turn the truck off?" Kyle said.

Hughes huffed. "Let me see that map."

Kyle passed the map forward.

Hughes yanked it out of Kyle's hands and scrutinized it. "We're too far east," he said. "We don't need to be all the way over here. We should just go back to 59 and head down into Missouri from there."

"I was just trying to get us a safe distance from Hamburg," Kyle said.

Annie had a sour taste her mouth. "To hell with all this."

"To hell with what?" Hughes snapped.

"Everything," Annie said.

"Not now, Annie," Hughes said.

Her companions couldn't see it. What if they were to wade across that creek and find an encampment of suspicious survivors, hunkered down in barns or whatever, and announce that they were from the government and had a vaccine? What would happen?

They'd most likely be shot. That's what would happen.

They'd certainly be shot if they banged on the gates of the walled city of Hamburg.

Whatever remained of American civilization in its former heartland had atomized. Everybody was paranoid, and everybody was dangerous, including Annie herself and her friends. She'd reach for her gun the moment she saw anyone upright on two legs, and she'd want to shoot them if they so much as twitched wrong.

Hughes turned the ignition back on, made a U-turn, drove back a couple of miles, and made a left on Route 59, threading the needle between Hamburg and whoever had blown the bridges.

The way ahead was clear. Annie saw nothing but frozen fields and derelict farmhouses surrounded by clusters of shade trees. The fields were vast, stretching almost from the asphalt to the horizon, and Annie was astonished at the staggering amount of food that must have been produced here. She wondered what the landscape would look like after a couple of years without anyone tending crops. The shade trees, presumably, would reproduce. After a couple of decades, Iowa would be blanketed again in forest and prairie.

The border between Iowa and Missouri appeared at the top of a small rise, with a sign that read: MISSOURI WELCOMES YOU. Next to it was a State Line Discount Tobacco store in what used to be a small house, advertising cartons of Marlboros and Old Golds for less. Just past the border loomed a half dozen high-tech windmills as silent and unmoving as everything else.

Annie scratched another state off her mental list: Washington, Oregon, Idaho, Wyoming, Nebraska, and now Iowa. So long, Iowa. Nice seeing you, but we'll never be back.

Kyle peered at the map. "Turn right on 136 toward Rock Port," he said.

"I got it, I got it," Hughes said, as if he'd memorized the map and didn't need or want any more bumbling directions from Kyle.

Annie leaned toward Kyle and peered at the map. Kyle pointed at Rock Port and traced his finger down along the Missouri River toward Kansas City a few hundred miles to the south. She doubted they had any real chance of finding a marina and a usable sailboat before reaching the next large city.

"Goddammit," Hughes said.

Annie looked up from the road and out the front windshield. The first thing she noticed was a large line of trees roughly a half mile away, which in this part of the country seemed to indicate a town was ahead. Then she saw people. Several of them. Moving out of the trees and onto the road. They were far away and small at this distance, but she could tell they weren't infected. They formed a line with deliberation and purpose.

Hughes slowed the truck to a crawl.

"What do we do?" Parker said.

"We need to talk to them," Hughes said. "Ask for directions."

The people in the road had rifles. Annie could see them now. One man stepped ahead of the others, his rifle pointing at the sky.

Hughes pumped the brakes and slid on the snow to a stop.

The man in front fired a warning shot into the sky.

Hughes powered down the driver's side window and placed both of his open palms outside the truck, as if to say he wasn't armed. But of course he was armed. The Suburban was full of weapons—hunting rifles, handguns, a pump-action shotgun, crowbars, and hammers. Nobody left alive in this world was unarmed anymore, and the Missouri militia up ahead knew it.

The man in the road fired another warning shot into the sky, then pointed his weapon at the Suburban.

"Shit," Parker said.

Hughes waved his left arm outside the window in a wide quarter circle, indicating *message received* in long-distance sign language. He backed up a few dozen feet, made a U-turn, and drove slowly away, north again toward the state line.

So much for scratching another state off the list. Annie thought she'd never see Iowa again, but she was heading back within minutes.

"Now what?" Parker said.

"We're boxed in on three sides," Hughes said. "Those assholes to the south, the blown bridges to the east, that Great Wall of Hamburg to the west. All we can do is drive north."

"Into Iowa," Kyle said.

"The wrong direction," Parker said.

"Either that, or go back to Nebraska," Hughes said.

"No!" Annie said. "We can't go back there." Not for any particular reason except that she didn't want to subtract yet another state from her list. Nobody argued. Returning to Iowa after five minutes was a setback, but driving all the way back to Nebraska would feel like a defeat.

Now that Annie was actually in the Midwest, looking around and taking it in, she realized something about the place that wasn't obvious on a map. This part of the country had few natural barriers. The western United States had mountains, canyons, inhospitable deserts, and incredible distances between cities. The Midwest had none of those things. Hence the perceived need to blow bridges and build walls: to create, with human effort, a weaker version of what nature provided elsewhere.

Getting any real distance from other people wasn't possible. Annie and her companions couldn't get more than a couple of miles from the nearest small town, nor could they get much more than a thousand feet from the nearest house. The landscape repeated itself with numbing regularity: large field, small house, large field, small house, large field, small town, large field, big city, all the way to the Appalachian Mountains.

"How much daylight do we have left?" Annie said.

"Two hours," Kyle said.

"We're not finding a boat today," she said.

Hughes sighed. "No, we're not." He sounded as frustrated as Annie felt. She realized she was grinding her back molars and forced her jaw to relax.

"We can loop around in a big arc," Kyle said. "Drive north to 35, then take the 71 south into Missouri."

"That won't put us anywhere near the river until we follow the road to St. Joseph," Hughes said, "which is practically Kansas City, which'll be even bigger and more fucked up than Omaha."

"Why don't we just drive across Iowa to the Mississippi River?" Parker said.

Hughes slouched at the wheel. "Yeah, right."

"It's a bigger river," Parker said. "More boats."

"There might be a marina in Kansas City," Kyle said.

That's what we thought about Omaha, Annie thought.

Kyle traced his finger on the map along the Mississippi River, all the way on the other side of the state. "Shit," he said. "Shit, shit, shit."

"What now?" Hughes said.

"We are so stupid," Kyle said.

"What?" Hughes said.

Kyle folded the map into quarters, shoved it onto the floor beneath his feet, and looked out the window.

"*What?*" Hughes said.

Kyle groaned, defeated. "It doesn't matter."

"What doesn't matter?" Annie said.

Kyle shook his head. "We can't sail to the Gulf of Mexico from here even if we do find a boat."

Annie sank into her seat. There was only one thing Kyle could have seen on the map that would block their path to the Gulf of Mexico on a boat. "The river is dammed," she said.

"Of course it is," Kyle said. "I don't know why none of us thought of it."

Hughes slowed the Suburban, pulled over to the side of the road, and stopped.

Of course they hadn't thought of it. They'd sailed from Olympia, Washington, to Orcas Island without any trouble. Puget Sound was a vast ocean inlet, not a river. No point damming it. And besides, before everything went sideways, anyone could have sailed down the Missouri and Mississippi Rivers to the Gulf of Mexico because a guy at the dam would open the locks and let boats through. But there'd be no guy at the locks anymore and no way past the dam.

"We're fucked, my friends," Hughes said. "We're going to have to drive."

"We can drive to the Gulf of Mexico," Parker said. "Sail to Georgia from New Orleans."

"No point," Kyle said.

"Why not?" Parker said.

"Because, believe it or not," Kyle said, "we're already closer to Atlanta than we are to New Orleans."

So we drive, Annie thought. We drive through a maze.

2

They spent the night in Riverton, Iowa, one of the empty village-like towns they'd already passed through. It was the most logical place they'd eyeballed all day. Bordering the settlement to the north and west was the East Nishnabotna River and the Riverton Wildlife Management Area, a large swath of wetlands that only birds would bother to navigate through. Immediately to the east lay another swampy area. Riverton had natural borders of sorts on three sides with only the southern approach exposed to open farmland.

So they parked the Suburban on Q Street, a gravel road on the town's northern fringe next to a compound of storage facilities and grain elevators. It wasn't pretty, but it was as secluded a spot as they were going to find even with downtown—just a handful of buildings, really—only a few streets away.

Kyle opened the door on his side and stepped out of the Suburban as twilight was turning to dusk. "I need to walk."

"Not by yourself, you don't," Hughes said.

"I'm not going more than a hundred feet," Kyle said. "I just need to move my legs."

"I'll come with you," Annie said, which partly delighted him—he still had a thing for her, even if she didn't reciprocate—but he needed to be alone with his thoughts. He blamed himself for the predicament they were in even though he could logically see that it was no more his fault than anyone else's.

"Sure," Kyle said to Annie, "but give me a couple of minutes to myself first, okay?"

He gently closed the door without saying anything else or waiting for a response.

A relatively warm and humid wind was coming in from the south. The air must have been ten degrees Fahrenheit warmer than it had been the last time he stepped outside even though night was falling. Iowa was a foreign country with strange meteorology. Strange to Kyle, anyway. The Pacific Northwest never warmed up at night. In this part of America, devoid of mountains and so far from large bodies of water, the air temperature seemed to be dictated as much by wind direction as by night and day, with frigid fronts from Canada battling it out with tropical fronts from the Gulf of Mexico.

He should have known about the dams on the river. Well, he did know, actually. He just hadn't thought about them as obstacles. They weren't obstacles in the old world, the one he'd spent most of his life in, and he was so accustomed to being able to sail unimpeded on Puget Sound that it hadn't occurred to him that he wouldn't be able to do the same thing on Midwestern rivers.

Over and over again for the past several months, he'd made different versions of the same mental mistake. Everyone did. He'd lost track of how many times he absentmindedly flipped on a light switch before remembering that light switches didn't work anymore. He'd forgotten how many times he thought, for a half second before catching himself, that he should look something up on the Internet. When the Suburban ran low on gas, he still had to remind himself that they'd have to siphon more out of somebody else's tank rather than pull into a fuel station. So it likewise hadn't occurred to him until today that American rivers were no longer navigable with no one left alive to operate the dams.

This was a brutal new fact of geography, brand new to the planet.

American rivers had always been navigable, even before there were people to navigate them. The United States had more navigable river miles than any other country on earth, which was one of the reasons it became such an economic powerhouse after the industrial revolution. Kyle remembered his high school geography teacher, Mr. Kampe, telling his class that any group of people in the world with the good fortune of straddling the North American continent would become among the richest on earth after industrialization as long as they were decently governed. Yet today, America's rivers were clogged arteries.

Kyle unzipped his coat, walked in a wide circle around the truck, and noticed that his boots didn't crunch in the snow anymore. The stuff was turning to slush.

One of the Suburban doors popped open, and Kyle remembered that Annie wanted to join him.

"Hey, Annie."

"It's Parker."

Kyle's face flashed hot. "Oh," he said. "Hey."

He had to admit, though, that the two of them had gotten along better since leaving Wyoming. Parker seemed, for the first time, almost like a normal person.

"Warm outside," Parker said.

"Yeah," Kyle said. "Weird, huh?"

Parker said nothing.

"I was thinking," Kyle said, "that this town is a good place to scavenge for supplies. We're stopped here anyway." Kyle could see Parker's dark shape against the starry night sky, but he could not read his face. "Pretty sure there's nobody here. No infected either." He kicked a bit of slush with his boot.

"You want to go now?" Parker said.

"Sure," Kyle said. "Why not? We could go together." Kyle wasn't sure he should have said that.

"Let's go in the morning," Parker said. "First light."

Kyle felt a twinge of relief. "Okay. Sure. In the morning."

First light took an eternity to arrive. Kyle kept waking up and fidgeting in his sleep until finally, at long last, a cold blue light tinted the sky. He eased himself out of the truck and closed the door without quite latching it so the others could sleep.

The snow was mostly gone, the morning air only a few degrees cooler than inside the truck. Iowa in midwinter felt temperate and humid now with tropical air on its way in from Texas.

Parker stirred and shook the sleep from his head. Kyle waved a silent good morning. Parker nodded and emerged from the truck a little clumsily to greet Kyle. "Want to head out now?" he said in a low voice.

"Want to wake up first?" Kyle said.

"I'm awake," Parker said. "Been in and out for the past couple of hours. If it weren't for the snow, I'd have slept on the grass."

Kyle understood. Human bodies were designed to sleep horizontally, not in car seats.

"Get your stuff," Kyle said and titled his head sideways toward the truck.

Parker opened the front passenger door and retrieved his Glock, a claw hammer, and a crowbar. Kyle had his own handgun tucked into his pants. Parker handed Kyle the crowbar.

Kyle popped open the back of the Suburban and lifted the hatch quietly.

"It's okay," Annie said. "We're awake."

Kyle shrugged. He still needed to be quiet in case they had neighbors they had not seen or heard yet. Anything was possible. That was the whole point of going out scavenging early, when anyone still alive in Riverton was most likely still sleeping.

Kyle and Parker donned empty backpacks and set out. Aside from food, they weren't looking for anything in particular. They simply made a point of scavenging when the opportunity arose, when it seemed safe enough, and Riverton, Iowa, seemed as safe a place as they were likely to find for a while.

"We could use one of those giant atlas books," Kyle said as he and Parker walked. "You know, the kind that has fifty pages of maps just for one state."

"Should look for those at a gas station," Parker said.

"Sure," Kyle said. "I'm just saying. If you see one, you know, grab it."

They followed Q Street to Apple Avenue, both of them gravel. After another two blocks, they came to K Street, the highway through town, with countryside to the right and houses to the left. They turned left. Downtown, so to speak, was just a few blocks ahead.

There wasn't much to the place. Just brown grass, bony trees, and off-white houses that hadn't been painted in years. There was nothing green or apparently even alive in any direction. Kyle had never seen such a colorless place.

Parker stopped in the middle of the road. Kyle held up.

"Shh," Parker said. "Hear anything?"

Kyle listened hard. And heard absolutely nothing at all.

"I don't hear anything," Kyle whispered. The town looked, sounded, and felt like it had been empty for years. He didn't get the creeping feeling that they were being watched.

"Me either," Parker said, in a normal tone of voice this time.

They walked until they came upon the Duck Pond Café on the right, a sad diner that had started its life as a mobile home. The sign out front had a drawing of a burger and a box of fries on it, each with a pair of eyeballs as if the two food items were cartoon characters. A red Chevy pickup in the lot provided the only vibrant color in any direction.

Kyle gestured toward the café with his crowbar. Parker nodded and headed toward it.

"I'm worried about Annie," Kyle said.

Parker said nothing.

"She seems different now," Kyle said.

"She is," Parker said.

"What do you think's going on?"

Parker raised his eyebrows and looked away. Kyle could only

imagine what the two of them had been through. As far as he knew, they were the only human beings on earth who had recovered from the infection.

Parker seemed to be in better shape now—a bit more agreeable and a lot less anxious—but Annie was worse. She seemed depressed, even despondent, after what happened to her in Wyoming.

"She's—" Kyle said, but Parker shushed him and placed his finger on his lips before pushing open the café's front door. It wasn't locked. Anyone, or anything, could be in there.

Inside, the place looked like a typical diner with a blue and white checkerboard floor, plastic chairs that almost matched the blue squares, round silver tables, and a chipped Formica counter with a soda fountain and a coffee warmer and pot next to the cash register. It smelled like dust and nothing else.

Parker gestured with his head toward the kitchen and pantry in back.

Kyle heard a door slam, not inside but outside, and not far away. Perhaps from the house down the street they'd just walked past. He and Parker looked at each other. Someone had seen them walk down the street and head into that diner, and whoever it was was coming.

Kyle swapped the crowbar into his left hand and drew his handgun with his right.

"Behind the counter," Parker said in a low voice.

Kyle and Parker stepped behind the counter. The diner still felt empty, undisturbed, and a layer of dust coated the Formica countertop, but they hadn't searched the kitchen area yet, and knowing that at least one person was out there on the street made Kyle feel like his back was exposed. There could be a hundred people out there converging all at once on the diner with only one of them dumb enough to draw attention to himself by slamming a door.

He and Parker crouched low. Kyle couldn't see a damn thing from down near the floor, but he knew better than to raise his head, so he peered around the side of the counter instead. He couldn't see the street from that angle, only the tops of the nearest trees.

"I don't think anyone can see inside," Parker said, "with the glare on the windows."

Probably true, Kyle thought, so he and Parker stood. The street looked the same as it had before: forlorn and empty with nobody out there.

"They know we're in here, though," Parker said. "They saw us walk in."

Kyle heard something else now, something farther away, a large vehicle, like a truck or a bus of some kind. "You hear that?"

Parker nodded.

"It's not Annie and Hughes," Kyle said. Whatever it was sounded larger than the Suburban, and it was coming from the east—the opposite direction from where they'd camped for the night.

Kyle's mind turned to flight, but he didn't dare run. He had no idea how many people were out there, no idea who or what he'd be facing, no idea which way to go. His eyes darted from the coffee pot and the cash register to the tables and chairs. Everything looked vaguely dangerous now.

The rumbling from the distant vehicle stopped, and Riverton fell into silence again.

Reinforcements showing up on the outskirts? Called in by radio?

"Stay down," Parker said and made a downward motion with his hand. "I'll keep watch. No sense both of us risking getting shot in the head."

Kyle crouched again and held his breath. He still didn't hear anything.

"You've got to be fucking kidding me," Parker said. He wiped his forehead with the back of his hand and raised his gun toward the glass.

"What?" Kyle said.

"Get up," Parker said.

Kyle stood up and saw it. One of those things. An infected man with a bald head, a gray overcoat, stained pants, and muddy boots staggering down the street past the diner.

"It doesn't know we're in here," Kyle said.

Parker exhaled loudly and kept his gun trained on the infected. He wasn't going to shoot through the glass. He'd probably miss at this distance with a handgun anyway, and besides, shooting a single oblivious infected would be a waste of ammunition and a reckless summons to everyone and everything in the area. There was still a truck or bus up the street, after all.

"Did that thing just randomly come out of the house after we passed?" Kyle said.

"Must have heard us but didn't see us," Parker said. "At least it didn't see us come in here."

Kyle gripped his crowbar. Whoever was in the vehicle he'd heard didn't seem to be around. Could have just been someone passing through. At the very least, it wasn't anyone's backup.

"Let's go out and take care of it," Kyle said.

"Wait up," Parker said. "There could be more."

"Doubt it," Kyle said.

"Just wait," Parker said. "We don't know who's up the road either."

The infected staggered toward a dingy square house on a corner lot with a child's bike on its side in the yard. It wasn't heading there in any kind of a hurry.

"We could just let it pass," Parker said.

"It could swing back around," Kyle said. "Cause trouble for us later."

"Could also cause trouble for whoever is up the road."

"Do we want that?"

Parker shrugged, shook his head, crept toward the front door, and pushed it open as slowly and quietly as he could.

The infected did not hear the door. It had no idea Kyle and Parker were there. The thing was a good 150 feet ahead, though, and would hear them coming.

Parker seemed to have the same thought, but he didn't care. "Fuck it," he whispered. "Go loud."

Kyle nodded, and they both took off running.

∼

HUGHES WAS DIGGING AROUND in the back of the truck for breakfast bars when he heard the scream. An infected. No question about it. Somewhere in the center of Riverton.

Annie was busy boiling water water on a camp stove for tea. She blew out the flame and stood up, wide-eyed.

Hughes slammed the Suburban's back door and fished the keys out of his pocket.

He heard the scream again, followed by a faint smack. Then nothing.

"We'd better go," he said.

Annie nodded. "In the truck or on foot?"

"Truck," Hughes said. He got behind the wheel and turned the ignition key as Annie zipped up the camp stove in her backpack and climbed into the passenger seat. Tires crunched over gravel as he pulled away from their camp site amid the grain silos and storage facilities.

He rounded a C-curve, made a hard left onto the paved road that went through the middle of town, and saw two things directly ahead: Kyle and Parker standing over a body and an RV approaching at a leisurely pace with its hazard lights on.

Kyle and Parker stood there waving at the RV. They were not running, nor were they pointing guns at the vehicle. Hughes had missed something. A friendly announcement of some kind signaling a lack of hostility.

Hughes pulled alongside Kyle and Parker and stopped. "Stay in the truck," he said to Annie and climbed out with his shotgun. He didn't point it at anybody, but he had no idea who the fuck was in that RV, and he wasn't going out there unarmed.

The RV came to a stop. At least two men were inside, a driver and passenger. The driver turned off the engine and stepped out with nothing in his hands. He was partly balding and appeared to be around fifty. He smiled and waved. Too friendly. Either that or oblivious to the danger of randomly encountering four strangers, but the man would not still be alive if he were oblivious to that danger. A younger man with darker skin waved hello and remained in the vehicle.

"Howdy," the driver said and shook hands with Kyle and Parker. "Name's Roy."

Kyle and Parker introduced themselves.

Hughes just said hi.

"You all know each other?" the man who called himself Roy said.

"We do," Hughes said.

"Looks like things went a little catawampus here," Roy said and looked at the body of the infected on the road, the back of its skull bashed in, a pool of blood spreading around its head.

"No trouble," Parker said. Drops of blood dripped from the hammer in his hand.

Hughes glanced at the RV's license plate. South Carolina. Which told Hughes that this Roy character might not be familiar with Iowa either.

"Strange, isn't it?" Roy said.

"What's that?" Hughes said.

"These stragglers," Roy said, gesturing toward the dead infected in the road. "Not part of a herd or a horde. And this far north too, out in the cold."

"You drove here from the South?" Hughes said.

"Sure did," Roy said.

"Long way," Hughes said.

"Not as far away as where you're from," Roy said, with his eyes on the Suburban's plates. "All the way from Washington?"

"Seattle," Parker said.

Roy glanced behind him at the RV and made a summoning motion. "Come on out, Lucas. These folks are friendly."

The man Roy called Lucas stepped out. He was younger, perhaps around thirty, and seemed vaguely Hispanic, though "Lucas" didn't sound to Hughes like a Hispanic name. Both of these men stood there in the road like meeting four complete strangers over the body of a brained infected in the middle of an Iowa village was no big thing.

"You seen many of these on the road from Seattle?" Roy said.

"Infected?" Hughes said, surprised by the question.

"Stragglers, I mean," Roy said.

"Not part of a herd or a horde," Hughes said.

"Exactly," Roy said. "Most folks who get bit turn quick, but there's a delayed response in some people."

Hughes shook his head. "He wasn't necessarily bit." The poor bastard could just as easily have been infected by a contaminated water supply, just like what had happened in Wyoming.

Roy squinted. "Not bit? Makes no sense. How would you know that, anyway? You strip him down naked and check him for bites while I wasn't looking?"

"There are other—" Hughes said, then stopped himself. He had no idea what on earth to make of these people except that he wanted to get far away from them. His danger signals were pinging. Roy and Lucas weren't behaving correctly at all under the circumstances. They were far too trusting of strangers. Then again, nobody had threatened or menaced anybody. And Hughes had to admit that running into two people willing to talk, for whatever reason, was a relief. Hughes needed information about the road ahead, information that Roy and Lucas would have if they'd really driven to Iowa from South Carolina.

"Why don't we get out of the road here?" Hughes said. "Maybe sit in that diner. We'll tell you what we know if you tell us what you know."

Hughes glanced at his friends to gauge their reaction. Parker shrugged and nodded. Annie was still in the truck and looked like she didn't want to get out. Kyle looked straight at Roy while Roy glanced at the diner.

"A fine idea," Roy said. "We'll have coffee."

"They're out of coffee," Parker said. "Probably been out for months."

"We have coffee," Roy said.

∽

They relocated to the Duck Pond Café. Rather than crowding six people around a four-top, they spread themselves out across two tables, with Roy and Lucas at one and everyone else at the other. Hughes leaned his pump-action Persuader against a chair at a table behind him, a polite distance from himself yet even farther away from Lucas and Roy.

Parker and Kyle placed their own weapons—the crowbar and the blood-spattered hammer—onto the table. Hughes knew that each of them had handguns in their coat pockets. Roy and Lucas most likely did too.

"I'll run to the RV and grab that coffee," Lucas said. "But first I wanted to say that we're really glad to meet you folks." He looked at Annie when he said it, then headed outside.

Hughes sat with a clear view out the front of the diner and watched Lucas disappear inside the RV. For all Hughes knew, there was somebody else in there that he hadn't seen yet. And if Lucas emerged from it with anything but coffee, Hughes would know.

He squinted at Roy.

"Penny for your thoughts," Roy said and smiled.

"Just wondering what you guys are doing out here," Hughes said.

Annie rubbed the back of her neck.

"Same thing y'all are, I assume," Roy said. "Out surviving."

"You seem surprisingly at ease," Hughes said, "considering you don't know us from Adam and Eve and we just splattered one of those things before you showed up."

"Just a straggler," Roy said and shrugged. "We run into them sometimes. Assume you have too. If there was a horde nearby, we'd know it by now, way that thing hollered before y'all thwacked it."

"Probably," Parker said. "But what about other people?"

Roy scratched his cheek. "What about other people?"

"You don't know us," Hughes said.

"Lucas and I been running into all kinds of folks between here and South Carolina," Roy said.

Annie sat up straight. "You're from South Carolina?"

"Yes, ma'am," Roy said.

Hughes saw Lucas climb out of the RV with a zipped-up backpack in his hands. He walked toward the diner as cool as a freshly picked apple in October. Hughes kept his eye on him.

"I'm from South Carolina," Annie said.

Roy beamed. "Whereabouts?"

"Georgetown, originally," Annie said, "though I think of Charleston more as home now."

"Charleston is a lovely city," Roy said. "Greenville is my stomping grounds. Lucas is from up in Charlotte. North Carolina."

"Heard of it," Hughes said. "Never been there."

Hughes did not want to stay and shoot the shit with Lucas and Roy any longer than he had to. He just wanted to know about the roads. He resisted the urge to drum his fingers and folded his hands on the tabletop instead.

Lucas came back inside.

"Annie here is from Charleston," Roy said.

"That so?" Lucas said and smiled. He set the backpack down on an empty neutral table.

Hughes stared at the backpack. "Thought you went to get coffee."

"In the backpack," Lucas said. "First, though, let's get a photo."

"A photo?" Parker said.

Annie's mouth opened slightly, and she flashed Hughes a look that said, *Get me out of here.*

Lucas pulled a smartphone with a cracked screen out of his pocket.

"You taking pictures with that?" Kyle said.

"Have been all along," Lucas said.

"What for?" Parker said in a raised voice.

Lucas shrugged. "Passes the time, I guess."

"How are you charging it?" Kyle said.

"Solar," Lucas said. "We got panels on the RV."

Kyle had some kind of a portable solar phone charger somewhere for his own gadgets, but Hughes hadn't noticed him using it lately.

"Why do you want a *picture*?" Annie said.

"Ma'am," Roy said. "We don't meet nice folks like yourself more than once in a while, and when we do, Lucas likes to memorialize the occasion with a nice photograph."

Hughes groaned to himself. Annie curled her lip. Parker looked at the ceiling.

Lucas tapped his phone's screen a couple of times and stood near and over Annie. She huffed and turned partly away from him.

"Come on, darlin'," Lucas said and held up his phone with the screen facing him, apparently in selfie mode. "Indulge me here for a minute."

Kyle indulged Lucas by looking at the phone, but no one else did.

Lucas tapped the screen, and the device made an electronic snicking sound. The picture must have been terrible.

"Alright now, sit down, Lucas," Roy said.

Lucas nodded and unzipped his backpack. He pulled out what looked like cans of beer. Hughes noticed some other things inside too. A hunting knife in its sheaf, loose boxes of ammunition, and a black leather pouch with the word "Southord" stamped on it in gold. Hughes knew exactly what that was, and he didn't like it.

"Thought you said you had coffee," Parker said.

"This is coffee," Lucas said and gently shook what still looked to Hughes like a beer can.

"Cold brew," Roy said as Lucas passed the cans around.

"What's up with the lockpicks?" Hughes said. He'd seen the exact same Southord set once or twice.

Lucas froze for just the briefest of moments. "To open doors with," he then said and shrugged. "What else would they be for?"

"Mmm," Hughes said. Lucas didn't need a set of lockpicks to open doors. Not anymore. Crowbars and axes worked faster. Hughes wouldn't bother picking up a lockpick set if somebody threw it at him. Lucas had it from the time before, when witnesses frowned on breaking down doors with crowbars and axes and were inclined to call the police.

Parker handed Hughes a coffee can that looked like a beer can.

Hughes scrutinized it. The label read STUMPTOWN COLD BREW

with the word NITRO across the top of it, whatever that was supposed to mean.

"This stuff is from Portland," Kyle said. "Where on earth did you get it?"

"Grocery store in Atlanta," Roy said.

Hughes held his breath. Parker wiped his mouth with the back of his hand. Annie exchanged startled glances with Kyle.

Nobody moved. Nobody said anything. Hughes could have heard an ant nibbling on a sugar crumb.

"I say something?" Roy said.

Annie gulped. "When were you in Atlanta?"

"Two weeks ago," Roy said.

Hughes glanced at Annie. She was looking right at him and leaning forward slightly, propped up on her forearms, with her eyes open more than usual, as if she were imploring him not to say a damn word. But Hughes couldn't say nothing.

"How is Atlanta, anyway?" he said, as casually and disinterested as he could manage.

"You haven't heard?" Lucas said.

"Heard what?" Hughes said.

Roy and Lucas looked at each other.

"They don't know," Lucas to Roy.

"You—" Roy said, then stopped himself, as if he wasn't sure what to say next. "You're coming from Seattle. Right?"

"Right," Hughes said.

"This is as far east as you've been?" Roy said.

"This is as far east as we've been," Hughes said.

"Alright," Roy said and cracked open a can. "Y'all better sit back and get comfortable."

3

Annie did not like these people. Didn't like them at all. They were strangers, and that by itself made them dangerous, but that was the least of it. For all she knew, she was the first living and breathing noninfected woman Lucas and Roy had seen in months.

They wanted to fuck her. It didn't take an expert in human psychology to figure that out. Which was no doubt why they took her picture. So they could take turns whacking off to it. And they were trying to determine which of her friends she belonged to. Perhaps she belonged to all three of them. Maybe they were willing to share. And if not, they could take steps.

Annie had been careful around men her whole life. A small percentage were always dangerous, which made all men she didn't know at least potentially dangerous. That was during the best of times. These were the worst of times, and the worst of times brought out the worst in people, men and women alike, including herself.

She hadn't hooked up with anyone since the world ended. Parker and Hughes weren't her type. Kyle seemed at first like her type, but his immature and vindictive feud with Parker on the San Juan Islands put her off. None of them had ever threatened her. She trusted them completely.

Roy and especially Lucas, however, screamed *rapist* after taking that photo.

∼

"Let me ask you folks something," Roy said. "What are you doing out here, exactly? Where you fixing to get to?" His pronunciation of "get" sounded liked *git*.

Hughes was not going to tell Lucas and Roy about Annie. Wouldn't be as dangerous as telling the mayor of Lander, Wyoming, about Annie. Lucas and Roy weren't going to tie her up and keep her for themselves—not for the antibodies in her blood, anyway. There just wasn't any point telling Lucas and Roy about Annie, and Hughes didn't want anyone to know where they were going. He didn't want anyone following them. He needed information, though, and he'd need to give if he was going to get.

"The West Coast," Hughes said, "is a disaster."

"Everywhere's gone to hell in a handbasket, my friends," Roy said.

"We were hoping the East Coast is in better shape," Hughes said.

"Well, it is," Roy said. "Parts of it, anyway, for the time being."

"Which parts?" Kyle said.

"Washington, DC, for starters," Roy said.

Hughes felt a flush of adrenaline in his chest, face, and hands.

"Least, that's what we heard," Roy said. "All kinds of bunkers and shit around Washington. Army bases, too, down in Virginia are still up and running. Atlanta—"

"Best place in the country," Lucas said, "is San Juan. If you consider that part of the country."

"Puerto Rico?" Parker said. Hughes both chafed at and appreciated Parker's diversion from what Roy was about to say about Atlanta. He wanted to hear it, but he didn't want Roy to know he wanted to hear it.

Lucas nodded. "It's an island," he said, referring to Puerto Rico. "Supposedly still intact."

Kyle sat forward in his chair, listening intently.

"Lots of places in the Caribbean are still intact," Lucas said.

"All kinds of people heading from here to there on boats," Roy said. "Like a reverse migration. Americans are beating feet to Cuba and Haiti now instead of the other way around. But mostly Puerto Rico, since it's American."

"So how come you guys aren't going there?" Hughes said.

"No point," Roy said.

"No point in what?" Hughes said. "You just said Puerto Rico is intact."

"How long you think that's going to last?" Roy said.

"Could last indefinitely," Hughes said.

"It won't," Roy said.

"Why not?" Hughes said.

"Because the universe is committing suicide," Roy said.

∼

THE UNIVERSE IS COMMITTING SUICIDE. Lucas and Roy were certifiable. Hughes was tempted to warn them to stay off the tap water unless they boiled it first, walk out of the diner with the others in tow, climb back into the Suburban, and figure out the way forward on their own without any directions or even advice. They could head north into the unknown from Riverton, then pick a road at random and head east again. They'd figure it out and get to Atlanta eventually. Probably. Roy and Lucas had done it. They'd picked up cold cans of coffee in an Atlanta grocery store two weeks ago.

There was nothing to be gained, though, from walking out of the diner if these two were willing to talk, and they hadn't yet said a word about Atlanta except that they'd been there.

"You ever hear of Julian Huxley?" Roy said.

Hughes shook his head.

"Interesting guy," Roy said. "Brother was Aldous Huxley. You know, *Brave New World*."

"I read it in college," Kyle said.

"Okay," Roy said. "So you know what I'm talking about."

"Not a clue," Kyle said, sounding a little exasperated.

"After a million years of evolution," Roy said, "the universe has become conscious of itself. Huxley was the one who first said that. And he ought to know. He was an evolutionary biologist."

"Roy—" Hughes said.

"Hear me out," Roy said. "You want to know what's what, I'm telling you."

Hughes spread his arms wide with his palms up, as if to say, *knock yourself out*.

"The universe," Roy said, "is full of all kinds of dead stuff like ice planets, asteroid belts, black holes, you name it. But parts of the universe are conscious. We are. You and me. Annie and everyone else. And we're aware of the ice planets, asteroid belts, and the black holes. We're like the universe's eyeballs and brains, taking in everything else the way a baby looks at and ponders its hands."

"Roy—" Hughes said.

"Now, hang on," Roy said.

Hughes had no interest in Roy's pop philosophy. He just wanted to know what to expect on the road to Atlanta and in Atlanta once they got there.

"You don't know Julian Huxley, but I assume you know Carl Jung," Roy said.

"Heard of him," Hughes said and sighed.

"Then you know about the collective unconscious," Roy said.

Lucas nodded as Roy talked. He'd heard this before.

"Sure," Hughes said.

"We're all linked together," Roy said, "in a kind of hive mind."

Hughes noticed Parker staring at the ceiling again. Annie looked like she would rather be just about anywhere else.

"So, you put Huxley and Jung together and *boom*," Roy said.

"Boom, what?" Hughes said.

"Think about it," Roy said. "The universe doesn't die when we die. It goes on."

"Sounds like you two have had a little too much time to think about this stuff lately," Parker said.

"Oh," Roy said. "I haven't just been thinking about this stuff lately. I've understood all this for a long, long time."

Annie gave Hughes another one of her looks. *Get me the fuck out of here and away from these people.* He nodded at her, but he needed a couple more minutes.

"What does this have to do with why you and Lucas aren't in the Caribbean?" Parker said.

"Let me ask y'all something," Roy said. "You want to live forever?"

"I suppose not," Hughes said and sighed again.

"And why not?" Roy said.

"I don't know, man," Hughes said. "I never really thought about it that much. Just always assumed I'd die like everyone else and was fine with it."

"You never really thought about it," Roy said. "Yet you know that living forever isn't something you'd want."

Roy seemed to Hughes like a wannabe cult leader. Maybe that's what he was doing. Prowling around the apocalyptic countryside looking for converts and followers. Maybe that's who and what Lucas was. The surviving pockets of humans were filled with bandits, warlords, strongmen, and militias, so it stood to reason that there'd be some apocalyptic cults here and there. Perhaps this was how they got started.

"Imagine being alive for a hundred thousand years," Roy said. "Eighty years is a long time, right? Doesn't seem like it sometimes, but it is. You grow up, go to school, work for four or five decades, then retire for a couple more if you're lucky. What would you do if you had to work for a hundred thousand years? You'd be bored out of your mind after a hundred, and then what?"

"What's your point, Roy?" Hughes said.

"Listen," Lucas said. "This is where it gets interesting."

This time, Hughes couldn't stop himself from rolling his eyes.

"You'd go crazy with a hundred-thousand-year life span," Roy said. "What if you didn't even *have* a life span? What if you were going to go on forever? You'd be here after the climate changes five or six times. After forests turn into deserts and deserts are covered in jungle. You'd be here after the moon drifts so far away you'd need binoculars to see it and after Antarctica is back on the equator."

Roy leaned forward in his chair and looked intently at Hughes. "You get what I'm saying?"

"Sure, Roy," Hughes said. "People think they'd like to live forever, but they actually don't. That's why you're not going to the Caribbean."

"That's part of it," Roy said.

"You have a death wish," Hughes said.

"We all do," Roy said.

"You're world-weary," Hughes said.

"It's not so much that I am," Roy said. "The universe is. Thanks to us, the universe has been self-aware for a hundred thousand years, and it wants to go to sleep now."

"Jesus Christ," Annie said and turned away from Roy in disgust.

"That's why *all* this is happening," Roy said. "The infection is a suicide pill."

Hughes stared at Roy. Guy was crazy. Like a schizoid who needed industrial-grade medication. But he'd been to Atlanta. "I hear you, man," Hughes said. "It's an interesting theory."

"An interesting theory," Roy said. "That's what everyone says. But they still don't get it. You don't get it."

"What don't we get?" Annie said. Her voice reeked of contempt.

Roy turned his attention to her the way a snake looks at a mouse. "There is no hope," he said. "And deep down, you don't want there to be."

Annie flared her nostrils. Hughes shushed her with his eyes, then turned to Roy and drummed his fingers on the tabletop. He'd heard enough of this crap. "How's Atlanta?"

"What's in Atlanta?" Roy said.

"Annie has family there," Hughes said.

Annie and Parker shot Hughes a look. He ignored them.

"Walled off," Lucas said.

Hughes felt a rush. Annie sat bolt upright in her seat.

"Walled off," Hughes said.

Roy laughed and shook his head. "They don't get it any more than you folks do."

"Who doesn't get it?" Hughes said.

"The government," Roy said.

"The government walled off Atlanta?" Hughes said.

Annie crossed her arms over her chest, but for the first time in a long time, Parker's face seemed to shine. Kyle clasped his hands together under his chin as if he were praying.

"They're still hoping they can find an antidote to the suicide pill," Roy said.

"The CDC is in Atlanta," Parker said.

"That's why they walled it off," Lucas said.

"Walled off a whole section of town," Roy said, "including the CDC."

"How?" Hughes said.

"Same way they walled off parts of Washington, DC," Roy said and shrugged. "With a wall. No point going there, though. They won't let you in. They won't let anyone in."

"You've been there?" Hughes said.

"Not inside the wall," Lucas said, "but yeah. We been everywhere."

"How did you get here from there?" Hughes said.

"We drove," Lucas said, like Hughes was an asshole for asking.

"I mean," Hughes said, "we've had a bit of trouble in this area." He didn't want to tell these people any more than he had to, but he had to tell them something to get them to talk.

"Trouble everywhere," Lucas said.

"Not out West," Hughes said, which wasn't strictly true, but it was sort of true. One could still roam mostly free in the western United States. "Most roads out there are open and clear."

Lucas turned to look at Roy and Roy squinted at him. "Maybe we should head that way," he said in a low voice, as if it were a private comment meant only for Roy. He then sat up straight and leaned forward toward Hughes. "Tell us about it."

Hughes told Lucas and Roy about their journey from Seattle to Iowa, how the only roadblock they encountered that forced them to detour was in the eastern Oregon desert. He made no mention of their adventure in Lander, Wyoming, except to warn them about drinking unboiled tap water.

"Now tell us what you've seen on the roads east of here," Hughes said.

"Completely different story east of here," Lucas said, as if they were having a perfectly normal conversation and the previous weirdness never happened. "Everything's carved up into checkerboards, some parts controlled by militias, some crawling with bandits, and other places overrun with infected. Other sections are quiet and basically dead."

Hughes wondered if they'd draw him a map if he asked. "How'd you get through?"

"Wasn't easy," Roy said and widened his eyes.

"How can we get to Atlanta?"

"Impossible to give directions," Roy said.

"You know the way, though," Hughes said.

"Sure," Roy said. "But like I said, impossible to give directions. And like I said, no point. They won't let anyone in."

Hughes said nothing for a moment and weighed his options. He saw Annie staring at him in his peripheral vision, but he did not meet her eyes. She seemed to know what he was thinking, though, and she proved it by standing up and storming out of the diner.

∽

ANNIE WAS ALMOST certain that Hughes would follow her outside into the cold Iowa morning, and he'd better. She knew exactly what he was thinking, and she would have none of it. She waited for him with her hands on her hips, eyeballing the dead infected in the road and resisting the urge to walk up and kick it. The Suburban and Roy's creepy RV seemed ludicrously out of place among the abandoned houses.

Hughes came out a few moments later, shotgun in hand, the diner's door banging shut behind him.

"Don't you dare," Annie said.

"Don't I dare what?" Hughes said.

"I know what you're thinking."

"Do you?"

"It's obvious."

"Is it?"

"You want to tell them."

"I don't."

"But you're going to anyway."

"You heard what they said. The CDC is still up and running. They were just there two weeks ago."

"They weren't at the CDC."

"They were in Atlanta. They know the geography, the roads. They know how to get there."

Annie crossed her arms over her chest and shivered. "Why do you think they're even sitting there with us?"

Hughes looked at her and said nothing.

"You think they'd be all chatty and friendly if I wasn't here?" she said. "If it was just the three of you guys?"

"Look," Hughes said.

"No, you look," Annie said. "I don't even want to do this, okay?"

"You've made that abundantly clear for the past three days," Hughes said.

Annie darted her eyes at Hughes for a moment but couldn't stand a long look at him.

"You said you doubted the CDC was even still there," Hughes said. "Now you know that it is."

Annie glowered at the RV and fantasized about setting it on fire with a Molotov Cocktail. "You seriously believe that it's worth it." She sucked down her guilt and faced him.

Hughes threw his hands into the air. "Christ, Annie, sometimes you sound like those two in there with their *universe-is-killing-itself* nonsense."

"Maybe God's doing it," Annie said. "Like a second flood. Maybe God has a point."

She didn't actually believe God was doing this, but she'd understand if he were.

"Those two in there?" she said. "They want to kill you and drive off with me in their rapey RV. That's what they're doing, you know. Driving around and looking for women."

"You don't know what they're doing," Hughes said.

"Women know these things."

"They touch you, they lose a hand."

"They'll kill you first," Annie said. "They'll poison your food or shoot you in the head while you sleep."

Hughes just looked at her. She was right, and he knew it.

"Annie—"

"Don't," she said.

"This whole thing was your idea," he said.

She shook her head, but he was right. The whole let's-go-to-Atlanta-and-save-the-world thing really was her idea. It made sense back on the San Juan Islands, which seemed like a lifetime ago now. Get to the CDC. Help out the doctors. Make the world like it was again.

She'd been in denial. There was no making the world like it was. Not anymore. It took her months and thousands of miles before she could accept it, but it was obvious now. The world was dead, and most people still left alive deserved to die with it.

"You heard what they said," Hughes said. "Atlanta is holding on. Washington, DC, is holding on. Puerto Rico is holding on."

Annie closed her eyes, but she could not close her ears.

"That's more than we dared to hope," Hughes said.

Annie felt a glimmer of something. Just the tiniest twinge in her belly. She wasn't sure what it was. Not hope, surely, but something. It was drowned out, though, by images of herself in the RV with Roy on top of her and Lucas grinning over his shoulder, two nihilists getting in some last kicks before the world finished shutting itself down completely.

"You have to get there, Annie," Hughes said. "The world can heal itself if there's a cure and everyone left alive knows it. You think Roy and Lucas would be out here trolling for women if they knew there was a cure? You think they'd be spouting off about the universe committing suicide if there was a cure?"

Annie didn't know what to say.

"You think they'd still want to haul you off if they knew who you really are?"

Annie considered that. She had to admit that it was an interesting question. Because of her immunity to the virus, Parker had once called her the most precious person alive. Everyone should want to protect her. Nobody should want to rape her.

The diner's door opened, and Roy emerged. "You two okay?" he said.

"Fine," Annie said dismissively.

"Let's go in, Annie," Hughes said. "Okay? Can we do that?"

"Give us a minute, Roy," Annie said.

"Yes, ma'am," he said, smiling like they were old friends, and went back inside.

Annie waited a moment before saying anything else. "You want to ask him to guide us."

"I do."

"He might not agree."

"He might not."

"They might make their move right here."

"Already factored that in. There are four of us and two of them, and we're armed. What are they going to do?"

They'll come at me in the night, Annie thought. On the road. When we're all asleep.

"We're not going with them in their RV," Annie said.

"Of course not," Hughes said.

"We sleep in shifts."

"No question."

"They will not be in charge."

"Guides only."

"If they even agree."

"If they even agree."

She took a deep breath and held it for a moment. "We sleep in shifts even if they say no. In case they try to follow us."

"In this part of the country, we have to sleep in shifts anyway."

"Okay then."

"Okay then. Let's go inside and see what he says."

4

Hughes and Annie returned to the diner. Roy and Lucas sat at one of the tables as Parker fished around behind the counter for something.

"Where's Kyle?" Annie said.

"Commode," Roy said and jabbed a sidewise hitchhiker thumb toward the bathroom.

Hughes sat at his old table and placed the shotgun on the floor next to him. He had this under control. He didn't trust Roy any more than Annie did, and he agreed with her assessment of what Lucas and Roy probably wanted, but he didn't sweat it. If Roy said yes and agreed to lead the way to Atlanta, Hughes, Annie, Parker, and Kyle would take their own vehicle. If Lucas or Roy pulled a weapon, they'd be down within seconds.

Hughes heard a toilet flush somewhere in back. So, the plumbing still worked.

Kyle emerged and sat back down next to Annie and Hughes. Parker joined them.

"You two okay?" Kyle said, looking at Annie.

Annie nodded.

"We have a proposition for you," Hughes said to Roy and Lucas.

Kyle squinted. Parker snapped his head back a little.

"A proposition," Roy said.

"Yep," Hughes said.

"What you two were talking about outside?" Roy said.

"Yep," Hughes said.

Kyle leaned forward and flicked his eyes back and forth between Annie and Hughes. Parker clenched his jaw. Hughes ignored both of them.

"We're on a mission," Hughes said.

Kyle's mouth went slack. "Wait."

"Just—" Hughes said.

"Now hang on," Parker said.

"Y'all need a minute?" Roy said.

Hughes sighed. He was in a bit of a bind here. He could pull Parker and Kyle outside, but he wanted eyes on Lucas and Roy at all times, and he sure as shit wasn't going to leave them alone with Annie. That wasn't the right way to play this anyway.

So he stared at Parker and willed the man to understand the situation and figure it out by himself. "Do we?" he said to Parker. "Need a minute?"

Parker leaned back in his chair with his arms crossed over his chest and stared at a point in space. Hughes gave Parker a moment to weigh the options and the pros and cons in his mind. Come on, man, Hughes thought. They were like blind rats in a maze in this landscape with no idea how to get where they were going. Parker finally nodded to himself. "Okay."

"Kyle?" Hughes said.

Kyle fidgeted in his chair, glanced around at everyone else, then nodded a little and cleared his throat. "Okay, I guess."

"Alright," Hughes said. He loosened his shoulders and tried to take up as much space as possible at the table. "Annie here is immune." He paused. "She's immune to the virus."

He stopped to let that sink in.

Roy and Lucas looked at each other, no real expressions on their faces.

"She was bit," Hughes said. "A couple of months ago. And she recovered."

Roy rubbed his chin and his mouth. Lucas tilted his head to one side and looked at Annie as if he were seeing her for the first time.

"You saw this happen?" Lucas said.

"No," Hughes said. "But we transferred her immunity to Parker. He was bit too. We watched him turn. And we watched him recover."

Roy stood up so fast that he knocked his chair back. His eyes moved from Annie to Hughes, then to Parker and Kyle. "Are *all* of you immune?"

Hughes shook his head.

"Just me and Annie," Parker said.

"Why just you?" Roy said, suspicion in his voice, his legs far apart.

"Because I share her blood type," Parker said.

"We injected him with Annie's blood," Hughes said. "Now both of them are immune. Both of them recovered."

Roy looked dizzy. He sat back down in his chair, presumably to process what he was hearing.

Hughes thought he should give them a couple of moments. The ramifications were obvious, but they wouldn't sink in all at once.

Roy figured out one of those ramifications and snapped his head toward Hughes. "You're going to Atlanta," he said. "That's why you drove all the way out here from Seattle. You're on your way to Atlanta."

Hughes nodded. "To the CDC."

Roy and Lucas looked at each other, shock on both of their faces.

"Can we step outside for a minute?" Lucas said to Roy.

Roy nodded. "Give us a minute please, folks." He and Lucas headed out into the cold, and the diner's door banged shut behind them.

"The fuck did you tell them that for without consulting Kyle and me first?" Parker said.

"I could have taken you two outside," Hughes said, "but I couldn't leave Annie in here alone with them, and I didn't want to leave them alone by themselves either."

"You could have taken us aside individually," Parker said.

"Nope," Hughes said.

"Why not?" Parker said.

"Think about it, man," Hughes said. "How would that have looked?"

Parker shrugged and shook his head.

"Pretend you're them," Hughes said. "How would it have looked if I had a private conversation with all three of you before springing a bombshell on them?"

Parker said nothing.

"They'd think we were up to something," Hughes said, "but now they know that we're not."

"How do they know that?" Kyle said.

"Because we each told them a part of the story," Hughes said, "and you guys put on a great show of being upset and nervous about it. Only it wasn't a show. You weren't acting. It was your genuine no-bullshit reaction."

"They're outside talking about us right now," Annie said.

"I've got my eye on them," Hughes said. And he did. They were a safe enough distance away from the RV and whatever weaponry they had inside. They weren't going for any weapons, though.

"Aren't you suspicious about what *they're* talking about?" Parker said.

"Course I am," Hughes said. "I know what they're saying, though. I know what they're debating, anyway."

"What's that?" Kyle said.

"We scrambled their plan," Hughes said.

"What was their plan?" Kyle said.

Parker looked at Annie.

"Me," Annie said.

Kyle froze for a moment, then frowned.

Hughes watched Lucas and Roy nod to each other and head back toward the diner.

"They're coming back," Hughes said. "Nobody ask them what they were talking about. Like everything's fine."

Lucas held the door open, and Roy entered first.

"We were discussing," Roy said, "whether or not we should believe you."

"And?" Hughes said.

"We want you to prove it," Lucas said.

"If the two of you were bit," Roy said. "You should have scars."

These two were in no position to demand proof of anything, Hughes thought. Nor, if they were just two disinterested strangers, would it even occur to them to demand proof. They wanted proof not to satisfy some idle curiosity on their part. They wanted proof because it would change something they had already planned. Otherwise, why bother?

That was obvious to Hughes, and it all but proved Annie was right. They had an agenda, and they weren't going to junk it without evidence.

"Annie?" Hughes said. "You okay showing them your scar?"

She relaxed and nodded. "I'm okay with it." She seemed to see things the same way Hughes did. Lucas and Roy were more likely to leave her alone if they knew the truth. "The scar is on my back. So I'm going to turn around and lift up my shirt."

Roy and Lucas looked at each other.

Annie turned around, took off her jacket, laid it on the back of a chair, and pulled her sweatshirt up around her neck. Hughes could see the bite mark almost as well as he could when it was still fresh, right there on the back of her shoulder, just above her bra strap. It was the perfect shape of human teeth, top and bottom, slightly smaller than an egg.

Roy and Lucas stepped forward to get a closer look.

"Don't touch me," Annie said.

Neither Lucas nor Roy answered, but they didn't touch her either. Lucas traced the shape of her scar in the air with his finger.

"Okay?" Hughes said.

Roy nodded. So did Lucas.

"Now him," Roy said, meaning Parker.

"My scar is less obviously a bite mark than hers," Parker said. He unlaced and slipped off his boot, pulled down his sock, and rested his foot on one of the chairs, exposing a newer scar on his ankle. Parker was right. It was less obviously a bite mark. It could have been anything, really.

"How'd you get bit on the ankle?" Lucas said.

"Long story," Parker said and pulled up his sock.

Roy nodded. "Okay. So now what? You said you had a proposition for us."

"We do," Hughes said. "We'd like you to lead us back to Atlanta."

Roy squinted, then nodded and stuck out his jaw. "We've been back and forth between Atlanta and Kansas City three times. There are some weird turns that wouldn't make any sense to you, some of 'em off-road. Can't promise we can get you there in one piece."

"Why go back and forth?" Hughes said, though he was pretty sure he knew the answer.

"Only effective way to scavenge for supplies is if we're on the move," Lucas said.

"And like I said," Roy said, "we like being on the road. Anyway, we take you to Atlanta, what do we get in return?"

"In return?" Hughes said.

Annie twisted up her face.

Roy shook his head. "You misunderstand me, ma'am."

Annie relaxed a little, but only a little.

"If he's immune," Roy said and gestured toward Parker, again with his thumb like a hitchhiker, "we want immunity too."

"It will only work," Annie said, "if we have the same blood type."

Roy made a grunting sound. "Why's that?"

"Your body will have an allergic reaction," Kyle said, "if you don't."

"How many blood types are there?" Roy said.

"Eight," Annie said.

Roy went stone-faced.

"You don't know yours," Hughes said, "do you?"

"I know mine," Lucas said. "Type A positive."

"Same as mine," Annie said.

"Really?" Lucas said, beaming.

Annie nodded. "Really. Kyle, we still have that needle kit in the truck?"

Kyle nodded.

"Kyle can draw my blood," Annie said, "and inject it into your arm. It'll hurt because he's not a professional, but he's done it before and it works."

"What about me?" Roy said.

"If you don't know your blood type, it's a shit idea," Hughes said.

Roy put his hands on his hips and turned to look out the window. "How can we figure out what it is?"

"We can't," Hughes said. "But the doctors in Atlanta can. If you take us."

Roy looked at Hughes again, his face tightening. "And if we don't have the same blood type?"

"Then you'd better hope they can develop a cure after studying Annie," Hughes said.

Roy started pacing back and forth. He would say yes. Hughes knew it. Anyone would. There was no good reason for even an apocalypse nut like Roy to say no. Still, the fact that he hesitated told Hughes everything he needed to know about the man's character.

"Come on, man," Lucas said. "It's totally worth it."

Any halfway decent person would agree to help Annie, not because there was anything in it for them, necessarily, but because she might save everyone. These two didn't give a flying fork about anyone else.

"There's one thing you're forgetting," Roy said.

"What's that?" Hughes said.

"They walled off Atlanta," Roy said.

"They'll let her in," Hughes said, "when they find out she's immune. We'll yell through a bullhorn if we have to."

"Where are we going to find a bullhorn?" Lucas said.

"We'll figure it out!" Hughes said. "You in or you out?"

Roy took a deep breath and looked hard at Lucas for a long moment, then nodded. Lucas nodded back.

"We're in," Roy said. "You can follow us in your vehicle."

Hughes almost said thanks but stopped himself. He nodded instead. "You need to do anything here before we head out?"

Roy shook his head. "Long as the creek don't rise, trip should take us four days. Normally we could do it in two, but we can't go there straight, and we can't go at night."

"Understood," Hughes said. "And I need to make one thing clear. I'm only going to say this once, and I wish I didn't have to say it at all. I'll even apologize in advance for saying it."

"I know what you're going to say," Roy said. Hughes imagined he did. "But go ahead and say it, so the air between us is clear."

"You raise a finger against any of us," Hughes said, "and I'll kill you both. I'll shoot you first and then beat you to death."

Roy swallowed and nodded.

"Kyle," Hughes said. "Go get the blood draw kit out of the truck."

∼

KYLE DREW a full syringe of blood from Annie's arm and plunged it into Lucas's triceps. Lucas did not flinch and did not appear to be grateful. He just sat through the procedure as though it was nothing. Annie considered saying *you're welcome* unprompted but decided against it.

Lucas did, however, give her something in exchange—the set of lockpicks—on their way out of the diner. "You never know," he said as he handed her the black leather pouch. "Might come in handy someday."

Annie doubted it, but she took the set anyway. She resisted the reflexive urge to say thanks and followed Hughes outside to the truck.

She sulked in the Suburban, in her usual place in the back behind Hughes, as Roy climbed into the RV and started the engine. Her arm ached where Kyle had drawn her blood. Lucas was immune now, too, thanks to her. She'd feel better about that if she could convince herself that the world was a better place with him in it.

Hughes followed Roy onto the road. Annie thought about rolling down the window on her side and dropping Lucas's lockpicks but tossed them at her feet on the floor instead.

"You okay?" Parker said. He was in his usual spot in the front passenger seat.

"Good as I'm going to be," Annie said, which she supposed was the truth. She wasn't okay, though. Not in this world, not anymore, and especially not on a road trip with Roy.

They would head south now, toward warmer weather, greener trees and grass, and more danger where the infected were less likely to freeze to death. She wished the Suburban were outfitted with a plow on the front and spikes on the sides.

She took a last look at Riverton, Iowa, as they drove through it for a second and final time, past the plain white houses, a now-decrepit Max's Mart with gas pumps in front, an appliance repair shop, and a brick house with a forlorn For Sale sign pounded into the dead-looking lawn.

∽

Parker paid close attention to the route they took out of Riverton. It started with a left turn, northward and away from the Missouri border, up and down Iowa's rolling hills, past soggy fields dotted with empty farmhouses and grain silos, all the way to the outskirts of Council Bluffs across the river from Omaha.

"How far north are we going?" Kyle said from the back seat.

Hughes shook his head. "They're retracing their steps. Not going to be any kind of a logical path, but that's why we need them."

They eventually turned right, just before Interstate 80, and soon saw mileage signs to Des Moines.

Parker understood why Roy and Lucas spooked Annie. He'd be wary of them too if he were a woman, but they bothered Parker for a different reason. Roy's creepy-ass philosophy about the universe killing itself was dark even for Parker. Even when he was at his worst back in Wyoming, when he feared the virus had permanently rewired his brain, it hadn't occurred to him that the entire *universe* was turning on itself. What must that kind of worldview do to a person's sense of morality? Nothing good.

Parker's own sense of morality was limping along now at best. No, he wasn't afraid anymore that he'd snap and sink his teeth into somebody's throat, but his behavior had been generally terrible for a long time and wouldn't get better if he refused to admit it. He had to get it together, partly because he was sick of wallowing in self-loathing, but mostly so that his friends wouldn't abandon him if they ever finished this mission. He didn't deserve Hughes, didn't deserve Kyle, and especially didn't deserve Annie, but they were all he had anymore.

The Suburban slowed and brought Parker's attention back to his surroundings. Roy's RV had its turn signal on, indicating a right onto a gravel road leading up a gentle rise between two fields to a stately farmhouse amid a cluster of bare trees.

"We're turning?" Annie said, an edge in her voice. "In the middle of nowhere?"

Parker pictured it now. Roy leading them to an armed camp, a sex-starved militia surrounding the Suburban, taking Annie by force, and murdering everyone else.

"We could be going around something," Hughes said. "Something they know is up ahead."

The RV turned onto the gravel road, and Hughes followed.

"We see anybody else up there," Parker said, "and we hightail it."

"Of course," Hughes said. "Watch the trees."

Parker did, but he saw only the house, a traditional red barn, a John Deere tractor, and a rusted blue pickup truck. Parker realized he was holding his breath.

The road ended at the barn, and Roy continued driving on the grass behind it. Parker saw faint tire tracks there. Someone had been through recently.

"The fuck are we doing?" Parker said. He powered down his

window and held his Glock two-handed in front of him and ready to fire.

They drove past the barn and still saw nobody on foot. After another hundred feet or so, they came to a wire fence. A twenty-foot-wide section had been flattened down. Faint tire tracks in the grass continued beyond it.

Hughes followed Roy over the fence.

A few hundred feet later, another farmhouse appeared.

Parker sat forward in his seat again and scanned for anything out of the ordinary in every direction. Again, he saw nothing but a house, and beyond it, another paved road.

"Shortcut," Kyle said.

"Work-around," Hughes said.

Tension unspooled from Parker's body.

"Well," Hughes said. "They seem to know what they're doing."

"You say that like it's a good thing," Annie said from the back.

∼

They camped that night on the outskirts of the small city of Burlington, Iowa, in the parking lot of a Sinclair gas station, a chain Kyle had never heard of before with a green brontosaurus as part of its logo. He found the sign mildly amusing, as oil and gasoline were supposedly made from dead dinosaurs.

Contact with Lucas and Roy was blessedly minimal. Just a heads-up from Roy that they were heading south tomorrow and that with a little luck they'd make it as far as Mark Twain National Forest down in Missouri and into Arkansas the following day. He did not say good night before climbing back inside the RV and closing it up for the evening.

"I'll take first watch," Kyle said. Figured he might as well since he wasn't tired and would just sit awake in his seat for the first couple of hours anyway. Besides, first watch and last watch were better than second or third. At the price of staying up late or getting up early, he could sleep uninterrupted.

Even so, he found staying awake challenging after full dark. Nights were far longer in winter than the eight hours of sleep a person needed, and the complete lack of artificial light could make alertness elusive. Two hours after sunset, though, the moon rose and lit up Roy's RV clearly enough to put it under easy surveillance.

Staring at the RV like it was a sleeping dragon that might rear up at any moment was hardly necessary, so Kyle spent a long time looking at Annie instead. She was right next to him in the back, her head resting against the window on her side, her faced bathed in moonlight. She was so beautiful, so close, and Kyle sensed she might be more open to him now than she had been before. She'd avoided him for a while—didn't want to talk to him and at times would not even look at him after things went south between him and Parker—but she got past it when Kyle and Parker got past it.

When it was time to shake Hughes awake for his shift, Kyle wished so hard that he could reach over and shake Annie instead that it hurt.

~

PARKER JERKED awake in the passenger seat to the sound of an incoming vehicle.

His mind was fogged by sleep inertia, and the dry air needled his eyes, but he managed to find the Glock at his feet without any trouble. Hughes snored in the driver's seat, but Kyle and Annie were already awake in the back.

"Hey," Parker said and shoved Hughes in the shoulder. "Somebody's coming."

Hughes blinked himself awake and squinted at the RV parked in front of them.

"Somebody on the road. We need to get down."

Parker turned in his seat and looked out the back window. A stand of trees blocked his line of sight to most of the road. Whoever was coming was still a healthy distance away, but sound carried far in a world gone quiet.

He and the others crouched down. As long as Lucas or Roy didn't bumble outside, whoever was coming wouldn't see anything. The RV and the Suburban would appear as just two more abandoned vehicles out of literally millions.

The approaching sound drew closer, and Parker could tell now that there were two vehicles, not one, and they sounded like SUVs or trucks. They slowed and then stopped in the road, barely fifty feet away.

Parker stared at his feet. Shit, he thought. If whoever was in those trucks got out and looked around, things could get ugly.

One of the truck doors opened. Parker did not hear it close. He just heard the engines rumbling in the street. He thought he heard a boot crunching road grit.

"What do we do?" Annie whispered from the back seat.

"Don't move," Hughes said quietly. "Don't even breathe."

Parker had no idea who was out there, yet he was afraid of them. Afraid of them for stopping. Afraid of them for getting out. Afraid of them for existing. He imagined them first as rough men in their forties with jailhouse tats on their arms and bats in their hands. Then he pictured them as twenty-something wildlings, roving around on joyrides during the day and drinking themselves stupid at night. He wasn't sure which group in his mind was more dangerous.

No matter. He was entirely wrong about who was out there.

"Is that them?" A woman's voice, with a hint of anger and impatience.

"Yeah." Another woman's voice, louder and closer. She must have been the one who'd stepped out of the truck.

Then a barrage of semiautomatic rifle fire shattered the morning. Parker heard what sounded like baseballs punch through the side of Roy's RV.

"God!" Annie shouted from the floor of the back seat as a hole the size of a grapefruit blew out the side window over her head and exited the window over Kyle's. Another round exploded through the door next to Parker's face and embedded itself somewhere below the dashboard. A third ripped through the passenger-side door in the back and went God-only-knew where. Several hit the gas station and at least one smacked into a fuel pump.

Parker held his head in his hands and braced himself for an impact that never came. All was quiet.

"Annie?" Hughes whispered.

"I'm okay," Annie said in a low voice. "I think."

"Me too," Kyle said.

Parker heard Kyle rustling around back there, perhaps patting himself down for holes.

Then the truck door slammed shut, and both vehicles hauled ass toward Burlington.

"Fuck me," Parker said and sucked in air as if surfacing from deep in the ocean.

Annie and Kyle sat up in back.

"Stay down!" Hughes said.

"They're gone," Kyle said.

Parker sat up. His head swam with dizziness, and he thought for a moment that he might pass out. He patted his chest, his abdomen, and even his neck. He didn't have any holes in him. "Everybody okay?"

Hughes sat up. "Yeah. At least we are."

Parker couldn't believe they'd just been shot at by women.

"Who do those bitches think we are?" Parker said.

"No," Hughes said. "Who do they think Lucas and Roy are?"

Roy stepped out of the RV. Hughes powered down the window. "You and Lucas alright?"

Roy nodded, then furtively turned toward the road in the direction the trucks had gone.

"What the fuck, man?" Hughes said.

"Don't ask me," Roy said, eyes wide.

Hughes stepped out of the vehicle. Parker stayed right where he was.

"What did you do, Roy?" Hughes said and stormed forward.

Roy took a step back and held his palms up in the air. "Hey, man. No idea." He shook his head.

Hughes stopped two feet from Roy, close enough to punch him or worse.

"You've been through here before," Hughes said. That was clear.

"Yesterday," Roy said. "And a month back. We didn't see or hear anybody." He widened his eyes again, as if seeing and hearing nobody in this part of the country was hard for even him to believe. "It was like no one had been here for years. That's why we came back this way."

"So those ladies just randomly shot at us?" Hughes said.

"The fuck should I know?" Roy said.

"They shot at your RV," Hughes said.

"They shot at your truck," Roy said.

Hughes stared hard at Roy. Stared holes through him. He thought about blasting the sonofabitch to pieces right there in the parking lot with the pump-action Persuader. It wouldn't do any good. Wouldn't get Annie to Atlanta any faster. Would fuck up their mission more than just about anything else he could do short of killing Annie herself.

"Must have seen us from a distance," Roy said. "Lucas and I drove through here yesterday, then again today. *Nobody* around here is friendly."

Perhaps, Hughes thought. America's heartland wasn't as hospitable as it used to be. That was for goddammed sure. But women shooting at strangers just for existing? Really? Hughes doubted that's what had happened. He didn't believe Roy for a minute, but they had to get back on the road. They could dump the bastard on the outskirts of Atlanta, which they should be able reach in a couple of days.

"Alright," Hughes said and squinted. "Let's just get out of here."

"Okay then," Roy said, sounding more relieved than he should.

∾

ANNIE DIDN'T BELIEVE Roy and didn't waste half a second before saying so once they got back on the road.

"I don't believe him either," Hughes said.

"You think it was some kind of revenge hit?" Parker said.

"Undoubtedly," Annie said.

"What for?" Parker said.

"You really have to ask?" Annie said.

"You think Lucas and Roy raped those women?" Parker said.

Of course they did. "Why shoot at them otherwise?"

"Lucas and Roy could have stolen something," Parker said. "Looted the wrong house or bunker."

"They're rapists," Annie said.

"You can't possibly know that," Parker said.

"I know it," Annie said.

"I'm sorry," Parker said, "but you don't. They're creepy for sure, but if they're rapists, why are those women still even alive?"

"Most rapists aren't murderers," Annie said.

"Maybe they're neither," Parker said.

"Parker has a point," Hughes said.

Annie felt herself get red in the face.

"I don't trust them any more than you do, Annie," Hughes said, "but we don't know what's going on. None of this would hold up in court."

Annie crossed her arms over her chest. "There aren't courts anymore."

"You know what I mean," Hughes said.

"No, actually I don't," Annie said.

Hughes huffed. "Look. They're creepy. I get it. I agree. And I don't trust them for shit. But we don't have to."

"We don't *have* to?" Annie said.

"I trust that they know where they're going, more or less, and that's enough," Hughes said. "We will never sleep in a room with them. We will never give them our weapons. We will never take all our eyes off them, not for five seconds."

"That's not good enough," Annie said.

"Okay, Annie," Hughes said. "What do you want to *do* then? Ditch 'em? Shoot 'em? Steal their RV and leave them for dead?"

Annie said nothing.

"Can I take that as a no?" Hughes said.

Annie had nothing to say.

"They try anything," Hughes said, "and they're dead. Both of them. That's a promise."

Annie nodded, but she still wouldn't say anything.

PART II
SOMETHING ELSE IS GOING ON

5

Traveling south through Missouri was almost straightforward. They zigged and zagged roughly parallel to the Mississippi River without ever actually driving alongside or even seeing it, bypassing the small and medium-sized cities that formed a necklace of pearls along the riverbank: Burlington and Keokuk in Iowa, then Hannibal, St. Louis, and Cape Girardeau in Missouri.

Hughes sulked at the wheel with his eyes and his mind on Lucas and Roy in their RV at all times. Cold air whistled through the bullet holes and flapped the plastic sheeting they'd taped over the busted window.

As promised, they made it to the Ozark highlands and Missouri's Mark Twain National Forest, a blend of leafless oaks and southern conifers across gentle rolling mountains too far south and far too smooth to have ever seen the underside of a glacier. Even now, with the winter sun low in the sky, the air felt warmer and damper than Iowa's, almost like Seattle's in April. Southern Missouri seemed the kind of place where a person could live outside for much of the year without too much trouble, which also meant encounters with the infected were more likely.

Roy pulled into an empty campground at the edge of the forest a few miles shy of the city of Poplar Bluffs, a place Hughes had never heard of, but judging by all the road signs he'd seen, must have been the most important place in the area. Hughes saw no reason for the campground to exist. It was not alongside a lake or a river but in a partial clearing in a random part of the forest.

They had their pick of sites. Roy chose one that was exactly like every other, with a green picnic table and a firepit under a canopy of evergreen branches.

Hughes parked the Suburban at the next campsite over and killed the engine. Everybody scrambled out and stretched. The air smelled of hardwood and pine and felt almost, but not quite, warm enough to sleep outside on the ground.

"Y'all holding up okay?" Roy said as he and Lucas stepped out of the RV.

"Fine," Hughes said without making eye contact. He twisted at the waist, first to the left and then to the right, to ease the tension in his lower back.

"Warmer here," Parker said.

"Gonna be even warmer tomorrow," Roy said, "when we get to Arkansas."

"Where are we, exactly?" Kyle said.

"Missouri," Roy said.

"I mean," Kyle said, "is this the Midwest or the South?" A bird flitted from one tree to another above Hughes's head.

"Both," Roy said. "Neither. This is the Ozarks."

Hughes thought the Ozarks looked more like large hills than mountains.

"Greater Appalachia," Roy said. He pronounced *Appalachia* so that that last two syllables sounded like *atcha* rather than *aitcha*. "More hillbillies than hayseeds."

At least there used to be, Hughes thought, not that it mattered. Whatever regional cultures had once existed were gone and would stay gone, even if the human race someday recovered. Any reemerging pockets of civilization would be defined far more by surviving a near-extinction event than whatever came before.

"Why don't you folks come on over and drink some beers?" Roy said. "We got lawn chairs."

"I'll pass," Annie said and gazed off into the trees.

"Come on now," Roy said. "Lucas, go fetch the lawn chairs."

Roy sat on a small boulder the size of a tree stump next to the fire pit.

Lucas went back inside the RV.

"You stayed here before?" Hughes said to Roy.

"Coupla times," Roy said.

"Any trouble?" Hughes said.

"Wouldn't be back if there was trouble," Roy said.

Hughes wasn't sure he believed that. Not after Iowa.

Lucas returned with two fold-out camping chairs.

Roy waved his arm in a summoning motion. "Come on and have a beer. Won't be full dark for another hour."

Hughes supposed that was true. They were farther south now than they had been at any point on their journey, and the sun would set later.

He didn't want to have a beer with these people but couldn't think of a polite reason not to. They'd be traveling together for at least another couple of days, and those couple of days wouldn't be any easier if Hughes and the others were standoffish. So he shrugged.

Annie shot him a look.

Lucas fetched a six-pack of longnecks and two more chairs from the RV and placed them in a semicircle around the firepit.

Roy stayed put on his boulder, but Lucas took one of the chairs. Hughes took a chair next to him. First Parker joined them, then Kyle, and finally Annie. She sat stiffly with her ankle over her knee and her hands in her lap.

Hughes took a longneck from the six-pack, twisted the cap off with his fingers, and passed the remaining beers to Parker.

"You still think the universe is committing suicide?" Kyle said.

Roy nodded. "Why wouldn't I?"

"How does Annie fit into that theory?" Kyle said.

"Not sure I follow," Roy said.

"She's immune," Kyle said. "So is Parker. Lucas now too. Three out of six of us are immune. That doesn't change anything for you?"

Lucas rubbed the back of his neck.

Roy narrowed his eyes. "I don't know that she's really immune."

"I showed you the scar on my back," Annie said.

"Anyone could have bit you," Roy said. "I didn't see it happen. I didn't see you recover."

Hughes wondered if Roy was accusing Annie of lying or if nothing was real in the world unless Roy had seen it himself. If a tree fell in the woods and Roy wasn't there to hear it, did it make a sound?

"So, what are we doing then?" Kyle said.

"I'm taking you to Atlanta," Roy said. "Case I'm wrong."

"You think this is some kind of big show?" Hughes said.

"The hell do I know?" Roy said.

"Why would we lie?" Hughes said.

Roy shrugged.

"Why else would we be driving from Seattle to Atlanta?" Hughes said. "You think that makes any kind of sense otherwise? We'd be living in tents on the roof of a Walmart two thousand miles from here if she wasn't immune."

Roy sized up Hughes as if the two men had never seen each other before. He and Lucas had been prowling all over the country, and they weren't entirely honest about why. It made sense then that he didn't entirely believe Annie's story. It was a classic case of projection. Pickpockets kept their cell phones and wallets close, and liars didn't trust other people.

"Not saying I don't believe you," Roy said. "Figure there's a halfway decent chance you're telling the truth."

"Terrific," Kyle said.

Nobody said anything for a couple of moments. Then Roy leaned forward on his boulder. "You ever try to kill yourself?"

"No," Kyle said.

"Any of you?" Roy said.

Headshakes all around.

"Neither have I," Roy said and sat up straight again. "You ever wonder what a man who throws himself off a building thinks when he's halfway down? Probably not *so far, so good*. Know what I'm saying?"

Nobody answered.

Hughes swallowed hard. His wife had been morbidly depressed for years and had killed herself after the outbreak. Sometimes he understood. The end of all things was finally too much for her, even though they had a child together. Most of the time, though, he could not understand. For years she'd made no effort whatsoever to fight the disease that poisoned her mind. She surrendered to it completely, as if she'd forgotten that she'd ever been happy and therefore could be again, as if cognitive therapy worked for other people but, for some reason that she never even tried to explain, would not work for her. She was lost in a dark maze, and she gave up trying to find the way out. Hughes had tried to lead her out plenty of times, but she would not take his hand.

"You want to die, Roy?" Hughes said.

"Not today," Roy said. "But I've seen enough to know I don't want to spend an eternity here."

"Why are you taking us to Atlanta then?" Kyle said.

"Flinch response," Roy said.

"Flinch response?" Parker said.

"That *oh shit* feeling a jumper gets when he's halfway to the ground from the top of his skyscraper."

∽

THEY MADE it as far as Jonesboro. A smallish city in northeastern Arkansas and home to Arkansas State University. Twenty miles southwest of the Missouri Bootheel. Incorporated in 1859, humid subtropical climate, population just shy of eighty thousand before the global shitstorm wiped almost everyone out.

Plan was to keep going east into Tennessee, less than an hour away. If they hadn't needed gas, they wouldn't have stopped. And if they hadn't stopped, more of them would have survived.

6

Despite their vast differences in culture, history, and politics, northern Arkansas looked exactly the same as southern Iowa—wide and flat, open fields studded with farmhouses, deciduous trees shorn of leaves for the season, and a foreboding sky threatening a grainy landscape with rain. If it weren't for a sign saying WELCOME TO ARKANSAS, Hughes would have had no idea they'd put Missouri behind them and officially entered what was once considered the South.

He had never been to Arkansas, nor anywhere else in that part of the country, and he wasn't sure what to make of the fact that it appeared—so far anyway—indistinguishable from up north. He hadn't expected banjos to start playing all of a sudden, but he somehow expected . . . something . . . though he couldn't rationally think of what that might be.

Hughes followed Roy's RV by a comfortable two hundred feet. It was eleven o'clock in the morning, and they'd already been on the road for four hours. Farmhouses gave way to homes set back among bare broadleaf trees without much land behind them, suggesting that Hughes and his crew were leaving agricultural country and heading into a small city or town. After passing a trailer park, Roy indicated a turn to the left with his signal.

Hughes slowed the Suburban and flipped his own signal on out of habit. There was no one behind him. There probably wouldn't be another vehicle behind him ever again, but he still used his turn signal.

Roy made a left into a dirt lot surrounded by ragged chain-link fencing and littered with transportation detritus from various collapsed industries—a cement truck, two rusted backhoes, and a half dozen semi truck cabs without trailers attached. Immediately south of the truck yard was a medium-sized warehouse of some kind, also ringed by chain-link fencing, with a paved lot around it.

"Kyle," Hughes said. "Where are we?"

"Just north of Jonesboro," Kyle said from the back seat, hovering over his map.

"North of Jonesboro, middle of nowhere, what's the difference?" Parker said as Hughes pulled the Suburban into the lot. "The hell are we doing here anyway?"

"Roy probably needs gas again," Hughes said and glanced at the dashboard. The Suburban still had half a tank. He didn't know how big the RV's tank was. Had to be huge, easily three times the capacity of a regular car's, but most RVs got less than eight miles to the gallon going downhill on a freeway.

Hughes killed the engine and climbed out with his pump-action Persuader in one hand and a crowbar in the other. The others stepped too, each with a pistol and a hand weapon—a hammer for Parker, crowbars for Kyle and Annie.

Roy got out of his RV with a hunting rifle. Hughes thought it might be a Tikka T3 Lite, but he couldn't be sure. Lucas appeared with a far more formidable weapon that Hughes recognized instantly —a Bushmaster M4 Type Carbine. Not the civilian model either. This one was military grade, a true weapon of war, illegal in all fifty states, with three-round burst and automatic fire capability. It took .233 NATO rounds and came with a six-position stock and a flash suppressor out of the box.

Hughes hoped he'd never get into a fight with Lucas while the man had that thing anywhere near him. Lucas leered at Annie and chuckled to himself at the look of disgust on her face. Scrapping with him at some point did not seem a remote possibility.

"Out of gas already?" Hughes said to Roy.

"Quarter tank," Roy said. "Don't want to go any farther with less than half. Shit's about to get interesting."

Hughes flicked his shotgun's safety into the *fire* position. Parker retrieved the siphon hose from the back of the Suburban. Lucas ran his own hose from one of the semi truck cabs into the RV as Parker sucked gas out of another into the Suburban.

Hughes noticed that neither Roy nor Lucas carried hand weapons. "Don't you guys have crowbars or something else quiet?"

"Roy has a sword," Lucas said. Then he shrugged. "Won't be here long."

"More bandits in these parts than infected," Roy said.

"Get your sword," Hughes said. "And a hammer or a knife or whatever else you've got."

"We've made more than enough noise already," Roy said, "just pulling in here and parking."

"Not half as much as we'll make if Lucas fires that Bushmaster," Hughes said.

Roy and Lucas ignored him. Hughes made a face. Lucas saw it but didn't react.

While Parker and Lucas siphoned fuel, the others stood guard at the four points of a circle, with Hughes facing the road, Annie facing the warehouse next door, Roy watching the trees to the north, and Kyle keeping watch toward a denser thicket of trees beyond the fence line. Hughes did not like that fence. It offered only the illusion of protection. He saw three ripped or cut gaps that anything smaller than a giraffe could barge right on through.

"Guys," Kyle whispered. "I hear something."

Hughes held his breath. He heard nothing but gasoline pissing out the hoses into the gas tanks.

Then he heard Roy's boots in the dirt behind him, heading

toward Kyle at the fence line, and he didn't like it, didn't like Roy doing anything at all that he couldn't see. Hughes had to keep his eyes on his sector across the road, but he briefly checked his six and saw Roy next to Kyle, his eyes off his own sector and looking intently through the fence into the trees.

"There," Kyle whispered. "You hear that?"

Hughes still didn't hear anything.

"I don't think so," Roy said in a normal tone of voice.

Hughes shushed him.

Then he heard it. Someone—or something—moving at a casual pace in the trees behind the truck yard.

"Lucas!" Hughes whispered as loud as he could. Lucas was still siphoning fuel into the RV. "Pull out that hose and get a hand weapon."

"I've got a Bushmaster, man," Lucas said, not even trying to be quiet.

The movement in the trees sounder faster now, not urgent but more deliberate than before.

Time to move.

"Everybody out of sight," Hughes whispered and dashed toward the Suburban. Annie and Parker joined him as Kyle and Roy headed toward the RV.

Too late.

A warlike scream belted out from the trees.

"I got this," Lucas said and raised his rifle toward the foliage.

"Hand weapons!" Hughes shouted.

He heard a surge of movement in the bush followed by another scream.

Then he saw them. First two infected, then three, two of them male, one of them female, all dressed in rotting clothes and covered in blood spatter and gore. They hadn't turned recently. They'd been out there for some time.

Lucas, not even trying to stay out of sight, stepped toward a gap in the fence with his rifle.

"No!" Hughes shouted. No point whispering now.

"You got this?" Lucas said with a lopsided grin. "You sure?"

"Out of my way," Hughes said and pushed past him toward the gap, shotgun and crowbar in hand.

Parker, Annie, and Kyle rushed to his side.

"Annie," Hughes said and waved her away with the crowbar. "Stay back." He handed her the shotgun. "And take this." He needed his hands free.

Annie took the shotgun and backed up toward the Suburban, away from the fence and away from Lucas and Roy.

Hughes saw five infected now, rushing through the trees toward the gap in the fencing.

"Spread out!" Hughes said.

Parker backed up. Hughes and Kyle converged on the gap in the fence, Hughes to the left and Kyle to the right, as the five infected were about to funnel through it.

Parker smashed his hammer into the side of the first infected's head with a ferocious scythe. Hughes swung his crowbar into the face of the second. Kyle swiped at the third and broke its arm. It went down screaming, and Kyle split open the top of its head.

The remaining two rushed toward Parker like juggernauts.

Parker hammered the first in the temple, then backhanded the second in the shoulder.

Six or seven more stampeded through the trees toward the fencing.

Lucas and Roy might as well have been standing there with their dicks in their hands for all the good they were doing. "Hand weapons!" Hughes bellowed at them. "Now!"

Hughes focused on the hostiles coming at them and in a quick backward glance saw Roy amble inside the RV. Annie stayed back near the Suburban. She had Hughes's shotgun but couldn't use it without spraying everybody with buckshot.

Roy returned from the RV with an axe in one hand and—Jesus—a gently curved sword matted with dried gore in the other. He kept the sword for himself and handed the axe over to Lucas.

The infected surged through the fence. Hughes, Parker, and Kyle felled them one after the other, with blood, sinew, and tissue spattering their clothes and their faces.

"Roy!" Hughes shouted. "Lucas!"

Hughes was tiring fast. Adrenaline be damned, the average human being couldn't swing a weapon in a life-or-death struggle for more than a minute or two. If Lucas and Roy didn't haul ass to the fence, Hughes and his friends would have to switch to their firearms.

Roy strode over to the fence with his sword.

Lucas stepped away from the fight toward the road. "I'll cover the rear!"

Fucker was useless. Lucas and Parker should take point in these fights. They were *both* immune now, thanks to Annie. She was the only one who should hang back. She could handle herself well enough and survive a bite, but she was the most precious person alive, and no one was immune to bleeding to death.

The infected were thinning at least. Just a handful remained. Hughes and Parker took care of most of them.

Roy dropped just one, decapitating it with a ferocious swing of his sword, spinning his entire body halfway around in the process until he faced Lucas and the road. He squinted and dropped his mouth open slightly. He saw something.

Hughes turned around and saw it. An infected converging on Lucas from behind, from the road, somehow making almost no sound.

"Look out!" Hughes shouted.

Too late.

The infected tackled Lucas and sank his teeth into his neck.

Lucas went down screaming.

Hughes rushed forward, kicked the diseased thing off Lucas, and broke its neck with a furious stomp of his boot.

One last infected made it through the fence. Parker dispatched it, and the truck yard went quiet.

Roy approached Lucas as his friend squirmed on the ground with his hand over the wound on his neck. "Well," he said.

"You motherfucker," Hughes said.

"We got a first-aid kit," Roy said and jerked his thumb toward his RV.

"Go get it!" Hughes said.

Roy ambled toward his vehicle.

Hughes was covered in blood. Everybody but Roy was covered in blood. And there were infected bodies all over the place, almost two dozen of them. The air smelled of sweat, copper pennies, and shit.

Parker stood next to Hughes and gasped for air.

"He did that on purpose," Hughes said in a low voice.

"Did what on purpose?" Annie said.

Hughes hadn't heard her come up behind and didn't mean for her to hear that. "He let Lucas get bit."

Lucas kicked the ground hard with the flat of his feet, back and forth, one after the other, and winced through the pain, seemingly trying as hard as he could not to yell out.

They had to patch him up and move him. Right now. Into one of the warehouses with some rope and something to tie him to.

"Kyle!" Hughes said. "Get the duct tape and rope out of the truck!"

"Why would Roy do that?" Parker said, astonishment in his voice.

"He's testing us," Annie said. "Isn't he? He wants to know if Lucas is really immune. If I'm really immune, then Lucas is too, and if Lucas isn't, then I'm not."

"Son of a bitch," Parker said.

Lucas had a nasty wound in his neck that bled down into his shirt, but it probably wouldn't be fatal. The bite missed the jugular. Lucas was going to turn, though, possibly within minutes.

Roy jogged back from the RV with a red pouch in his hand. "Got it."

Parker snatched the first-aid kit out of his hands as Kyle returned from the Suburban with a long length of rope.

"What's the rope for?" Roy said.

"You idiot," Hughes said.

"What?" Roy said.

"I saw what you did," Hughes said.

Roy said nothing.

"He's going to turn," Hughes said.

"He turns," Roy said, an edge in his voice, "we aren't going to Atlanta."

Hughes closed his eyes and took a deep breath. This was his fault. In his aversion to wasting any more time talking to Roy than he had to, he'd neglected to fully explain what immunity meant in this world. Parker had spent *three days* as one of those things before returning—sort of—to normal. Annie herself turned too before coming back in a temporary state of amnesia. He'd found her wandering around the ruined Pacific Northwest, forgetting not only that she'd been infected but that the world had ended at all. Parker suffered post-traumatic stress for weeks after he came back. God only knew how fucked up Lucas would be when he came out of it.

"Lucas is going to turn before he gets better," Hughes told Roy. "He'll recover, but he's going to be infected for *days*."

Roy said nothing.

"We need to move him," Parker said softly.

"Into that warehouse," Hughes said. "Roy, help us carry him."

"Just drag him," Roy said.

"Carry him!" Hughes said. "Kyle, shoot anything you see that isn't us."

Hughes and Roy each grabbed one of Lucas's arms, Kyle and Annie took one of Lucas's legs, and they hoisted him off the ground. Blood pulsed gently from the wound in his neck.

"He's going to bleed out," Roy said and grunted as they hauled him toward the warehouse.

"You'd better hope not," Hughes said. "We'll clean him and bandage him properly ... after we tie him up."

The warehouse was an industrial behemoth, effectively three stories high, fronted by a loading dock with a metal roll gate, accessible on foot by only a single visible door and topped with an exterior ladder leading up to the roof. Hughes liked the idea of spending three days on top of the building, but they didn't have time to haul Lucas up there, and he wasn't sure there'd be anything suitable to tie him to anyway. Besides, the ladder didn't reach ground level. The bottom dangled twelve feet up and would only slide down if somebody released some mechanism that Hughes couldn't see.

The loading dock was closed and probably locked, but the solitary door leading into the warehouse had been busted open already. Looters must have kicked it in. That door wouldn't lock or even close properly. It would have to be barricaded.

When they hauled Lucas inside, though, Hughes saw at once that there was nothing in there worth stealing. The place was a textile warehouse. Rolled carpets the size of living room couches covered the first half acre of the warehouse floor. Shelves a dozen feet high stocked with smaller rolled carpets took up the back half.

There was a mezzanine level at the far end with doors leading into a couple of offices.

"Take him upstairs!" Hughes said, hoping they could find a desk or something to tie Lucas to so they wouldn't have to hog-tie him on the floor.

Lucas's eyes rolled back in his head. The bleeding from the wound on his neck was slowing down now, though. He'd be okay. Probably.

They carried him past the giant rolls of carpets on the floor, through the rows of shelves in the back, and up a flight of metal stairs into one of the offices, a spare and utilitarian place, dark and windowless, with a battered wooden desk, a high-backed office chair, and a set of mismatched filing cabinets.

"Sorry, man," Parker said as they dumped Lucas into the chair.

Lucas slouched to the side, his mouth open.

Kyle handed Parker the duct tape and rope.

"We can't tie him to that," Annie said.

Hughes sighed. The chair had wheels on its feet. Lucas would thrash back and forth and bounce himself off the walls in there like a damn bumper car.

"Kyle," Hughes said. "See if there's a chair in the other office."

Kyle headed out.

Parker tore off a strip of duct tape and stretched it across Lucas's mouth.

"Make sure he can breathe," Hughes said.

Parker held his hand in front of Lucas's nose. "He's breathing."

Roy just stood there. "What should I do?"

"You can start by fucking yourself," Hughes said. "When you're finished with that, go downstairs and move some carpets in front of that door so nothing else can get in."

Roy ignored the insult and went downstairs.

Lucas slumped over one of the chair's arms, and his cell phone fell out of his jacket. Hughes picked it up and turned it on. It opened right up without a passcode or biometric ID. Not much point worrying about a stolen phone anymore, he supposed, except that he was now stealing it. He turned it off to conserve the battery and placed it in his pocket.

Kyle returned. "No chairs without wheels."

"Fine," Hughes said and looked around. "Who has the hammer?"

Parker had it and handed it over. Hughes used it to smash the wheels off the chair's feet. "Now tie him."

"I got it, I got it," Parker said, seemingly impatient with Hughes barking obvious orders.

Parker uncoiled the rope and lashed Lucas's ankles to the now disabled chair feet, his hands to the armrests, and his torso to the chair back. He wasn't going anywhere. He wouldn't be the least bit comfortable, but so what?

Annie produced a piece of gauze from the first-aid kit, wiped Lucas's neck clean, then affixed a fresh piece over the wound with medical tape.

Hughes heard footsteps on the metal stairway. Roy was coming back up. "Can't move the carpets in front of the door by myself," he said, out of breath.

"I'll help," Kyle said. "Come on."

Hughes groaned to himself and wished the warehouse were stocked with machine parts instead of carpets. Would be a whole lot easier to barricade the door.

"We're not going to be able to lock him in here," Parker said, examining the knob on the door.

"Don't need to lock it," Hughes said. "He won't be able to open it."

"He'll make a hell of a racket, though," Parker said.

Hughes opened his eyes wide and nodded. Lucas would indeed make a terrible racket. Hughes would never forget the unspeakable sounds Parker had made when the infection turned his own nervous system and mind into a furnace. They hadn't gagged Parker. Didn't strictly need to since they'd been sheltering on a tiny island without any infected on it. They'd have to gag Lucas, though. In a world gone quiet, anyone or any thing immediately outside the warehouse might hear him even with tape over his mouth.

Kyle and Roy came back up the stairs.

"Door's barricaded," Kyle said, catching his breath. "And the loading gate is locked. There's a back door just below us, and that one's locked too."

Hughes nodded.

"Good," Annie said.

"So, now what?" Roy said.

"We wait for your friend here to turn," Hughes said. "Then we wait for him to recover. I strongly advise you to wait outside this room."

7

Annie would rather have been just about anywhere on earth except in that warehouse. The best she could do was move as far from Lucas and the others as possible, all the way to the far side of the building in a corner by herself amid rolls of carpets. Kyle tried to follow, but she waved him off.

Lucas turned moments later. If Hughes hadn't gagged him, his furious cries would have echoed off the walls and the looming ceiling above.

Annie sat on a roll of beige carpet as high as her waist and buried her face in her hands. God, these people. She didn't want to wait for Lucas to recover. She wanted out of there, to leave this place with her friends, to head north into Canada and keep on going until the shattering cold killed all but the Inuit. The infected would leave her alone then, and so would everyone else.

Her friends wanted to save the world. What world? She'd transferred her immunity to that creep up there in the office, and for what? The bastard emphatically didn't deserve it, and now she and her friends were stuck there because a monster who should have been dead wasn't.

She loved Kyle, Parker, and Hughes. The world shined with them in it. But what about everyone else she'd met since Seattle?

There'd been Lane, Bobby, and Roland in Washington who'd taken her and her friends prisoner and stripped them of their weapons. All dead now, and the rest of the world better off.

Then there was Joseph Steele and his goon squad in Wyoming. All dead, and the rest of the world better off. Only one person in a town of thousands, Doc Nash, had redeemed himself, but he was dead too.

And finally, Lucas and Roy, both of them meatheads and probably rapists, and one a deranged idiot who let the other get bit to see what would happen.

She closed her eyes. Were she and her friends any better? Were they *really*? She, Kyle, and Hughes didn't "let" Parker get bit to see what would happen. They arranged it. They planned it. And nobody had told them that he would recover.

Annie would go to Atlanta. And she'd go there with Lucas and Roy. She *wanted* to wrest the sword from Roy's hands and slice off his head with it. She'd be doing the world a favor. No question about it. And she knew, because she believed that, that the person she used to be was gone and was not coming back.

~

Hughes, Parker, and Roy hauled all their supplies from the Suburban and the RV into the warehouse. They couldn't go in and out the front door since it was broken in and barricaded already, so they used the back door, secured with a simple dead bolt, as Kyle stood watch with a pistol in one hand and a crowbar in the other. Annie sulked somewhere by herself.

On the off chance that the main floor might be breached, they brought everything into the second office on the mezzanine level and emptied it onto the desks: canned food, jugs of filtered water, sleeping bags, blankets, pillows, first-aid kits, the set of lockpicks Lucas had given to Annie, a box of medicines including antibiotics and narcotic painkillers, rope, duct tape, a battered toolbox that was heavier than it looked, bottles of beer and cold brew, night vision monocles, a flint firestarter, five cigarette lighters, six camping chairs, two Leatherman multitools, knives, binoculars, a hatchet, eight flashlights, a box full of batteries, two portable solar charging kits, a couple of hammers, six handguns, two hunting rifles, a Bushmaster assault rifle, Hughes's Mossberg pump-action Persuader, a half dozen boxes of ammunition, and a supposedly unbreakable Brooklyn Smasher Cold Steel baseball bat.

Good to go, Hughes thought.

⁓

As Lucas screamed himself raw into tape over his mouth, Parker sat on the floor near the front door of the warehouse, far away from the offices on the mezzanine level, and plugged his ears with his fingers. That thing tied to the chair was not even Lucas any longer, as if his body had been taken over by a demonic spirit determined to explode his body outward from his lungs and his guts.

Parker had been there. Oh, had he been there. Most of the time, he remembered it only faintly, like a dream that half fades into the mists upon awakening. Hearing Lucas wailing and thrashing brought it all back, the malevolent rage of a hungry hungry predator chained by its food, by its prey. Parker could not bear to hear it. He couldn't even bear to share the same cavernous building.

Breathe, he told himself. If he breathed slowly enough, he could slow down his heart and his mind.

He couldn't sit for three days on the floor, though. His back would cry out in agony. So he lay on the concrete and gazed at the high ceiling with his fingers in his ears.

There were skylights up there, embedded in the roof of the warehouse. Bright shafts of afternoon sun slanted in through those portals. He imagined himself floating up and out into the light. Perhaps that's what dying would be like.

Parker felt better on his back, as if he were somehow farther away from Lucas's trauma. He unplugged his fingers from his ears. Lucas's heaving and groaning wasn't actually all that loud, not with his mouth taped. Now that Parker thought about it, he doubted anyone or anything would be able to hear it from outside unless they were standing right below the office windows in back. The sound still disturbed him, but he forced himself to listen to it. He needed exposure therapy. Sound couldn't actually hurt him. It might not even bother him much if he could habituate himself to it, the way people with tinnitus eventually stopped noticing the ringing in their ears even though it was still there. Surely it was what Betty the therapist back in Wyoming would tell him to do. Besides, he couldn't keep his fingers in his ears for three solid days.

He wondered what kind of person Lucas would be when he snapped out of it. Annie had succumbed to temporary amnesia. Parker had suffered panic attacks. Perhaps Lucas wouldn't fully recover, emerging instead as a full-blown homicidal psychopath that Parker and Hughes would have to put down. Anything was possible.

If anything was possible, though, Lucas might forge himself into a better man after recovery. That's what Parker was trying to do, after all. He'd never forget what Hughes had asked him when he resurfaced from his own ordeal. *What kind of man do you want to be?* Parker was too traumatized then to even consider the question, but he knew the answer now. He wanted to *earn* the privilege of being one of the last survivors on earth.

Almost everybody was dead, so why was he, of all people, alive? It was mostly a matter of random chance—he understood that—but at the same time, he couldn't entirely shake the feeling that the universe had a moral center, that terrible things happened for a reason. At the very least, he could make something good follow tragedy that would not have been possible otherwise.

He ought to go upstairs and check on Lucas. Face his own demons. Make sure the bandage on the man's neck hadn't come loose and that Lucas hadn't tipped himself over.

Parker rose from the floor and headed toward the back stairs. He saw that the others were sitting almost in a circle on the floor in the middle of the building with Annie a healthy distance from Roy.

"You okay?" Hughes said to Parker as he approached.

"Heading up to check on Lucas."

Hughes nodded. Kyle tipped his head back.

Annie opened her mouth a little. Parker could read her face. She knew this would be hard for him.

Roy didn't react, didn't seem the least bit interested in how his supposed friend was doing, and didn't betray even a twinge of guilt for putting him there.

Parker felt flushed when he reached the bottom of the stairs. He could hear Lucas's groaning and clamoring as clearly now as if they were together in the same room. Lucas was heaving himself forward and backward. Parker could tell without even looking that the chair Lucas was tied to was, somehow, still upright.

He ascended the stairs, pausing again outside the door. He made fists with his hands and cracked his knuckles with his thumbs, told himself that anxiety was just a feeling, that it would pass, that a welling up of panic wasn't medically dangerous, that he could settle down later, perhaps in his sleep, and talk about it afterward with Annie because she, of all people, would at least understand.

Parker opened the door and saw not Lucas but himself strapped to that chair, the fury of a hundred suns exploding behind pitiless eyes.

∼

PARKER JOINED the group in the center of the warehouse. They sat mostly in a circle on the floor with Annie opposite Roy and outside the circumference, as if she'd rather be somewhere else but didn't want to be by herself. Parker took a spot on the floor next to her and wondered why no one had busted out the camping chairs yet.

"How's Lucas?" Annie said.

Parker knew what she meant. Annie was not asking about Lucas's well-being. Lucas had no well-being. She wanted to know how Parker was doing after getting a look at him.

He answered by opening his eyes wide.

Kyle craned his head back and looked at the ceiling. The sun was lower on the horizon now and no longer slanting in through the skylights. "I'm really liking Arkansas so far."

Roy chuckled. Parker was surprised the man had a sense a humor.

"Wish I could show you folks Fayetteville," Roy said. He paused. "Best warehouses around."

"You know," Parker said to Roy, "he's going to be royally pissed at you when he recovers."

"More pissed than he is now?" Roy said and laughed at his own joke.

"Seriously, man," Parker said. "What are you going to tell him?"

Roy shrugged. "I don't have to tell him anything."

"He knows you let him get bit," Parker said.

"He doesn't know anything," Roy said. "Not right now he doesn't. And he might not even remember our names when he comes out of it. If he comes out of it. Isn't that what y'all said happened to Annie?"

"My memories came back," Annie said, "after a couple of days."

"Lucas didn't see it happen," Roy said. "He won't know if none of you tell him."

Parker doubted that, but he supposed it could be true. Hughes had seen what happened, but Parker hadn't. Kyle or Annie hadn't seen it either, so Lucas also might not have. "We should tell him."

"The hell for?" Roy said.

"Because it's the right thing to do, asshole," Kyle said.

"You people," Roy said. "The right thing to do."

Kyle gave Roy some side-eye.

Parker liked Kyle now, especially with these jackasses around for comparison. Kyle has been a punk when Parker first met him, but he was more of a man now and less of a child. Kyle was, at his core, a decent person and always had been. Parker hadn't seen that at first because it hadn't yet occurred to him that it mattered.

"Roy?" Parker said.

"Yes, sir," Roy said.

"What do you plan to do when all this is over?"

"All what?" Roy said.

"When the doctors find a cure," Parker said.

Roy shrugged. "Hope they'll cure me."

"Then what?"

"Depends."

"On what?"

"Don't know," Roy said.

"What did you do for a living before all this?" Parker said.

"That's a peculiar question."

"How's that?"

"Because you're the first person to ask it."

"How many people have you met since this happened?"

Roy rolled his shoulders. "Dozens maybe."

"And nobody asked you?"

Roy jutted his chin slightly and shook his head.

"We're stuck in this place for days," Parker said. "Might as well be friendly, don't you think?"

Roy didn't respond.

"I built cabinets for a living," Parker said. "Hughes here was a bail bondsman. Annie was a college student. Kyle did something with computers."

Roy said nothing at first, clearly uninterested, but he played along in the end. "I installed home security systems."

Parker wondered if that meant Roy had known, or had access to, the passcodes his customers used to disarm their security systems.

"What did Lucas do?" Hughes said.

"Hell if I know," Roy said. "Didn't know him back then. Never asked him."

"You guys have been wandering around the countryside together for how long?" Parker said. "And you haven't asked him?"

"The person I was is dead," Roy said. "The person Lucas was is dead. The people y'all used to be are dead too."

"I'm still me," Annie said, sounding more defensive than she should.

"Bless your heart, ma'am," Roy said, "but I doubt that."

Annie got a little red in the face. Parker saw anger there and something else too.

"Doesn't matter who Lucas was," Roy said. "Only matters who he is."

Parker shook his head.

"These people," Kyle said, "are the best friends I've ever had." He looked Parker right in the eye when he said that. Parker nodded, slowly and deliberately, and saw out of the corner of his eye that Annie watched it happen.

"We've all lost people," Kyle said. "Hughes lost his wife and child. Annie lost her sister. Parker never heard from his ex-wife again. She's a missing person now, basically. She left him before all this, and he did everything he could to get her back."

Parker's throat ached as he listened to this. His friends didn't know why Holly had left him. He never told them and never would. Holly left him because he hit her. He only hit her once, and he'd *hated* himself for it since. A single act that lasted less than a second permanently changed who he was. Roy's nonsense be damned, not even the end of the world could change that searing fact about Parker.

"I wouldn't be here," Hughes said, "if I hadn't lost my wife and my child."

"That's how y'all define yourselves now?" Roy said. "By what you've lost?"

Hughes threw his hands in the air. "I don't get you, man. I truly don't. My wife and child made me who I am. I'd bet my life that you weren't ever married. I'd bet my life that you never loved anyone."

Roy stared at a point in space at the back of the warehouse.

～

NIGHT FELL. Kyle went upstairs to check on Lucas. He took the tiny LED flashlight on Parker's keychain, the one that emitted the faint blue glow. It barely illuminated his feet. No chance that anyone or anything would see it from outside even if they were squinting up at the windows.

Kyle was worried because Lucas had gone quiet. The man was probably just down for the night—the infected had to sleep too—but there was always a chance that something had happened. Lucas could have had a rage-induced heart attack or a stroke. Maybe he bled out from the wound in his neck or got some kind of infection aside from the obvious one.

Kyle didn't care about Lucas per se. He didn't even like the guy, couldn't help but see him through Annie's eyes at least some of the time, but Lucas and Roy were helping Kyle and his friends get to Atlanta, something they did not have to do, something that could save the lives of many thousands of people. Lucas himself was one of the few remaining survivors and had value for that reason alone. If Kyle expected Lucas to have his back, he was duty-bound to reciprocate.

The metal stairs shuddered under the weight of a person, so Kyle took them slow. He didn't want to wake the poor bastard and felt relief that the infected, despite everything, still needed to sleep.

He reached the top of the stairs, stepped into the office, and aimed his faint light toward the chair. Lucas's head slumped sideways, and his chest rose and fell. He was still upright. The bandage, though, was thick with dried blood. At some point, Lucas's screaming and thrashing must have reopened the wound, but it seemed to have sealed again. Tomorrow, Kyle thought, they should wash his neck and dress him with a fresh bandage.

He had a low opinion of Lucas, but he'd had an even lower opinion of Parker when they'd first met, and Parker was well along the path of redemption. Parker seemed to be an even better person *because* he'd been infected. A certain amount of suffering was good for us, Kyle thought. It was a crucible that burned away the impurities and left only the things that matter most—family, friends, and the sheer wonder of being alive. It helped us see the suffering in others and feel something for them. Parker would never be the same after everything he'd been through, and Lucas was now being tormented in the same inferno that had burned away the darkness in Parker.

Kyle thought back to when he met Annie. It felt like ten years ago even though it was only a couple of months ago. How different he was now. He hadn't changed so much so quickly in the whole of his life. He wondered, then, if Roy had a point. Was the person Kyle used to be dead?

He didn't think so. He wouldn't be who he was today if he hadn't once been somebody else. In his distant future—and he could believe again that he had a distant future ahead of him—he'd no doubt change again, but he'd change from where he was now, the various versions of Kyle strung together in time like links in a chain. Whoever and whatever Lucas once was, he would not be the same after recovery. Whether he'd be a better person or a worse person was anyone's guess. Not even Roy could know the answer to that. It hadn't even occurred to Roy to ask the question.

Kyle crept silently down the stairs and found Annie waiting for him below.

"Hey," she said.

"Hey, yourself," he said.

He saw her smile in the faint blue glow from his light.

"Come on," she said and held out her hand to him.

Warmth spread in his chest as he took her hand. She led him toward the dead-bolted door in the back, far away from the others.

What was she doing? He didn't dare get his hopes up, but . . . was she doing what he thought she was doing?

She spun around when they reached the far wall and kissed him full on the mouth.

It took him a moment to respond, but he got there after a moment and leaned into the kiss, placing his hands on her waist as she rested hers on the back of his neck. She probed his mouth with her tongue and pressed her body into his.

She pulled back for a moment, took a breath, and said, "I've wanted to do this for days."

I've wanted to do this for months, he thought.

Then Lucas woke up. At first, he just grunted, and Kyle paused and turned his ear toward the office upstairs.

"Forget him," Annie said and kissed him again, harder this time.

Lucas went quiet again, and Kyle all but forgot about him.

He luxuriated in Annie and thought, I am the luckiest person alive.

"How far do you want to take this?" Kyle whispered.

Annie let him go for a moment and lifted her shirt over her head. That answered the question. For the briefest of instants, he considered saying they should make sure the others went to sleep first, but Kyle wasn't about to pull the plug on this moment. Not a chance.

Lucas screamed into the duct tape and rattled the office chair. The worst sort of distraction possible, but also the best. The others wouldn't hear him and Annie.

He reached behind her back to unhook her bra strap. He couldn't figure out how. He was never any good at this and doubted he ever would be.

"I got it," Annie said and laughed. She reached behind herself, unlatched the strap with a single motion, and let her bra fall to the floor.

Kyle cupped her cool right breast in his left hand. He wished he could look her in the eye when he did it, but the warehouse couldn't be darker.

Then Lucas screamed again, louder this time, and managed to topple his chair to the floor. The sound of metal and plastic and human weight crashing onto concrete echoed throughout the warehouse.

Kyle willed himself to ignore it. The others would handle it if the situation had to be handled.

He dropped to his knees and kissed Annie's breasts. She cooed and grinded her hips. He felt himself go hard and ignored the chatter from the others inside the warehouse.

A new ruckus now from the office: in addition to Lucas's screaming, blessedly muted by the tape over his mouth, something was banging repeatedly against metal.

"Kyle!" Hughes's voice. "Annie!"

Goddammit.

Somebody shushed Hughes. Probably Parker.

More banging and shaking. Lucas was down for sure and slamming himself into a filing cabinet.

"Kyle!" Hughes said again, quieter this time.

Why was Hughes calling his name? Couldn't he go up there himself?

Then he remembered. He had the LED light, the only one they could use in that warehouse at night without drawing attention from outside through the windows twenty feet up.

Kyle reluctantly pulled away from Annie. "Can I get a rain check?"

Annie answered him with a quick kiss, then squatted and fussed with her bra and her shirt.

"Kyle!" Hughes said, angrily but still quietly.

"Coming," Kyle said. He used the blue glow to find his way back to the others.

Lucas banged his chair into the cabinet some more.

"What are you and Annie doing?" Hughes, his face faintly cobalt. "Never mind. We need to get up there."

Kyle led the way, and the others followed, including Annie—bra and shirt in place again—up the stairs and into the office.

Lucas had indeed tipped himself over and was slamming himself hard against one of the metal cabinets.

"Parker," Hughes said. "You and Roy get that thing out of here. Kyle and I will take care of Lucas."

"Stay back, Annie," Kyle said.

Lucas heaved his lungs into the tape over his mouth as Hughes grabbed him by the ankles and dragged him across the floor. Parker and Roy hauled the filing cabinet out of the office and onto the mezzanine's walkway. A desk and a bookshelf were still in there. They'd have to come out too. Lucas could still, theoretically, slam himself into a wall if he tipped himself over again, but he'd only make half as much noise if he did.

Kyle and Hughes hauled the desk out of the office, and Parker and Roy removed the bookshelf. In a single motion with one arm, Hughes yanked Lucas off the floor and set him upright.

"He'll just tip over again," Annie said.

"Why don't we take him off the chair," Kyle said, "and hog-tie him on the floor? Tie his wrists to his ankles."

"We could do that," Hughes said.

"He'll be in more pain," Parker said. "When he wakes up, I mean."

"We need to shut him up," Roy said.

"You got us into this," Hughes said, "so stay out of it."

Kyle heard a loud bang from downstairs, something firm slamming hard against metal. "The hell was that?"

Nobody moved. Nobody said anything. Lucas wailed into the tape.

Bang. There it was again, at the far end of the warehouse.

Nobody moved.

"What is that?" Annie said. Fear in her voice.

BANG. Louder this time. Lucas screamed and thrashed like he had a parasitic creature inside him struggling to burst out.

"We need to shut him up now," Roy said.

"Shh!" Hughes said.

Kyle then heard a new sound, somewhere between a grunt and a moan, faint but clearly perceptible. Something was out there. Something that heard them. Something that wanted in.

Lucas thrashed some more and howled into the tape. The volume wasn't particularly loud, all things considered. If it were summer, and if crickets were singing outside, the sound might not have carried. Even the low roar of distant nighttime traffic probably would have muffled the noise. But in a world gone quiet, it didn't take much to alert whoever and whatever was prowling around the perimeter if it was up close and personal, right at the edge of the building.

Something pounded three consecutives times on the door, more urgently now and making all kinds of noise of its own, the kind that could be heard for a quarter mile in every direction.

8

Hughes saw them through the second-floor windows, coming in the moonlight, sometimes as stragglers, other times in pairs or in threes.

They did not run. They heard the commotion and were drawn toward stimulus as they always were, but they didn't seem to know what they'd find once they got there. They did not know there were people inside. One of them thought it had heard something in the warehouse, and the rest were drawn by its response. One after another started banging on the walls of the warehouse, raising an even louder ruckus that could be heard from farther and farther away. An enormous mass—a horde—eventually congealed outside the building, the sound of its assault on the walls mushrooming into a horrendous encircling thrum. Hughes couldn't even hear Lucas over the din anymore.

"How much ammunition do we have?" Annie shouted. She leaned into Kyle. The two of them apparently were a thing now.

"Two dozen shotgun shells," Hughes said, "a few dozen cartridges for the rifles, and a hundred or so rounds for the handguns."

Annie seemed to relax. They weren't okay, though. Not by a long shot.

"They can't get in," Kyle said.

"No, they can't," Hughes said. "But we can't get out."

"They don't know we're here," Parker said. "They haven't seen us or heard us."

"They heard Lucas," Hughes said and shot a glance toward Roy. The asshole was looking up in wonder at the skylights as if an escalator might magically descend and carry everyone up to a helicopter on the roof.

"They're reacting to each other," Parker said.

"None of them have screamed," Annie said.

"No, they haven't," Hughes said. And that meant something. The infected screamed when they saw prey. To alert others, perhaps. Or maybe it was involuntary, triggered by some kind of aggression reflex, the way cats couldn't resist chasing yarn. Lucas was different. He was screaming because he couldn't get loose, not because he wanted to eat. That was clear; he bellowed even louder and harder whenever he saw food on legs step into the office.

"We could distract them somehow," Roy said, still looking up at the skylights.

"Without drawing attention to ourselves?" Hughes said. "How?"

"I don't know," Roy said. "Just wonderin'. We could probably get onto the roof. One of us could climb down the exterior ladder, hop into one of the vehicles, and lead them away."

The bottom of the ladder outside the building dangled twelve feet up in the air. Anyone who descended would drop down into a melee.

Hughes shook his head. "Too risky."

"Not if someone else on the roof distracted them," Roy said. "With flashlights or gunfire or something."

It wasn't the worst idea possible, Hughes thought. They'd have to do it under cover of full darkness, of course, after the moon set. By then, though, even more of those things could be surrounding the warehouse.

Just getting onto the roof wouldn't be easy. Doable, but tricky. There were metal beams up there, crisscrossing below the ceiling. If they shot out a skylight, someone could inch their way across one of the beams, make their way underneath one of the lights, and pull themselves up. A fall from up there would probably kill a person, however.

"We could climb up there and shoot them," Annie said.

Hughes shook his head. "There are at least a hundred out there already. We have more than a hundred rounds, but we'll miss a lot with the handguns. Thinning them is the best we could do. And the noise would be catastrophic. Might as well shine a bat signal onto the clouds and tell every shambling psychopath for ten miles around where we are."

He did not like what he saw outside the windows. Didn't like it at all. Dozens more were converging on the warehouse from every direction. No way could they shoot all of them. And only a suicidal person would drop from the bottom of the exterior ladder even in total darkness. Hughes wished they had an air force.

Thank heaven the windows were far above the ground, ringing the warehouse at mezzanine level where the second floor would be if there were a second floor. The upside was that the infected outside couldn't break through the windows. The downside was that the elevated windows gave Hughes a terrible angle. He couldn't see straight down outside, couldn't count the number of infected out there. He could only guess by roughly how many he'd seen on approach and by the sounds they made. That inevitably led to an undercount. There could be another hundred down there that he hadn't seen.

"What if we get onto the roof," Annie said, "drop the ladder from above, then crack their heads one at a time as they climb up?"

"No dice," Hughes said. "More of them are showing up here every minute. I don't know if we can take them out faster than new ones arrive. And the last thing we want is to have them above us. If we can get onto the roof from the inside, they can get inside from the roof."

"So you don't want to shoot them," Parker said, "and you don't want to lead them away. You have a better idea?"

"I do," Hughes said.

It was simple, really. The infected behaved like alien beings, but they were still human organisms. They had the same survival needs that everyone else had. It was a simple fact of biology. They'd die if those needs were not met.

"We wait," Hughes said.

"Wait?" Annie said. "We can't just passively sit here."

"We can," Hughes said. "And we will."

"You want to just hope they get distracted and go somewhere else?" Parker said.

"It could happen," Hughes said. "It could happen five minutes from now. None of them have actually seen us. They don't know we're in here. One of them heard Lucas banging around and slamming his fist on the wall. Others showed up and started doing the same thing. So what? They're stupid, right? Just about anything could pull them away. A lightning storm on the horizon, a car driving down the road, even a rabbit hopping around."

"And if not?" Parker said.

"They'll die," Hughes said.

Annie narrowed her eyes and nodded. She saw it. Then Parker did too, followed by Kyle.

Roy didn't get it. Didn't seem to, anyway.

"We can survive in here longer than they can out there," Hughes said, "because we have water and food and they don't."

∽

They hunkered down for a long siege, long enough that Lucas might recover before it ended. They could keep him alive by pouring water down his throat if they had to. The infected outside, though, if they didn't wander off to find something to drink, would weaken and collapse over time. Hughes and his friends wouldn't even have to wait for them to die. They'd just have to wait for the infected to keel over and groan on the ground, and then he could step over them on the way to the Suburban.

Hughes saw a potential flaw in the plan, though. If the infected could find a nearby water source, this business could last a whole lot longer. Hughes doubted it, though. The infected would get distracted and drift away. Planning and strategy were beyond them.

The damn things were more likely to move first thing in the morning, when the sun came up. Night produced little stimulus. Even with a half moon in the sky, they couldn't see much without streetlights, headlights, or porch lights. Any number of things could draw their attention in daylight, though, so long as Hughes and his companions kept quiet and out of sight.

Hughes stood on the mezzanine and watched through the windows as more of them came, drawn by the noise of the others mindlessly assaulting the walls. The darkness inside concealed him, but he could see well enough outside in the moonlight. What he wouldn't give right now for some incendiary devices. The warehouse wouldn't burn. It was made of prefab metal. The infected would burn, though. He just needed a way to set them ablaze.

Annie and Kyle joined Hughes at the railing at the top of the staircase. Parker and Roy were still somewhere below.

"What if your plan doesn't work?" Annie said. "What if they never stop coming?"

Hughes had already thought of that. He tried his best to play out every conceivable scenario in his mind so that nothing that happened later would truly surprise him.

"Our best bet," he said, "would be to run outside with guns blazing and shoot our way through. Lead them away from the building, then come back and jump into the vehicles. We probably wouldn't make it. But some of us might."

Kyle nodded.

Annie shuddered.

～

THE BOOMING against the walls slacked off by one in the morning. A few infected were still slapping and kicking the building, but they sounded half-hearted and tired now. Some shuffled around and moaned outside the door, but the horde as a whole seemed to be retiring for "bed."

Annie couldn't stay awake any longer despite her fried nerves. None of them could. She and Kyle prepared a comfortable space for themselves of five carpets piled atop each other. They did not, however, find a private spot away from their companions. She wanted to cash in that rain check as much as he did, but the feeling of impending doom hadn't done her libido any favors.

Besides, she wanted the others—well, Roy, anyway—to see her and Kyle sleeping together. If Kyle publicly "claimed" her, Roy would be less likely to mess with her. No guarantees, of course, but another boundary was in place now.

Neither Parker nor Hughes said anything about or even seemed to notice her openly bedding with Kyle. They must have expected it. If Kyle and Parker hadn't gotten into that blood feud with each other, it would have happened a long time ago.

"I want to sleep for a week," she said and lay her head on Kyle's chest.

"I want to sleep for a month," Kyle said and wrapped his arm around her shoulder.

She heard his heart beating and felt the rise and fall of his chest as he breathed.

"Can I still cash that rain check?" Kyle said.

"Mmm," Annie said and answered his question by running her hand down to his stomach area. "Maybe tomorrow if those things leave us alone."

∾

HUMAN BEINGS COULD SLEEP through just about anything with enough time to get used to whatever they needed to sleep through. The first clap in a thunderstorm may startle a person awake, but they could probably sleep through the fiftieth without too much trouble. Residents of Manhattan didn't even hear the traffic when they went to bed, back when there was still traffic. Even civilians in war zones managed to drift off if exploding bombs weren't too close.

Likewise, Hughes, Annie, Kyle, Parker, and Roy slept almost peacefully even with a horde right outside. The threat-detection parts of their brains settled down after learning that the sounds, while angst-inducing and dreadful, didn't portend imminent danger.

A sudden new sound, however, such as breaking glass or a gunshot, could wake anyone who wasn't deaf or in a coma. That's exactly what happened at dawn when three things occurred almost at once. The busted door leading into the warehouse jerked open a couple of inches, the pile of rolled carpets barricading it slid across the floor, and Hughes bolted upright before he even knew what was happening.

Everybody was up—Annie and Kyle on their makeshift bed, Parker on the concrete next to Hughes, and Roy off to the side by himself. Hughes shook himself awake, blinked a couple of times, and figured out what had just happened. A surging mass of infected outside had shoved so hard against the door that they managed to budge it. And they were still shoving.

Hughes placed his index finger over his lips—*nobody make a sound*—but it was too late. One of the infected got a glimpse through the now-ajar door into the warehouse. It saw Hughes and the others, stirring from sleep, and it screamed. Moments later, two more of them screamed, and a chain reaction of shrieking and howling spread outward from the door like a concussion wave.

The infected had found the building's weak point, and now they knew prey was inside.

Kyle and Roy had amassed a four-foot-high stack of carpets in front of that door. It must have weighed as much as a car, but it still wasn't enough. They'd have to double it, stack carpets eight feet high, all the way to the top of the door.

Parker leapt to the top of the pile and leaned hard against the door while the others scrambled to lay on more weight. The carpets were large and awkward to move, but they didn't weigh all that much when they were laid inert on top of each other. If a vehicle or some kind of heavy machinery could have been parked against that door, everything would have been fine.

After ten minutes, the door finally seemed secure with what must have been two tons of weight—more than enough, about as much as a truck. The door had been shoved three inches ajar, though, and it remained stuck in that position. The infected couldn't squeeze in, but they could see in, and the howling derangement outside was louder than ever.

"They're not getting in," Hughes said.

"They aren't going away either," Annie said, "now that they know we're in here. Either they die or we die."

Roy retrieved his sword from his bedding area. "Out of my way," he said and pushed past Annie.

He jabbed the point of his blade between the door and the jamb and ran his steel through the faces of the infected peering inside. He stabbed and impaled almost expertly, as if he'd been practicing every day, until he couldn't reach any more live ones over the pile of corpses.

He turned and faced the others, blood dripping from his sword, his face set with grim determination as if he might run his weapon through his companions before finally thinking better of it. He shook his head violently from side to side as if to clear the gruesome chore he'd just carried out from his mind.

"Thanks, I guess," Kyle said.

"Won't help," Parker said.

"Didn't make it worse," Kyle said.

"So now what?" Annie said.

"Same as before," Hughes said. "We wait."

"We going to wait here for a week?" Annie said.

"As long as it takes," Hughes said.

∼

They sat in Roy's camping chairs in a sort-of circle, with Annie standing and hovering over Kyle. She could not just sit there and do nothing. Not for a week. Not with a mob outside hurling itself at the walls.

She forced herself to stop wringing her hands. "How long does it take to die of dehydration?"

"Couple of days," Parker said. "Almost happened to us at the prison in Lander. After maybe two days, though, they'll be so fatigued they'll hardly be able to move."

Annie relaxed a little. If the infected collapsed from exhaustion after two days, she and her companions might be able to stroll right on past them to their vehicles. But more could show up in the meantime. There were hundreds out there already.

"Where are they getting their water from, anyway?" Kyle said.

"There's creeks and rivers and lakes and ponds all over the place," Roy said. "There's a creek two hundred feet from here, just behind the trees in back of the warehouse."

Annie tensed.

"Wonderful," Kyle said.

The infected could take a break and wander on over there any time, lap up some water, and come right on back. If it occurred to them. If they knew the creek was there. If they'd seen it, crossed it, and remembered it.

"We can't just sit here," Annie said.

"I'm all ears," Hughes said.

"What if we disguised ourselves?" Roy said.

Hughes slowly turned his head toward Roy. "With what?"

"With nothing," Roy said. "The infected don't go after each other. They only go after us. Why?"

"Because they know we're different," Parker said.

"So, what if they didn't?" Roy said. "What if they thought we were them? They would if we moved and acted like them."

Annie had considered that months ago. They all had. The infected didn't just behave differently. They moved differently, more aggressively and spastically. Sometimes they even stood still at strange angles. Their body language would be hard to imitate, especially without any practice.

"You ever try it?" Hughes said.

Roy shook his head. "Never been trapped before."

"There's no way to test it," Annie said. She didn't like addressing Roy, didn't even want to look at him. "If we open that door and it doesn't work, we're all dead."

"You're the one who doesn't want to just sit here," Roy said. He scanned the warehouse walls with his eyes when he said it, refusing to make eye contact with her either.

"Look around," Parker said.

Annie looked around. They were surrounded by nothing but carpets, huge rolls on the floor and smaller ones stacked on a vast array of metal shelves.

"We've got plenty of rope," Parker said. "We could hoist those shelves through the skylights and onto the roof and toss 'em off. They must weigh fifty pounds apiece, if not more. We could take out lots of 'em that way."

There were easily a hundred shelves in that warehouse. No obvious way to hoist them onto the roof even with rope, but they could figure something out.

"Not the worst idea I've ever heard," Kyle said.

"Can't kill all of them that way," Hughes said.

"We wouldn't have to," Annie said. "We have guns. We could thin the rest with handguns, then pick off the last ones with rifles."

Hughes nodded. "Okay. What else you got?"

"Try to shrink the problem," Kyle said. "We don't need to kill or disable all of them. We just need a clear path to one of the vehicles. Just one person needs to get to the Suburban and drive off and lead them away."

Annie sighed. They should have parked the damn thing right at the door, but no one had thought of it.

Something was happening outside. The furor grew louder, as if even more infected had gathered on the other side of the door, but they were already jammed hip to hip. The sound was building and moving . . . higher. Up the exterior wall as if they were standing on some kind of platform.

"What is that?" Kyle said and leaned forward. "It's like they're on stilts."

"Are they climbing on top of each other?" Hughes said.

Annie heard a racking, sliding metallic sound.

"The ladder!" Parker said.

Oh, God. They pulled down the ladder that led to the roof. Like a fire escape, the lower part had been drawn up to keep trespassers and thieves off it when the warehouse was closed. One of the infected tripped the mechanism that dropped the bottom rungs to the ground.

"Onto the mezzanine!" Hughes shouted. "Now!"

Parker bolted for the stairs. Kyle leapt from his chair and grabbed Annie by the hand. They both followed Parker. She took the stairs two at a time as the roar outside rose toward the sky.

9

There were twelve skylights embedded in the roof of the warehouse, two rows of six running the length of the building. They weren't the smallish kind meant for houses. These were industrial scale. You could drop a car through them.

The two skylights at the front, where the exterior ladder crested the ceiling, went dim, the sunlight partially blotted out by more than a dozen infected announcing themselves with slaps on the glass overhead.

Hughes stood on the mezzanine in the back next to his friends. He knew without even thinking about it that they had a single possible option—barricade themselves in the office. But closing and locking the door wouldn't be good enough.

"We have to block the stairs!" he shouted and waved his hands toward the warehouse floor. "Cover the stairs with those shelves!"

He and the others ran back down to the main level. Tipping shelves over onto the stairs wouldn't stop the infected from climbing, but it would slow them down.

All the shelves were stocked with small rolled-up carpets. Hughes and Parker cleared and hoisted one of them while Kyle, Annie, and Roy took another. There were two sets of stairs leading up to the mezzanine level, one on the left and one on the right. Hughes and Parker carried their shelf toward the staircase on the right while the others took care of the left.

Another infected made it up the ladder every couple of seconds, and they spread across the roof and blocked out the overhead light like a dark slow-breaking wave. Hughes caught Annie looking up toward the swarming mass and shuddering.

"Come on!" he shouted. They could gaze at the ceiling in horror later.

Hughes and Parker hauled three more shelves onto the stairs, laying them down at forty-five-degree angles for maximum slow-down effect, with one edge touching the steps and the other resting against the railing. The stairs were a genuine obstacle course now. Passable, no question about it, but a pain in the ass. Hughes needed almost a full minute to climb to the top.

Annie, Kyle, and Roy did the same thing to the staircase on the other side of the mezzanine, and all five of them reconvened at the door to the office.

The warehouse was much darker now, the floor in shadow, the skylights in the roof filled with jeering and menacing faces. More than a hundred infected impotently slapped their palms on the glass.

The dark waters were rising, Hughes thought. The infected were coming in, and he and his friends weren't getting out. Hughes had long ago accepted that something like this would one day happen to him, and he knew that that day would come sooner rather than later, but knowing did not make it easier.

He wanted to scream that he and his friends were on a mission to cure them and everyone else. *Let us go*, he wanted to shout. *We can save you. We can save everyone.* But all he could do was take out as many as he could on his way out.

"Look on the bright side," Roy said.

"What's that?" Parker said.

"If they all go up there," Roy said and nodded toward the roof with his head, "we'll have a better chance if we run out the front."

An interesting notion, Hughes thought, but only if everything went perfectly. The roof might be large enough to hold all of them. What were the chances, though, that all of them would go up there?

Miniscule. Negligible. Vanishingly close to zero.

"It can't end like this," Kyle said.

Sure it could, Hughes thought. Every one of them knew that saving the world was the longest of long shots. They weren't even sure they could get to Atlanta. If they did manage to get there, odds were remote that the CDC would still be there. If it were still in business, the chances that the doctors would actually find a cure were abysmal. If those odds weren't bad enough, Annie had damn near convinced him that there was no point, that hardly anybody was left alive anywhere anyway and that those who were—like Lucas and Roy and Joseph Steele and his henchmen in Lander—arguably weren't even worth saving.

So, Kyle was wrong. It absolutely could end like this. And it was about to.

Hughes heard a sharp splintering *crack* in the ceiling above the far end of the warehouse. Then another crack, louder this time, and finally an explosive shattering of glass shards showering onto the concrete below.

Hughes felt resigned. Resigned to finally die but also to fight.

Parker flinched but otherwise watched the scene stoically. Annie seemed to steel herself. Roy's left eye twitched.

Just like that—and everyone had to know this was coming—one of those things fell through the broken skylight, its arms and legs flailing like a bug as it descended and smacked onto the floor. It did not move. Did not even twitch. The fall from above killed it instantly. Hughes thought he saw a small puddle of blood under its head.

Then another fell, this one screaming on its way down and twitching for just a moment after it hit.

Another skylight shattered and three infected plunged toward the floor all at once, feetfirst as if they'd jumped through the glass rather than falling or diving through it. All landed in a mangled heap at the bottom. None survived.

"I'll be goddamned," Parker said.

Hughes had been observing the infected's behavior for months. They were as predictable as the seasons, so he wasn't the least bit surprised by what happened next: all of them on the roof belted what sounded like a victory cheer, and within a matter of seconds, every remaining skylight shattered at once. Dozens plunged from the roof if they were diving down into heaven. They burst their skulls, snapped their necks, shattered their legs, and crushed their internal organs on the concrete. Some landed on the tops of the metal shelves and split their backs like twigs.

The universe is killing itself, Hughes thought.

The warehouse looked like the inside of a giant meat grinder with a steady stream of post-human bodies falling through holes and amassing themselves into twisted piles below.

"My God," Annie said and covered her mouth. She looked like she was about to throw up. But she couldn't take her eyes off the incredible scene before her. Nobody could.

It was the worst thing Hughes had ever seen. And yet—and yet—soon enough there would be hundreds of dead and broken bodies on the floor, far more than he and his friends could ever dispatch with their hands or their guns. And they kept coming, climbing up the ladder and hurling themselves lemming-like into the cavity below.

They fell at a slower rate now. They could only ascend the ladder one at a time. Most of them dropped through the farther skylights, the ones nearest the ladder, so the piles of bodies at the far end of the warehouse grew taller than the others.

Hughes braced for what was sure to happen eventually. It was a simple matter of physics and biology. A human being, infected or not, had a hell of a time surviving a forty-foot drop onto concrete. A forty-foot drop onto something much softer, though, was a different equation. A pile of bodies wasn't the softest thing one could land on, but it was softer than the floor. It was softer than grass. And the drop wasn't as steep anymore. Forty feet had been reduced, in the last couple of minutes, to just over thirty.

A plummeting infected landed feetfirst in one of the far piles, toppled to the floor a little bit awkwardly, and managed to crawl away. It seemed to have broken its leg but was otherwise fine.

"Should we bother with hand weapons?" Kyle said.

Parker shook his head. "Just shoot them. Before they get anywhere near us."

Hughes agreed. They might have enough ammunition now and the noise wouldn't make any difference. "Roy and I will take the staircase on the right. The three of you take the left."

They armed themselves, Roy with Lucas's Bushmaster, Parker with the hunting rifle, Kyle and Annie with handguns, and Hughes with his pump-action Persuader.

"You fire while I'm reloading," Hughes said to Roy. "And I'll take your place when you are."

Roy nodded.

"Get ready," Hughes said and set his weapon to *fire*. "Don't waste ammunition. Wait for them to reach the stairs."

The infected that broke its leg was crawling away, toward the far corner of the warehouse, apparently too injured and dazed to understand what was happening or where it should go. More began surviving the fall, though, some too injured to move, but first one and then another limped away.

Hughes counted seven of them on their feet and staggering around at the far end of the warehouse. "Hey!" he shouted. No sense delaying the inevitable, and besides, the last thing he wanted was twenty of them charging at the same time.

All seven turned in unison as another fell headfirst through the skylight and snapped its neck. The survivors made a beeline for Hughes, for their prey, four of them limping and three of them running.

"We just might get out of this," Parker said.

"Don't get cocky," Hughes said and descended the stairs as far he could without getting tangled up in the shelving.

His Persuader held eight 70mm shells, one in the chamber and seven in the magazine. He splattered the three runners with a single shot, then racked in the next round with an intimidating *ca-crunch* as more of them plunged from the sky.

He watched the four infected limping toward him as if he had tunnel vision. Everything else in the world—the walls, the ceiling, even the stairs at his feet—vanished into a peripheral fog.

The infected limping toward him came at their own pace, the first moving a bit faster than walking speed, the slowest barely moving at all. Hughes wouldn't be able to take out more than one per shot this time.

He waited until the first made it right to the bottom of the steps, then blasted it into a bloody mess. As he raised his eyes toward the next one in line, roughly fifty feet away, he saw at the top of his tunnel vision that two more were coming right toward him, and they were both running.

So he widened his view and saw four more charging at full speed toward Parker at the top of the left staircase, all running, none limping, as if the infected were dropping from a modest height onto mattresses now.

Two more hurtled down from the ceiling.

Hughes and Parker both fired until their weapons were empty. Hughes headed back up the stairs to reload in the office as Roy took his place.

"You okay?" Annie said as he reloaded the shotgun.

"Golden," he said. He wasn't really, but they had a chance of making it out now. It was a numbers game at this point. Would Hughes and his friends run out of ammo, or would this army of infected run out of bodies? That was the question. There was a finite number outside the warehouse. Every one killed or maimed on impact took itself off the board. Every one shot by Hughes and his companions was another removed from the board. And if Hughes and his friends ran out of ammo, they still had their hand weapons.

Now that it was Roy's turn to cover the staircase, Hughes could zoom out and watch the broader picture unfold. What he saw was not good. More falling infected were surviving, and fewer of them were limping.

Hughes swapped places with Roy when the Bushmaster needed a reload, and Kyle and Annie took over from Parker when he emptied the hunting rifle.

Bodies piled up like bloated, oozing anthills at the base of the staircases, but the goddamned things kept on coming. With a wide blast radius from the Persuader, Hughes barely had to aim and could fire almost an autopilot. His ears rang with tinnitus, his shoulder throbbed from the shotgun's kick, wafts of gun smoke stung his eyes, and the stench of blood, copper, shit, black powder, and propellant filled his nostrils.

He saw every infected he dropped as a victory and kept telling himself that there were only so many, but there were still more outside coming in. They just would not stop. At last he felt like a man on the beach trying to hold back a tsunami with sandbags. It just wasn't possible, and he finally ran out of shells. Roy took his place at the top of the stairs with his Bushmaster. Hughes darted into the office to retrieve the second hunting rifle, but there were only seven cartridges left in the box.

They weren't going to make it. He saw that now. But what else could he do? He dutifully loaded the rounds into the rifle and relieved Roy as Kyle and Annie popped their handguns at the top of the second staircase.

"I'm dry," Roy said.

"Grab your sword," Hughes said.

"I'm out too," Annie said, sounding resigned.

Hughes vowed not to waste a single one of his rounds. Each infected he hit in its center of mass was one fewer he'd have to take down by hand.

Four rushed the staircase as two more fell from the ceiling.

Hughes dropped all four incoming before they reached the staircase. Five more of them followed.

"How many of these fuckers are there?" Parker shouted.

Too goddamned many, Hughes thought. He fired his last three shots, threw down his rifle, and slowly picked up a crowbar.

10

Annie felt a strange sense of calm wash over her knowing that she was going to die. She should have died a long time ago, back at the beginning when she got bit. Her survival thus far was a pointless glitch of nature. She was never going to save the world. She couldn't even save herself or her friends. Roy was right. The world was better off going to sleep and not waking up.

Even so, she swung her crowbar and defended her ground on the staircase. The instinct to survive even a few more miserable moments wouldn't release. She wasn't even entirely sure what was happening. The world was a blur now. The infected making their way up the staircase with their snarling teeth and predatory eyes seemed almost hallucinatory. The sounds of weapons bludgeoning bone and sinew and flesh sounded as if under water, unintelligible shouts from her friends like recordings played in slow-motion. She finally reached the verge of total exhaustion and surrender when the gauzy state lifted and she returned to a state of partial alertness.

The back of the warehouse was clear. Nothing else was coming down from the roof.

Just three last infected on the stairs headed toward her and Kyle and Parker, bursting with a relentless energy that had deserted her some time ago. She felt a hand on her shoulder.

"I got this." Parker's voice, heavy and weary but determined somehow. He stepped forward, looking as depleted as she was, like he was about to topple over, but he saved her from expending her last drop, and she eased herself to the floor in a state of bewilderment that this was actually just about over, that she wasn't going to die after all.

Kyle stood to the left of the staircase, Parker to the right.

The three infected ascended the stairs, bounding over the obstacles in their path as if they'd been bred for it. All headed toward Parker.

He cocked the hammer back and swung a little too early and a little too slowly. The first of the three infected on the stairs flinched and changed direction.

Toward Kyle.

Kyle wasn't expecting it. Nobody was expecting it. He raised the crowbar to strike, but he did so limply, not quickly or adeptly enough, and the infected tucked its chin into its chest and drove its head into Kyle's stomach like a human-shaped pile driver. Kyle tumbled onto his back with a raging thing that was once a healthy twenty-something male on top of him. It raised its face toward Kyle's and lunged with its teeth bared.

Annie had no time to save him—nobody did—yet she struggled off the floor all the same. Parker was ready with his hammer, and this time he wouldn't miss, but it would not happen fast enough.

Kyle raised his arm to defend his face. Not that it would do any good.

Parker swung the hammer.

And the infected bit Kyle, clamped its teeth around his wrist just a moment before Parker's hammer split open the back of its skull.

"No!" Annie shouted, rising from the floor, unarmed because she'd dropped her own weapon, but energized and enraged now, scrambling toward Kyle as Parker, incredibly, shoved her back to the ground.

"Stay down!" he shouted.

There were two more infected right behind the first, coming straight at him.

Parker swung the hammer and took out the first one.

Roy appeared from somewhere behind Annie and dispatched the third by running his sword through its arm and its neck.

Hughes arrived too, barreling past Parker, as Kyle lay on his back clutching his wrist. Annie didn't know if he was screaming in pain or not. She couldn't hear anything but a high-pitched whine in her ears.

Why couldn't *she* have been bit on the wrist? Why not Parker? They were both immune and would be fine. She rushed to Kyle's side, careful of his arm, and stroked his cheek. He winced in pain and turned away.

The universe was a sonofabitch. Why couldn't *Roy* have been bit?

Kyle's wound as such wasn't serious. No major artery had been severed. It looked as if he'd suffer more from bruising than anything else if the virus hadn't entered his system.

"Somebody get a bandage," Annie said.

"The hell for?" Roy said.

"Just do it!" Annie shouted.

She heard someone step into the office, but she didn't know who, and she didn't care.

The ringing in her ears was subsiding. She could almost hear okay now.

"Kyle," she said.

"Annie," he said. "I'm sorry." He still wouldn't look at her.

She grabbed his chin between her thumb and fingers and turned his face toward hers. "No," she said. "I'm sorry. This shouldn't have happened." She kissed him, first on the forehead and then on the mouth.

Kyle coughed.

They never did get a chance to cash in that rain check.

"Does it hurt?" she said.

He nodded. "But I'll be okay."

No, Kyle, she thought. You will not be okay. None of us will be okay. Not herself, not Parker, not Hughes. Certainly not Roy by the time she finished with him.

Kyle closed his eyes then. He wasn't gone yet. She knew that. She doubted he'd even entered the short coma that would set in before the turn. He was simply exhausted.

"Kyle," she said and shook him. "Kyle!"

He slitted his eyes open.

Annie wanted to say she loved him. She wasn't sure that was actually true, and it would be far too soon to say so even if it was, but this was the only chance she had left.

She imagined herself in his place. If she were lying there instead of him, would she want him to hold her hand and tell her he loved her? Of course she would. What else does a human being want to hear on their way out of this world?

"Kyle," she said.

Kyle closed his eyes again.

"Kyle!"

She shook him. She slapped him. Shook him again.

He didn't respond.

"Kyle!"

"Ma'am," Roy said.

Annie ignored him.

"Ma'am," Roy said again. "Step back and I'll take care of it."

She whirled to face him. "Get the fuck away from us or I'll beat you to death."

Roy's nodded politely and took a step back.

"Roy," Hughes said. "Give them some space."

She turned back to Kyle. He didn't look asleep anymore. She didn't know how she knew. She just did. He wasn't gone yet, but he was gone.

"What do you want to do with him?" Roy finally said.

Hughes blew out his breath. "We'll bury him. Outside and with dignity. We can't leave him in here."

"I mean," Roy said, "what do you want to do before you bury him?"

Annie noticed his words. Before *you* bury him. Not before *we* bury him.

~

Hughes wanted to rip Roy's intestines out with his hands and spool them onto the floor. He'd made it all the way to Arkansas from Seattle with Kyle—eighty percent of the way to Atlanta—and now Kyle was effectively dead because Roy wanted proof that Annie was really immune.

Why the fuck did Roy think they were going to Atlanta if Annie wasn't really immune?

Liars never believed anyone else. They lied like they breathed and thought everyone else did it too.

Good God. Hughes could only imagine what Roy must have been thinking when he let Lucas get bit. At this point, though, what difference did it make? Hughes couldn't trust Roy to tell the truth. Nor could he trust Roy to have anyone's back in a fight.

He still had Lucas's cracked cell phone in his pocket. He doubted he'd find much of anything useful or even interesting on it, but he made a note to himself to scroll through it at some point before Lucas recovered.

First, though: Kyle. The poor kid was going to return within minutes as one of those things.

Parker and Annie knew what Hughes would do next. They'd seen it before. Roy was the only one with a question mark hanging over his head. So, Annie kissed Kyle one last time and got out of the way, moving to the steps and putting her head in her hands, not seeming to care that she was staining the bottom of her pants with even more blood.

Parker stepped into the office.

Roy hovered nearby as Hughes gently used his fingers to close Kyle's mouth and plug his nose. Kyle didn't struggle. He was far too deeply unconscious. Try that with even a passed-out drunk, and the victim would snap to attention and fight. But a man whose brain was undergoing the brutal transformation wrought by that virus was in no condition to resist. He just suffocated. Hughes held Kyle's airways shut for five long minutes. To ensure that his work was done, he felt Kyle's neck for a pulse that wasn't there.

Hughes knew all along that it could come to this, that he'd have to snuff out one of his companions. Ever since they left the Pacific Northwest, though, this could only happen to Kyle or to himself since neither Parker nor Annie could turn. At this point, Hughes was just grateful that he'd never have to do this to Annie.

The world went quiet again. Hughes heard nothing but his own heartbeat and a faint post-violence hum in the atmosphere. That meant something. On some level, he knew that the silence was important, but he was so physically and emotionally depleted that he wasn't sure what it meant, couldn't understand what his subconscious was trying to tell him.

Why did it matter that the warehouse was quiet again? Of course it was quiet. The infected were dead, and no more seemed to be coming. Some dim part of his mind found that astonishing, but the hush itself meant something else.

Then it hit him, ton-of-bricks style. Lucas was silent. After all that gunfire and shouting, after all that hell, Lucas did not make a sound. He couldn't possibly be asleep.

"Parker," Hughes said. "Can you go check on Lucas?" He looked at Roy as he said that. Roy looked at his feet.

Hughes could have checked on Lucas himself, but he didn't want Roy out of his sight.

Parker ducked into the office.

Annie turned her head toward the skylights, as if the heavens might offer her something if she only wished hard enough. Hughes knew she would grieve for a long time.

Parker returned from the office. "Guys," he said. "Lucas died."

∼

THEY BURIED Kyle and Lucas in the trees behind the warehouse.

Hughes would have made Roy dig the graves if they had a shovel, but they didn't, so they used crowbars. It took them four hours.

Nobody said anything over Lucas's grave, but they all said a few words over Kyle's. Hughes went first. "Rest easy, my friend."

"I'm sorry for everything," Parker said.

"This will be righted," Annie said. "That is a promise."

"Sorry for your loss," Roy said, not to Kyle, of course, but to the others, as if he hadn't even heard what Annie had said.

∼

Parker wanted a cigarette. He hadn't smoked for years, hadn't even thought about smoking for years, but he wanted a cigarette and considered scrounging around in a convenience store for some cartons. It would only take him five minutes once he found the right place.

A chemical addiction, though, was the last thing he needed. He wouldn't be able to feed that habit indefinitely. There were plenty of unsmoked cigarettes left in the world, sure, but they were all going rancid, and he doubted that more would ever be produced, even if the whole world one day recovered. Smoking was over forever. Doctors in Atlanta might extract a miracle cure from Annie's veins, but the odds that the cigarette or vaping industry would revive in his lifetime were zero. So he gnawed on his fingertips and let darkness overtake him.

∼

Annie felt shock and disbelief at the same time, like she might be able to scramble reality and run it again, perhaps with a different and better outcome, if only she could find a *rewind* button.

Kyle was gone, but he couldn't be. He'd been perfectly fine a couple of hours ago.

She had only known him for a few months, but it felt like years, and she couldn't imagine going forward without him. Once she and her companions had set out for Atlanta, win or lose, succeed or fail, she'd never imagined her future without any of them. If they saved the world, they'd do it together. If they failed, they'd fail together, dying at once in a calamity or finding a niche somewhere to live out whatever remained of their lives.

Annie still had Parker and Hughes. They were friends—no, they were *family*—but they weren't potential life partners as Kyle had been.

Her mind was erecting guardrails against reality to protect herself. The enormity of what had happened was too much to process at once. She was not in denial, though. No. Psychological guardrails couldn't keep the truth out entirely. Rather, she found herself in a surreal kind of limbo state, where Kyle was somehow alive and dead at the same time, where the future she had imagined for herself was still a real possibility despite what had just happened, as if one part of her mind knew that Kyle was gone while the other continued as it had before.

The guardrails fell, though, one at a time. The first went down when Hughes gently suffocated Kyle. The second slipped when Annie helped carry Kyle out of the warehouse. The third tumbled when she helped Parker dig Kyle's grave, a fourth when they lowered the body, and a fifth when they covered him up.

"We're leaving," Hughes said. There wasn't much daylight left, and the area was almost certainly cleared of every infected for miles, but none of them could tolerate another night near that warehouse.

So she and her friends got back in their Suburban as Roy returned to his RV alone. Annie was shocked to realize that she had the entire back seat to herself now. Somehow, and for no rational reason, she hadn't expected that. She'd gotten into the back seat and shared it with Kyle so many times.

Another guardrail down.

Hughes drove the Suburban behind Roy's RV out of the lot and back onto the road heading farther south into Arkansas.

Annie had no idea where they were going and didn't care. Into Tennessee, presumably, since it was only a couple of miles away, but she just wanted to curl up in the back seat and sleep. She couldn't do it, though, in case she accidentally sprawled onto Kyle's side. Instead, she leaned her head against the glass and willed herself to slip away from the wretched world for as long as she could. Just being awake at all was excruciating.

She had only two friends left now, and it raised a terrible question. What would she do if she also lost Parker and Hughes?

She wouldn't go on. Not to Atlanta. She was going there for Kyle, Parker, and Hughes now and not for anyone else. She couldn't lie to herself about that any longer. Soldiers who returned home from war famously said they no longer cared what they were fighting for once the bullets started flying. They fought for the men next to them. That's what she was doing. Gutting it out for the men next to her.

A vaccine couldn't bring back the world. Civilization was an abstraction, a collective thing in the head that had been flipped off like a breaker switch on a wall.

∼

PARKER MARVELED at the fact that he'd once wished Kyle was dead.

He'd seen Kyle as a stupid kid in a young man's body who was going to get them all killed, but Kyle could, and did, learn how to survive as a valued companion after the disintegration of practically everything. From here on out, Parker would have to be very fucking careful about what he wished for. And he shouldn't ever think he knew the future based on a single moment in time. The future was not like the present, only more so. Life rarely went in straight lines for long. It turned corners.

Kyle had fully matured, but Parker was still a work in progress—an irony since Parker was twice Kyle's age. Kyle's problem had been developmental; Parker's was chronic. He'd spent his entire life as a pain in everyone's ass, the sort of thing that, after the apocalypse, could get somebody killed. Others might kill you if you couldn't get along and they saw you as a threat. Parker's own friends damn near killed him when they experimented and infected him on purpose.

They never would have done that if he'd been a better human being.

The kind of person who saw God's hand in everything might nod and smile. Annie wouldn't even be on the road to Atlanta if she, Kyle, and Hughes hadn't conducted their mad scientist experiment on Parker. And if she wasn't on the road to Atlanta, she could not save the world. None of this would be happening if Parker had not done something terrible to deserve it. Seen that way, Parker's near-fatal flaw could bring salvation to all in the end.

Parker could imagine that, but he dared not believe it. He wasn't a Jesus figure. He'd been forced to shape up or die, so he shaped up.

What was Roy doing? That's what Parker wanted to know. Was he improving himself in some way? Becoming smarter, more capable, more decent, more . . . anything? Parker doubted it but forced himself to hold off. His experience getting Kyle wrong all but demanded it.

A sign on the side of the road startled him. WELCOME TO MISSOURI. "What the hell?" he said. He'd sensed they'd been heading north but dismissed it. He always knew which way was north, as if he had a scrap of metal in his head that pinged the magnetic pole.

His larynx spasmed when, for the briefest of moments, he thought about asking Kyle to check the map. He turned around in his own seat and saw Annie with her head against the window and her eyes closed.

"Why are we heading north?" he said.

"A little piece of Missouri juts down into Arkansas," Hughes said. "That's where we are."

Parker huffed. He should give Roy a break, though. Knowing the way was Roy's job. It was his only job. If they had to head north around some obstacle to cross the Mississippi River, then fine. Even so, he turned around in his seat again and fished Kyle's map out of the back.

He saw it now, there on the page. They were avoiding Memphis. Plenty of bridges spanned the Mississippi into Tennessee in and around Memphis, but Memphis surely had no shortage of problems better avoided. The only other bridge Parker could see over the river was up in Missouri between Caruthersville and Dyersburg.

Their route made sense, then, for a while anyway, but when Roy took them over the Mississippi River into Dyersville, he turned left and headed north again toward Kentucky. They were still going the wrong way on the map.

Annie stirred in the back. "Where are we?"

"Heading into Kentucky," Parker said.

"We're going *north*?" she said.

"We are," Hughes said.

"Where's the map?" she said.

"I have it up here," Parker said and passed it back to Annie.

"We're going around something," Hughes said.

"Going around what?" Annie said.

"No idea," Hughes said.

"We're just trusting him?" she said.

Nobody replied.

The light in the sky faded as they continued in silence. They finally reached a campground at the Land Between the Lakes National Recreation Area, a misnomer of park on a long and narrow peninsula between a lake and a river.

Roy pulled into a campsite, and Hughes took another two slots away, which Parker took as a not-subtle suggestion that they weren't going to sit around a fire pit drinking beer and shooting the shit before bed anymore.

Hughes got out of the Suburban and headed toward the RV. He walked angrily and with purpose. Parker stayed put, too exhausted to move. His body would have demanded sleep at gunpoint if it could. Annie seemed to feel the same way even though she'd already napped in the truck.

Roy met Hughes in the neutral zone, in the empty campsite between them.

"Why didn't we just cross into Kentucky from Missouri," Hughes said, "and skip that shitshow in Arkansas?"

"Can't," Roy said.

"Why not?" Hughes said.

"That border ain't friendly," Roy said.

"Which side is a problem?" Hughes said.

"Both," Roy said.

"Both *how*?" Hughes said.

"Bad as Arkansas was," Roy said, "the border is worse. Yes, we lost two people, but I still saved your asses. You don't want to follow me? Adios, motherfuckers."

"Everybody, just settle down," Parker said. He didn't want to hear any more. He had to sleep. Now. He would have slept for twelve hours if Hughes wasn't about to discover something as dangerous as a live grenade cooking off in the truck.

11

The cold sky faded to a dark purple. A light wind shook the evergreen branches overhead and whistled faintly in the Suburban's intake vents. The air in the truck, warmed from three living bodies, felt almost humid.

Hughes racked back the driver's seat and stretched out his legs. His two companions were conked for the night, with Parker snoring gently in the passenger seat and Annie curled into a ball behind him in back. She could have stretched herself out lengthwise, but grief and guilt seemed to stop her.

Hughes would miss Kyle, not just for his companionship but for his navigational role. Not that Kyle was uniquely brilliant at it. Parker and Annie could read a map just as well, and Hughes was simply following Roy in the RV anyway. Even so, consulting the map had been Kyle's job, and the fact that somebody else would now have to do it left another Kyle-sized hole in the world.

Roy would face the same problem since he did all the driving. Not once had Hughes seen Lucas behind the wheel, which meant Lucas must have done most or all of the navigating. And navigating in this part of the country was a vastly more complicated affair than what

Kyle had done out West where there were far fewer roads, almost all of them empty, and no known obstacles.

Obviously, Lucas used maps. Hughes wondered if Lucas also took notes. Lucas and Roy must have turned down one hazardous path after another, far too many to keep track of in their heads.

Rather than taking notes, Lucas might have annotated his maps. That's probably what Kyle would have done. He was a map guy. He seemed to enjoy poring over them, at times in a state of almost wonder.

If Hughes were in charge of essentially remapping an entire quarter of American territory, he'd be wary of now-outdated maps. Ideally, he'd create his own, though that, of course, wouldn't be possible. He wasn't a geographer. And the locations of cities, roads, and rivers weren't suddenly up in the air. So he would take notes.

He'd almost have to. Indicating most problems with red Xs on maps wouldn't cut it. He could cross out a blown bridge, sure, but he would not want to note the locations of militias, bandits, or hordes that way. They moved around. Didn't stay in one place unless something was pinning them there.

Lucas, therefore, probably had some kind of a notebook. If he did, it would be in the RV, in the glove box perhaps, or on the floor beneath the passenger seat. Hughes wanted it. He wouldn't need Roy anymore if he could make enough sense of it. He could ditch Roy pretty much anywhere. Wouldn't be difficult.

Hughes couldn't creep the RV without being seen, but he had Lucas's cell phone right there in the Suburban's glove box. Lucas had used that thing all the time. He had a portable solar charger just like Kyle did. Kyle hadn't used his since they left Wyoming, but Lucas had whipped his out at the diner in Iowa to take photographs. Maybe he'd used his phone to take notes. Why not? Before the world broke, Hughes used his phone all the time to make shopping and to-do lists because he had it in his pocket wherever he went.

He reached over, popped open the glove box, and took Lucas's phone out. He traced his finger gently over the cracked screen, feeling the fractures across its surface, and pressed the *home* button.

Nothing happened. He remembered that he'd turned the phone off after retrieving it to conserve the battery. So he pressed and held the *on* button until the device stirred to life.

The phone was a make and model he wasn't familiar with, which was fine. What wasn't fine was that the phone only had six percent of its battery left. He could fish Kyle's solar charging kit out of the piles of supplies in the back of the truck, but it wouldn't even start working until the morning, and the damn thing seemed to take forever to add even a bit of juice to a phone. He'd have to hurry if he wanted to find what he was looking for.

He scrutinized the icons on the screen and located a note-taking app. He opened it and found nothing inside, as if Lucas had never once taken a note about anything, at least not with that app.

So Hughes opened the map app. Nothing doing. Lucas's phone wanted an Internet connection and wouldn't display anything without one.

Nothing interesting in the email app either. Lucas hadn't received a single new message since early November the previous year.

Lucas had liked to take pictures, though. Hughes knew that much about the man and his phone. So, he opened the camera roll.

The first photo disturbed him. Lucas had taken a shot, in low light, of the Suburban parked in the Mark Twain National Forest back in Missouri. Hughes saw the dark outlines of two sleeping figures in the front seat of the truck, himself and Parker. What on earth had Lucas been thinking when he snapped that?

The battery charge was down to four percent now.

Hughes swiped the phone's screen with his finger and scrolled backwards through Lucas's camera roll.

He knew the next picture already. It was the one Lucas had taken in the Iowa diner. A terrible shot. Annie was front and center, her face a blur as she actively turned away from the camera. Parker was sitting in his chair and looking up at the ceiling. Hughes saw himself with his arms crossed and glowering off to the side. He remembered that moment, remembered deliberately sabotaging the photo because the whole thing weirded him out. Only Kyle was looking at the camera, though he wasn't smiling.

Hughes felt an ache in his throat. This awkward photograph, on Lucas's cracked phone, was the only picture of Kyle that Hughes would ever see. And there were no possibilities to take another now that Kyle was gone.

Perhaps not, though, now that he thought about it. Kyle probably had a few selfies on his own phone, and Hughes could recharge it. Annie would want those pictures. Hughes made a mental note to himself to make that happen when he had the chance.

Lucas's battery had only two percent left now. Hughes had to stop fucking around if he wanted to find anything useful. He scrolled backward through the camera roll and nearly vomited when he saw the next picture.

～

HUGHES HAD EXPERIENCED MORE horror and violence during the past couple of months than even most combat veterans. His entire home city of Seattle had been wiped from the earth, its people by the infection, its buildings and houses by fire. Not since World War II had soldiers anywhere in the world experienced more mass carnage and mayhem than he and his friends had. He'd become inured to it all as much as a human being could. The emotional switch in his mind wasn't off, exactly, but he no longer had the same capacity to be shocked and appalled.

He discovered, though, when he saw the contents of Lucas's camera role, that he could still be shocked and appalled. He'd been seeing everything wrong. This brutality, this hell, inflicted on the world by the hordes of infected wasn't at all like a massacre in a war, not even a nuclear war. It had more in common with mass casualties from an earthquake, a volcanic eruption, or an asteroid strike. The infected weren't evil. They had no agency and no culpability. They were a force of nature, not human wickedness.

Lucas's cell phone, on the other hand, was a chronicle of human psychopathy.

The first photo—a selfie of sorts—showed a grinning Lucas in the foreground crouching over the body of a young woman bound hand and foot, her throat slit from ear to ear, with a rat shoved headfirst into her mouth, the rodent's feet and tail protruding from her grimacing lips. Roy stood in the background with blood dripping from his sword. Lucas and Roy wore all-black contact lenses that made them look like demons visiting from another dimension to torment the living.

Next up in the camera roll wasn't a selfie. It wasn't even a photograph.

It was a video.

Bilious dread bloomed in Hughes's chest as he pressed the *play* button. He saw the dead woman still alive, tied on the floor and cowering as Roy loomed over her. Lucas was there, too, with a squirming rat in his hand. Hughes heard it squealing as its legs thrashed between Lucas's fingers. He fiddled with the phone and found the *down* button on the volume controls but not before the woman on the video screamed.

Annie stirred in the back. Parker sat bolt upright in the passenger seat. Hughes killed the video.

Parker swung his head from side to side, trying to figure out if they were under attack.

"What's going on?" Annie said. "Are you watching a video?" Bewilderment in her voice.

Hughes powered the phone down. Just before the screen went dark, he saw that only one percent of the battery charge remained.

"Whose phone is that?" Parker said.

Hughes just sat there, nauseated and shaking. He closed his eyes, took a deep breath, and willed his guts not to heave. No use. He opened the door and vomited onto the dirt. It was a full body experience. Every muscle from his toes to the top of his head contracted to expel the contents of his stomach. He took a breath and felt dizzy and disgusting and only partly relieved. His stomach wasn't finished with him yet, and he vomited up whatever was left. A wave of blackness washed through him.

"What on earth did you just watch?" Parker said. "Is that Lucas's phone?"

Hughes couldn't speak. He just nodded and struggled to hold himself up.

"Let me see that," Annie said. Fear in her voice this time.

Hughes shook his head, sat back upright, and placed the phone in his pants pocket. Then he stepped out of the truck, careful to avoid the puddle at his feet, and stumbled in the dark toward the trees, away from the Suburban and away from the RV and Roy. He heard, but did not see, Parker and Annie exit the truck and follow him. One of them brought a flashlight, and its beam created jagged fragments of light and shadows ahead in the trees.

"Hey," Annie said.

Hughes staggered away, his stomach calmed but his mind still reeling. He knew what he'd find if he continued scrolling through Lucas's camera roll. He'd find a picture of that woman alive and well, posing with the men who knew they were going to kill her.

"Hughes!" Annie said.

"Hey, man," Parker said.

Hughes turned around. It was Parker who carried the flashlight. He aimed it low at Hughes's feet.

Lucas had a picture of Annie on that phone.

"What's going on?" Annie said. "You need to tell us."

"Lucas did something," Parker said. "Didn't he."

Hughes nodded. He couldn't speak.

"Lucas and Roy?" Parker said.

Hughes nodded again.

"What?" Annie said. "What did they do? They took a video of it on their *phone*?"

Poor Annie. She thought the two men wanted to rape her.

"We need to know," Annie said again. "And you need to tell us."

"Let us see, man," Parker said.

Hughes shook his head and forced himself to speak even though he wasn't getting enough air. "You don't want to see. The battery is dead anyway."

"Give it to me," Parker said.

Hughes couldn't keep this from them. They had to know, but he had to process it first. He couldn't even say the words in his head without processing it first. He also wanted at least a minute to figure out what the fuck they were supposed to do now.

Roy could never come back from this. He and Lucas were worse than the infected. Much, much worse. The infected's minds were wiped, but they were redeemable. The proof was right there in front of him. Both Annie and Parker had been infected, yet there they were. Alive and healthy. Morally intact.

"Hughes!" Parker said. "You need to talk to us."

Hughes saw Roy's half-baked philosophy about the universe committing suicide differently now. It was a justification, a license, since everyone's lives were forfeit anyway and everyone secretly yearned to die anyway.

Yet Lucas and Roy wanted immunity. They'd apparently rather have *that* than an additional handful of victims. God, Hughes thought. That's what the two of them had been talking about outside the diner when they'd heard Annie was immune. They'd been out there in the parking lot scrambling their plans, shelving their plot to brutally dispatch four strangers.

"They raped somebody," Annie said. "Didn't they."

Hughes had to tell her. He did not want to tell her.

He shook his head.

"Killed somebody?" Parker said.

Hughes loudly exhaled. His way of saying yes without saying yes.

"You need to tell us what's going on," Annie said.

The RV door banged open.

"Shh," Hughes said.

Roy was coming out. "Everything okay out here?"

"No!" Annie shouted.

"We're fine," Hughes said, surprised at how normal he managed to sound.

"Anything I can do?" Roy said.

"Go back to bed," Hughes said.

Annie narrowed her eyes at Hughes.

"Just hang on," Hughes said, his stomach twisting into a knot again. He needed to get Annie away from Roy. "Let's take a walk."

"A walk?" Annie said. "In the woods at night? Are you kidding?"

They weren't armed. They'd need to be, though, if they were going anywhere.

"Hang on," he said. "Wait here a sec."

He walked back to the Suburban, the sour taste of bile in his mouth, and retrieved Parker's hammer. He wanted the shotgun, but they were out of ammunition. Restocking would be the first order of business tomorrow. Shouldn't be hard. They were in Kentucky, after all, where guns and ammo were widely available.

Hughes returned with the hammer and another flashlight in hand.

"Let's go," Hughes said.

"Just one hammer?" Parker said. "Man—"

"Just walk with me," Hughes said. He didn't want either Parker or Annie to be armed when he told them what he had to tell them. "We're not going far."

"Why are we going anywhere?" Annie said.

"To get away from Roy," Hughes said.

Annie stared hard at him for a moment. "Fine."

Hughes took them into the trees, far enough away that Roy wouldn't be able to hear anything anyone said.

"Spit it out," Annie said. "Or show us."

The phone still had a one percent battery charge. Hughes could show them but wouldn't. They had a right to see it, no question, but he didn't want them getting emotional yet. They had to keep their heads until they figured out what to do.

"Roy and Lucas murdered a woman," Hughes said. He expected some kind of reaction—a gasp from Annie or a curse from Parker—but nothing came. They'd already figured it out. What else would Hughes be making such a big deal out of?

"They photographed her body," Parker said.

"They did," Hughes said and nodded. "And they videotaped themselves doing it."

"Jesus Christ," Annie said.

"Looked like they'd done it before," Hughes said. "And in case there's any doubt, no, they weren't executing her for committing some kind of crime. They shoved a live rat in her mouth before slitting her throat."

A long silence followed as Annie and Parker processed what they'd just heard.

"So, they're serial killers," Parker finally said.

"Seems so," Hughes said.

12

Annie could no longer stand. She first tottered on her feet and then eased herself onto the ground. Her insides went cold, and her head swam with dizziness.

Roy and Lucas were serial killers? She shook her head. No. That could not be. She'd gotten a creep vibe off them from the very beginning, but serial killers?

"The fuck do we do?" Parker said.

"I don't know yet," Hughes said.

No way could they continue to Atlanta with Roy, Annie thought. She stood up, unsteady on her feet. "We have to go back there."

"And do what?" Hughes said.

"What do you think?" Annie said. She turned her head toward camp and saw nothing but blackness beyond the edge of the flashlight beam. She didn't have a light of her own.

"We need him," Hughes said.

"We don't need him that bad," Parker said.

"We don't need him at all," Annie said.

"He knows the way," Hughes said.

"He got Kyle killed!" Annie said.

"We might not have gotten this far without him," Hughes said.

"Bullshit," Annie said.

"Roy found his way on these roads," Parker said. "We can too."

"You want to chance it?"

"Damn straight," Parker said.

Thank God, Annie thought. She wasn't alone. "Me too."

Hughes huffed.

Annie couldn't believe it. What the hell was wrong with Hughes? They could just get into the Suburban and go. They had maps. They didn't need Roy. On the contrary. The world needed Roy gone.

"He's not going to kill us," Hughes said.

Annie blew out her breath.

"We're already halfway to Atlanta from Iowa," Hughes said. "If he and Lucas wanted to kill us, they would have done it back there. And now that it's three against one, Roy is even less likely to try anything. Especially if he wants to get vaccinated."

Annie shook her head. Hughes failed to see what was right in front of his nose. "He doesn't believe we're really immune," Annie said. "That's why he let Lucas get bit. And that's why Kyle is dead."

There. She actually said it. *Kyle is dead.* Another guardrail down.

"No," Hughes said. "You're wrong. He's a serial killer, right? And he found himself a buddy. He's not getting another one of those, and it's way too dangerous to be wandering around out here by himself. He wouldn't have let Lucas get bit if he actually thought Lucas would die. What is it that folks used to say? Trust but verify? Roy trusted us when he told us to follow him. Letting Lucas get bit was verification."

"Roy didn't verify anything," Annie said. "Lucas died."

"From blood loss and shock," Hughes said. "Not from the virus."

"He still doesn't know I'm immune," Annie said. "He never got his proof."

"So what?" Hughes said.

"What do you mean, *so what*?" Annie said.

"Who cares what he thinks as long as he takes us to Atlanta?" Hughes said.

"Okay," Annie said, "so let's say he takes us. Then what do we do with him?"

"We figure it out when we get there," Hughes said.

"The fuck's that supposed to mean?" Parker said.

"If Atlanta's still standing, they'll have security," Hughes said. "We turn him in."

"Lander, Wyoming, had security," Parker said, "and look how that turned out."

"We don't know what we'll find until we get there."

"What if there's no security?" Annie said. "What if there's nothing?"

"Then we handle it ourselves," Hughes said.

"We take him out?" Parker said.

"We take him out," Hughes said.

"And until then?" Annie said.

"We pretend like everything's peachy," Hughes said.

"Fuck," Annie said.

They stood around for another couple of moments saying nothing. Annie didn't even know what to think anymore.

"We sleep in shifts," Parker said.

"We're already sleeping in shifts," Hughes said.

Annie wanted to kick something. "Can we go back to the truck now?"

"Will you go to sleep?" Hughes said.

Annie snorted.

"Will you lay there and be quiet and not do anything stupid? At least until we've thought about this some more?"

Annie held up her hands in surrender. She was beyond exhausted and could hardly even stand, let alone think straight.

"Parker?" Hughes said.

"We're not done talking about this," Parker said.

"Of course not," Hughes said.

"Fine then," Parker said. "Let's go."

They headed back toward camp.

God, Annie thought as she made her way through the trees. She'd drawn her own blood and transferred her immunity to a monster.

PART III
THE LAST CITY

13

Menacing clouds threatened the Kentucky countryside with rain. At least one winter storm had already chewed up the area; snapped branches the size and shape of human limbs littered the highway. The Suburban's wheels crunched so many dead leaves that the pavement sounded wet, though the asphalt was as gray as the sky. Annie saw a few ditched cars here and there on the side of the road. A corpse sat behind the wheel of an old gray Peugeot with Arkansas plates parked half on and half off the shoulder.

The truck smelled of old food and unwashed bodies, and Annie's mouth tasted sour. She hadn't bothered brushing her teeth that morning and had refused reconstituted oatmeal when Hughes had offered her some. She would have turned down even coffee had it been an option.

Hughes swerved around a downed branch in the road. "How much farther is Bowling Green?"

Parker checked the map. "Fifty miles or so." They both spoke in a low voice, as if neither man cared whether or not Annie could hear them from the back seat.

"Should be just about there then," Hughes said.

Annie crossed her arms over her chest. She didn't like Parker taking over map-reading duties from Kyle. And neither of her friends wanted to talk about what they'd discovered about Roy and Lucas the night before.

"Here we go," Hughes said and followed the RV off the main highway past a sign that read MADDOX MUNITIONS and toward a security checkpoint with a drive-up hut. The steel arm that blocked unauthorized vehicles from proceeding was already raised. Beyond the hut rose a gray windowless building surrounded by an empty lake of parking.

According to Roy, Maddox Munitions was better than an ammunition store. Better, even, than an armory. Maddox Munitions was an ammunition factory.

"Hell of a thing," Hughes said.

"Man's earning his money," Parker said.

"So to speak," Hughes said.

Roy's RV came to a stop near the front door, a metal slab with a rectangular window at head level. Hughes pulled into a space more than a hundred feet away, with Annie's side of the Suburban facing the other direction.

"You two stay here," Hughes said as he killed the engine, "and guard the vehicles. I'll go inside with Roy."

Annie stewed. Hughes didn't want her "guarding" the vehicles. He wanted her the hell away from Roy. Not for her protection either. For Roy's. To stop her from bashing in his skull with the hammer.

Roy approached the Suburban and stopped a respectful distance away.

Hughes rolled down his window. "Be there in a sec." He reached under the driver's side seat. "Got something for you, Annie."

He produced Kyle's cell phone. Annie frowned.

"I looked through it last night when you two were sleeping," Hughes said. "Still has a thirty percent charge. There are some photos on there that you might like to have. Mostly nature shots but also a few selfies that turned out real good."

Annie took the phone from him and nodded in thanks.

"Back soon," Hughes said. He stepped out of the SUV with the hammer Annie wanted to brain Roy with and shut the door and headed into the factory with Roy. The door wasn't locked. Someone had already busted in.

"You okay?" Parker said.

"What do you think?" Annie said.

"I think," Parker said, "that I'm going to enjoy ridding the world of that sonofabitch when all this is over."

Annie felt some of the tension ease out of her body. She hesitated a moment before powering up Kyle's phone, though. Would looking at the photos make her feel better or worse? Both, probably, at the same time in different ways. She went ahead and pressed the *home* button. The device didn't require a passcode.

She found the camera app easily enough and scrolled through it. Like Hughes had already said, most of the pictures were nature shots from the Pacific Northwest: Oregon's Mount Hood, Washington's Mount Rainier, the Columbia River Gorge on the border between the two states, and a place on the Oregon Coast that she thought might be Cannon Beach. She also found a few photos of Kyle with a pretty young girlfriend on a boat in Puget Sound with a sweet-looking Labrador Retriever, a panoramic shot of glass apartment towers in Vancouver, Canada, and another shot with the same girlfriend on a beach with palm trees in a place Annie assumed was Hawaii. Annie had no idea what this girlfriend's name was. Kyle had never mentioned her.

She felt an ache in her throat. Kyle looked so innocent in these pictures, an optimistic all-American boy just out of college with a whole adventurous life in front of him. Thank God people couldn't see the future, that Kyle hadn't even a flickering notion of the hell that awaited him, that the most grueling journey of his life would end in a bloody warehouse in Arkansas.

Annie let herself cry. Parker couldn't see her in the back seat from his perch in the front, but he must have heard her sniffle.

"We're going to be okay," Parker said.

"Why would you even think that?"

"We're almost there. This will be over soon."

Annie wiped her face with the back of her hand. "Then what?"

"They might let us stay."

"We don't even know if they'll let us in. We don't even know if they're still there."

"They'll let us in." Parker turned around and faced her. "The minute they know who you are, they'll let us in."

Annie wasn't so sure. She couldn't prove that she was immune before going inside. For all she knew, plenty of people had already shown up at the gate, said they were immune, and were later found out to be lying. A common story, perhaps. And what did it say about the people who lived inside the walled part of Atlanta that they wouldn't take refugees? Even Joseph Steele, the sonofabitch who ran Lander, Wyoming, had taken refugees.

Even so, Parker was probably right. If they were protecting the Centers for Disease Control, leaving her and her friends outside to die wouldn't make any sense.

Hughes emerged grinning from the building and carrying what looked like two heavy shoeboxes. "Enough ammunition in there to outfit the Romanian army," he said.

Roy followed close behind with a third box. He and Hughes placed all three boxes into the back of the Suburban.

"Nothing for him?" Parker said.

"We're going back," Hughes said, "for another load."

Annie sighed and slumped in her seat.

Hughes and Roy finally returned a few minutes later with three more boxes, again with Hughes carrying two and Roy carrying one. Two went into the RV and one into the Suburban.

Parker stepped out of the truck and helped Hughes load ammunition into the weapons as Roy headed back toward his RV. Annie passed the Glock at her feet back to Parker. "Can you fill this one too?"

Parker nodded and took the weapon from her.

She stared at Roy as he loaded the Bushmaster. The man was barely a hundred feet away, and he had his back turned. He trusted the others too much. They didn't need him as much as he thought they did.

Hughes and Parker, weapons loaded, got back in the truck.

"How far to Atlanta from here?" Hughes said.

"Six hours if we were going straight," Parker said.

But they weren't going straight. They planned to spend the night in Tennessee near the Great Smoky Mountains. "Should make the city by noon tomorrow."

They were almost there. And they knew the route now.

Parker handed Annie her Glock. She checked it. Fully loaded.

She turned her eyes back toward the RV. Roy was inside now but not behind the driver's seat, fiddling around with something in back and blind to everything else around him.

"We'll be in Nantahala National Forest tonight," Annie said.

"I'm not sure if that's—" Parker said.

"That's the one," Annie said. "I've been there." She'd been there a number of times, actually, camping with her family when she was a girl.

"We're driving into Atlanta from the north," Annie said.

"We are," Parker said.

"Into Alpharetta," Annie said.

"What's that?" Hughes said.

"Northernmost suburb," Annie said. They were back in the South now, her part of the country, her homeland. She could guide them as well as anyone else.

"We know the way," Annie said.

"I guess so," Hughes said and racked the slide on this own hand weapon.

"We've restocked on ammo," Annie said.

"In spades," Parker said and chuckled.

Annie returned her attention to the RV. Roy was still in there, rummaging around in the back.

"Hey," Hughes said. "Don't even think about it."

"He's done enough already," Annie said.

"You could probably get us to Atlanta without even needing a map," Hughes said.

"I can," Annie said.

"I get that," Hughes said. "But he's the only one who has been there since the outbreak. If it had been up to you, you would have taken us in from the west. Am I right?"

Annie said nothing.

"We were originally going to come in from the south," Hughes said, "if we'd gotten a boat and sailed to the gulf down the river. Only Roy knew to drop down from the north."

"Sure," Annie said. "But now we know. And I know the way."

"You don't know what you don't know," Hughes said.

"You're forgetting what we do know!" Annie said. "He got Kyle killed. He got his own friend killed. And he's killed other people for sport."

"He's been more than useful so far," Hughes said.

"*Useful*," Annie said.

"Annie," Parker said.

"We wouldn't be where we are without him," Hughes said.

"Kyle wouldn't be dead if it weren't for him," Annie said.

"We might all be dead if it weren't for him," Hughes said.

Roy stepped out of the RV with a box of gear in his hands and headed toward the Suburban. "Finally found these," he said and shook the box. "Thought I'd lost 'em there for a minute."

Looked like he had some portable radios.

"Walkie-talkies?" Parker said.

"Yes, sir," Roy said and handed one to Hughes. "You know how to use 'em?"

"Sure do," Hughes said.

"Battery's mostly full," Roy said. He pressed the *talk* button on his own radio and said "yo." His voice crackled through the speaker in Hughes's hands. "We'll need these when we get where we're going."

∽

SLEEP CAME TO ANNIE UNBIDDEN. This was no shallow nap in the back of the truck. It was more like falling into a well. Darkness pulled her into the depths as if it had gripped her ankles with hands. There was no ring of light at the top of the well, not even stars.

Annie found herself in an ornate Victorian mansion, in her house that wasn't her house, in a time that wasn't her time, in a city that wasn't her city, unsure but uncaring how she got there, as if she'd drunk from the River Lethe. She glided through the living room, her feet just off the floor, the furniture antique Gilded Age pieces, heavy curtains pulled tight against the windows to keep the night out. There were people outside the house, gathering on the lawn, milling about on her porch, and wanting in. She could not see them or hear them, but she knew they were there the same way she knew the sky was overhead even though she couldn't see it. She did not want those outside to come inside. The walls were thick, the doors were locked, and as long as they didn't see her, as long as they didn't hear her, they would not come in through the windows.

Rather than pressing her weight upon creaking hardwood, she glided above the floor in bare feet—quieter that way—and headed through the dining room toward the kitchen.

She didn't make it.

He stood there in the doorway.

Roy. Big and stone faced, wearing work jeans and an olive drab jacket matted with mud and dried blood. He had a live, squealing rat in his left hand and a carving knife in his right. She knew that knife. It was the longest and most dangerous blade slotted into the block of wood on the counter.

He stood there, implacable and unmoving, no expression on his face, his eyes locked on hers.

Annie halted her glide.

She wasn't afraid of him. No reason to be. She had him right where she wanted him—a trap laid just for him—so she smiled. She could see herself smile too, as if she were disembodied and observing the room through a camera placed over Roy's shoulder, like she was watching a scene in a movie. Her smile was devilish, almost Satanic, her dark, wet hair hanging in front of her eyes like that of a nightmare apparition.

Roy would not jam that squirming rat in her mouth. He would not run the blade through her throat. He was in her house now. She had powers there that he still did not understand, and she had friends outside who would help her.

"Finally we get to play," Roy said and smiled.

She tilted her head to the side.

He did not know about her shadow self, that she could tap its dark, inner power whenever she wanted. Unlike Parker, she did not fear it. It had always been there, had always been real. The virus merely taught her how to unlock it.

Now was the time to unlock it.

Darkness filled Annie's mind and body like black ink poured into water. She felt energized, powerful, and transcendent. Her mind went to dangerous places. Not dangerous for her. Dangerous for Roy. She smiled again and imagined her teeth ripping flesh, her hands mauling internal organs, muscle and tissue and entrails engorging her stomach, and nothing but sticky, red bones left on the floor.

She lost her ability to articulate words, but no matter. She could still communicate all that she had to.

She dropped out of gliding position, lowered her feet to the floorboards, and felt the full weight of her body pressing down on the wood. She opened her mouth, not to speak but to scream.

To summon an army.

She belted it out, high in pitch, urgent and furious, like the shock wave from a bomb detonation, alerting the others on the porch and the lawn who waited for just the right stimulus.

Prey inside the house.

A roar engulfed the house like a stadium cheer. The windows blew in as if they'd been hit by a tornado as the others surged inside, a multi-bodied organism with Annie Starling as its queen, as its brain.

Roy twitched and backed into the kitchen, clenching his hands around the knife in his right and the rat in his left.

Annie raised herself up on the balls of her feet and surged forward with all her power, a *hungry hungry predator* with its teeth bared, fury in her heart and her throat.

Roy jammed the knife into her abdomen as she sank her teeth into his shoulder.

They toppled onto the floor, Roy on his back and Annie impaled on the blade, squirming on top of him like a fly stuck to a wall as hundreds of millions of viruses swarmed into his bloodstream.

You're one of us now, you sonofabitch.

She woke up screaming in the back of the truck.

14

They drove in silence the rest of the day, which suited Hughes fine. He did not want to talk, especially not to Annie. They'd just fight, about Roy, about Atlanta, about everything. He worried about her despondency, about losing her faith in a mission that had been her idea in the first place, about her waking up screaming from a goddamn nap in the middle of the day and refusing even to speak about it, and about her . . . bloodthirstiness toward Roy. Hughes wondered if the same demons that had tortured Parker after he recovered from the virus were having their way with Annie now too, if on some level the postinfected could never fully be cured. That would explain why she was losing her faith in Atlanta.

Parker had gotten over it. At least he seemed to, so perhaps Annie would be fine in the end, but he worried sometimes that she was going to snap and do something stupid or dangerous or both—something with irrevocable consequences for her personally and for everyone still alive—before they reached the end of the road.

Hughes and Annie agreed about one thing, at least. Roy could not be allowed to go free when they reached the city. Hughes just had to make sure that Roy didn't know what the others knew about him until it was too late to bail on the mission or to sabotage it. If Roy even suspected that the others knew his secret, God only knew what he'd do.

At least the drive was interesting. The highway plunging southward from Kentucky into Tennessee looked nothing like the Midwest. The landscape was hillier, more densely forested, and lined with little cliffs along the side of the highway, as if the roadbed had been blasted out of rock to smooth out the grade. The forest seemed almost impenetrable. Those woods had been hiding secrets for hundreds of years and no doubt concealed pockets of rugged survivors who had no need or inclination to erect man-made barriers to keep others away. Hunkering down in the hollows between the hills would be enough. No one with a lick of sense would go traipsing around in there without knowing exactly who and what lay at the end of the paths. Hughes knew there had to be paths, old ones, long hidden from outsiders.

They eventually crossed the Tennessee River between Old Washington and Decatur, bypassed the small town of Athens, and entered the forbidding Nantahala National Forest near the border with Georgia and North Carolina. Prairie and farmland country were long behind them now. Appalachia was another world entirely, and Hughes was relieved to have a guide here, even if that guide was Roy. Annie vaguely knew the area, sure, but she had never lived there, hadn't visited in years, and had no idea, really, what to expect after everything had violently changed forever.

Past the small village of Austral, the woods looked positively gothic with a jungle-like tangle of trees draped with moss, slashed by vines, and almost but not quite concealing imposing wood-framed houses rotting from years of neglect. Many of them looked haunted.

"Jesus," Parker said.

"He's taking us to his lair," Annie said.

A joke, surely, but Hughes thought the real joke was that Annie was only half joking. Just moments later, Roy pulled into a driveway that led to a weathered and peeling Victorian mansion with a collapsed porch, a decrepit balcony on the second floor that nobody would dare set foot on, a crumbling chimney topped with an iron lightning rod, and—most incongruously—windows that sparkled as if they'd just been cleaned yesterday.

"What did I tell you?" Annie said.

Roy parked in the driveway.

"Seriously?" Parker said. "We're staying here? And we're just going to leave the vehicles out front?"

Hughes didn't like it either. He wasn't going inside that house. No way. He kept the engine running and rolled down the window as Roy climbed out of the RV. The air smelled faintly of mold. "What are we doing here, Roy?"

"What's it look like?" Roy said.

"You want to sleep in there?" Hughes said, resting his arm on the top of the truck door.

"There's beds inside," Roy said.

"What on earth would make you pick this place?" Parker said.

"There's nobody anywhere near here, my friends," Roy said.

Hughes killed the engine, left the keys in the ignition, opened the door, and stepped out. "I don't like it. None of us likes it. And we need to get something straight here."

He took a step toward Roy. Roy did not move.

"I'm not your friend."

Roy's facial expression did not change.

"None of us here are your friends," Hughes said.

Roy looked at his feet for a moment, then made eye contact with Hughes again. "I'm real sorry about Kyle. I told you that before, and I'll say it again as many times as I need to."

"This isn't about Kyle," Annie said from the Suburban's backseat.

Hughes winced.

Roy looked at Annie with slitted eyes, icy and cold and reptilian. Annie stared back, righteous and angry and hot.

Goddammit, Annie.

Roy glanced at Parker and finally at Hughes again.

"She doesn't trust you," Hughes said, because he had to say something. "None of us trusts you."

Roy squinted at Hughes. Annie was fucking up in the worst possible way.

"Why are y'all doing this?" Roy said.

Hughes wasn't entirely sure what Roy meant by *this*.

"You like the world the way it is," Annie said. "Don't you." It wasn't really a question.

Roy said nothing.

"It suits you just fine," Annie said. "It suits you perfectly."

Parker opened the passenger door and got out. "Why don't we all take a step back here?"

Nobody said anything for a couple of moments.

"Roy wouldn't be here if he liked the world how it is," Parker said. "Isn't that right?"

Roy eyeballed Parker. Hughes stared hard at Annie and shook his head almost imperceptibly, telling her, *Don't*.

"He wants what you and I have," Annie said to Parker. *Immunity*. "And what Lucas had before he got killed. That's not the same thing."

Nice save, Hughes thought.

"You got me dead to rights, ma'am," Roy said. "I never denied it." He paused, as if weighing what to say next. "I don't expect y'all to think much of me after what happened. But we got a job to do, and we'll finish tomorrow. Least I will. And I'm doing what I can in the meantime. Lucas and I've stayed in this house. There's beds in there and water in the sink. Even the toilets flush. Nobody around here for miles. Nobody in these woods and nobody on the roads."

"We're sleeping in the truck," Hughes said.

"Suit yourself," Roy said and shrugged. "You want to make our final plan tonight or in the morning?"

Hughes exhaled. Roy had moved on. Disaster averted.

"What's to plan?" Annie said, her voice still edged with contempt.

"Atlanta ain't empty," Roy said. "It's overrun. We can't just drive up to the gate."

"I sure as hell hope you don't expect us to walk," Parker said.

"Course not," Roy said. "Question is how we make our way

through the suburbs. You want to shoot our way through? Get bigger trucks? Sneak in at night?"

"Maybe we should," Parker said.

"Should what?" Roy said.

"Sneak in at night," Parker said.

Hughes nodded. "We've got night vision. We can drive in the dark with the headlights off."

Roy nodded. "Okay then."

Hughes exchanged glances with Parker, then returned his attention to Roy. "Okay then? We're going to need a lot more than that."

"Sir," Roy said, apparently chastised at his earlier use of the word *friend*, "I don't know what else to tell you. I haven't been to the center of Atlanta in two and a half years. I can tell you, though, that the suburbs were swarming with infected less than two weeks ago."

Hughes glanced at his friends. Parker swallowed hard. Annie stared at a point in space and nodded to herself, as if she saw something no one else could. But Hughes knew what she was thinking. They truly didn't need Roy anymore. Once they reached Alpharetta, the northernmost suburb, they'd *all* be running blind. Annie could take the sonofabitch out the moment they got there.

Hughes wouldn't let her. Even vicious and murderous psychopaths were on the side of the angels against the infected.

"Let's go inside," Roy said.

Hughes glanced at the house again. It must have been abandoned twenty years earlier and looked like it had been beaten up not only by weather but also by a moderate earthquake. "Not happening."

"It ain't haunted," Roy said. "There's no body parts in the fridge."

Hughes exchanged glances with Annie, still ensconced in the Suburban's back seat and refusing to come out. She leaned forward and opened her eyes wide, imploring Hughes to deal with this somehow.

He checked his watch. The sun would be down in less than an hour.

"How far's Alpharetta?"

"Three hours," Roy said.

"What's stopping us from going tonight?"

Annie opened her mouth to say something, then shut it again. Parker looked around, as if wondering where Kyle was. Roy dropped his chin and shrugged.

"Why don't we just go?" Hughes said. "If we're driving through it in the dark anyway, what's the point of staying here for twenty-four hours?"

"We're going through the suburbs in the dark," Parker said. "You sure you want to drive *to* the suburbs in the dark?"

"Why not?" Hughes said.

"We've never driven anywhere in the dark," Annie said. "Not even once."

That wasn't true, actually. They'd fled Lander, Wyoming, at night. But Hughes took her point.

"We didn't do that out West," Hughes said, "because our headlights could be seen for miles in the empty countryside."

"Plenty of open countryside before we get to Atlanta," Roy said. "It ain't all woods from here."

"But we have the night vision," Hughes said.

"We've always had night vision," Parker said.

"We'd have used up the batteries if we drove all night every night," Hughes said. "Doesn't matter now, though. We only have to do it once. And the batteries last fifty hours," Hughes said. "We'll be fine."

"What about moonlight?" Parker said.

"It's a half moon," Hughes said. "It won't be up all night."

"Is it waxing or waning?" Annie said.

Nobody said anything. Nobody knew.

"Is is rising earlier each night or later?" Annie said.

Shit. Nobody knew.

Hughes looked at the sky. Still as cloudy as before, an uninterrupted gray slab and heavy as an iron lid over the atmosphere. "I think we'll be okay." And if not, he thought, we'll deal with it.

Nobody spoke. They just looked at each other for a couple of moments. Parker swallowed hard. Annie tilted her head a little bit sideways. Roy put his hands in his pockets.

"If the moon comes out from behind the clouds," Hughes said, "we'll hunker down or withdraw and try again tomorrow night. And we have enough battery power to go three nights in a row without a recharge."

Still, nobody spoke.

Annie's face turned ashen. She pressed her elbows into her sides as if trying to make herself smaller. Until now, she'd seemed almost fearless. Hughes knew she wasn't afraid of the drive. He wasn't even sure she worried about the infected out in the suburbs. She was afraid of the city itself and what they might find there, whether the CDC was really still up and running and what the doctors might do to her once she told them the truth. Hughes had promised her that he wouldn't let them mistreat her as the authorities in Wyoming had, but she knew as well as he did that he wouldn't be able to stop them.

"Let's get this over with," Hughes said. He locked eyes with Annie and turned so that Roy could not see his face. "Let's finally rid the world of this scourge." Then he pointed at Roy with his eyes.

Annie nodded. She understood. Parker nodded too. They were on the same secret page, right out in the open. The sooner they got to Atlanta, the sooner they could get rid of Roy.

"Or we could spend the next twenty-four hours in this haunted house," Hughes said.

"Severed heads in the fridge for dinner," Roy said.

"Alright," Parker said. "City's walled off, right?"

"Correct," Roy said.

"And they aren't letting anyone in," Parker said.

"That's what I've heard," Roy said. "Not that I've tried."

Of course Roy hadn't tried. Harder to get away with murdering people for sport inside a walled enclave.

"We just going to drive up to the wall and yell at whoever's inside to let us in anyway?" Parker said.

"We need to pull up at a gate," Roy said. "There's three of 'em. The White Gate, the Red Gate, and the Black Gate."

"They painted them?" Annie said.

"Those are just names," Roy said.

"Why have gates if they don't let anyone in?" Hughes said.

"So they can come out," Roy said.

"Who's 'they?'"

"The army," Roy said.

"The army's in there?" Hughes said.

"Army built the wall," Roy said, "just like around Washington, DC. Same kind of walls they once built in Baghdad."

"How many civilians are in there?" Hughes said.

"No idea," Roy said.

"So, we drive up to one of the gates," Annie said, "and tell them we're immune. They'll either open the gate or come out to get us."

"What if they don't?" Parker said.

"They will," Annie said.

"They might not," Parker said.

"What would you do?" Annie said. "You're the army commander who walled off the Centers for Disease Control, and you don't open the gate to people coming in from the wasteland who say they're immune? How does that make any sense?"

"They'll let us in," Hughes said. "The CDC has no reason to still exist otherwise."

"I'll lead in the RV," Roy said. "Keep your radio on."

"You know your way?" Hughes said.

"A bit," Roy said.

"Annie?" Parker said. "Do you know your way around Atlanta?"

"In the city," Annie said, "but not in the suburbs."

"Main roads are blocked," Roy said, "once we get past the outskirts. We'll have to find our way through on the surface streets."

"We'll need a detailed map," Parker said. "From a gas station or something. Unless you already have one."

Roy shook his head.

"Where are we going, exactly?" Annie said.

"CDC," Roy said, like she was stupid for asking.

"I mean," Annie said, "where are the gates?"

"Just follow me," Roy said.

"You don't know," Annie said.

"I know where one of 'em is," Roy said.

"So tell us," Annie said.

Hughes opened his mouth to tell her to drop it, then shut it again. She was right. They needed to know. "In case something happens to you," he said to Roy. "We're driving separately, after all."

"North Druid Hills," Roy said. "The Black Gate is at North Druid Hills."

"You know where that is?" Hughes said to Annie.

"It's just north of the CDC and Emory University," Roy said.

"Okay," Hughes said and nodded, satisfied. Annie never did answer his question about whether or not she knew that part of the city, but it wouldn't matter once they found a map.

Night was coming. The weak winter sun was below the trees now. "We could leave midafternoon tomorrow instead of right now," Hughes said. "Sleep in tomorrow and arrive just before nightfall. That would be the smart play. But I'm itching to go and will be awake for several more hours anyway."

"I don't like this place," Annie said and shuddered.

Roy rolled his eyes.

"We could get attacked here," Parker said.

"More likely to get attacked on the way down," Roy said.

"Not if we drive in the dark with the lights off," Hughes said.

"Should we eat first?" Parker said.

"We should eat when we can," Hughes said, "because we have no idea when we'll be able to do it again."

"I ate in the RV," Roy said, "so I'm good to go."

"You aren't the only person here," Annie said.

"We can eat in the truck," Parker said.

"Fine with me," Hughes said.

"Okay then," Roy said, as if Annie's opinion counted for nothing. "In the long run, we're all dead, and so is everyone else, but what the hell. Let's save the world."

Daggers flashed in Annie's eyes. "You aren't saving the world."

"Annie—" Parker said.

"You're only saving yourself," Annie said. "None of us have forgotten what you said in that diner."

The universe is committing suicide.

"You're no better than me," Roy said.

"We're all better than you," Annie said.

"Annie—" Hughes said.

"Because you're saving the world and I'm saving myself," Roy said.

"That's about the long and the short of it," Annie said.

"Alright," Parker said.

"I'm just more honest about it than you," Roy said.

"Let's go," Hughes said.

"How's that?" Annie said.

"I do what's good for me," Roy said, "and you do what's good for you."

"Bullshit," Annie said. "What's good for me is heading so far north into Canada that what's left of the world will leave me alone. That's what I want to do. This is a sacrifice."

"It ain't a sacrifice," Roy said. "It makes you feel good. Like a virtuous person. That's why you're doing it. And you want the old world back because you were comfortable in it. I'll believe in your altruism when you show me a jackalope."

"We're going," Hughes said, got behind the wheel, and shut the door.

Roy pulled his keys out of his pocket and headed toward his own vehicle. "I'm doing this for me," he said, "and so are y'all."

Parker opened the back of the Suburban.

"Don't worry," Annie said and nodded. "You'll get what's coming to you."

Hughes sucked down his anger and started the engine.

"Found the night vision," Parker said from the back of the truck. "We should all probably wear these."

Hughes closed his eyes and nodded. He couldn't drive in the dark otherwise, and everyone would need to see if they ran into trouble.

Parker climbed into the passenger seat with the box of futuristic monocles in his hands. An hour from now, he and his friends would look like cyborg cyclopses.

"Forgetting something?" Hughes said.

"Right," Parker said. He pulled one of the monocles out of the box and took it to Roy.

"Annie," Hughes said while Parker showed Roy how to use the device, "do everybody a favor, would you?"

Annie didn't reply. She had to know what Hughes was going to say.

"Quiet down until we're on the other side of the wall."

She sat sullen and silent in the back seat until Parker returned. "Sorry, guys," she said. "It takes everything I have right now not to set him on fire."

"Like you said," Parker said. "He'll get what's coming to him."

"Let's just get this over with," Annie said.

Hughes watched as Roy fiddled with the night vision monocle before placing it onto his face. "Don't turn it on yet!" he shouted. "With this much light in the sky, it'll blind you."

Roy nodded, rolled up his window, and put his vehicle into reverse. Hughes took one of the monocles out of the box, fastened it to his head, and rested the eyepiece on his forehead so he could see with both eyes as long as he could. Then he put the Suburban into reverse and backed up onto the highway.

"Don't let that bastard get into your head, Annie," Parker said. "Everything he just said is bullshit."

"He's a monster," Annie said, "but he isn't wrong about all of it."

"Yes, he is," Parker said. "About all of it."

"Going to Atlanta does make us feel better," she said. "Doesn't it? That's the real reason we're doing this. It makes us feel virtuous. And who are we kidding? The old world was a lot more pleasant to live in than this one."

Parker shook his head. "You have *got* to get him out of your head. He doesn't even pretend to care about other people. He's a goddamn psychopath."

"I get that," Annie said.

"Far as he's concerned, the rest of us are bugs under glass. You think he feels good if he helps other people?"

Annie didn't reply.

"That's not a rhetorical question," Parker said. "I'm actually asking you. Do you think he feels anything if he helps other people?"

Annie let him wait for a moment before answering no.

"But you do," Parker said.

"Of course," Annie said.

"That's why he's wrong, Annie," Parker said. "Roy's missing screws. Sure, we help other people because it makes us feel good. But it makes us feel good *because* we care about people."

Hughes followed Roy down the darkening highway, deeper into the forest, until every sign of human civilization finally fell away.

"Parker's right, Annie," Hughes said and moved the night vision monocle from his forehead to his left eye. "Don't ever forget who you are."

15

The night vision monocle was nothing at all like the military-grade goggles Joseph Steele's crew had used in Wyoming. Hughes hated the heavy, bulky thing. He had no peripheral vision, couldn't see anything at all that was not right in front of him. Even straight ahead, he perceived only the faint contours of a road through a forest rendered in a grainy, dark green on a background of black. Everything else, the woods especially, was shrouded in darkness. Nothing looked or seemed real. Phantasmagoric shadows moved along the thin green surface between the visible world and the hidden one beyond. And since he was using only one eye, he had no depth perception, as if he were watching it all on a flat screen. He didn't dare drive faster than twenty miles an hour. At least he could trust that no one would come around a corner and blind him with headlights.

"How you holding up?" Parker said.

"Exhausted," Hughes said. "This is exhausting."

"You want a break?" Annie said. "We'll be there in two hours, but the sun won't come up for ten."

Hughes shook his head. "Let's just get there."

"I can drive," Parker said.

"Takes some getting used to," Hughes said. "And I'm used to it now."

"You're also exhausted," Parker said. "Damn shame if we made it all this way just to get killed on the road."

Hughes checked the speedometer. He'd inched up the speed, without even realizing it, to twenty-five miles an hour. "I'm driving like we're in a school zone. We're not gonna die."

"Okay, man," Parker said. "But if you feel like you're falling asleep—"

"I'm fine!"

Hughes regretted snapping, but he didn't apologize. He had to keep his eyes and mind on the road.

He powered down the window and rested his elbow on the top of the door, half in and half out of the truck. It helped. Gave him a tactile connection to the world around him and made it all seem more real. And the temperature surprised him. Outside felt like midspring in Seattle, no cooler than the low sixties.

"Surprisingly warm," Parker said.

"Sometimes it's cold down here in the winter," Annie said, "but this is hardly out of the ordinary."

Which meant few, if any, of the infected in the Atlanta area would have frozen to death.

"Okay," Parker said, "so we know where the gate is, more or less. What do we do when we get there?"

"We need a bullhorn," Hughes said.

"Where are we supposed to get a bullhorn?" Annie said.

"No idea," Parker said.

"Who uses bullhorns, anyway?" Hughes said. "Cops? How about a police station?"

"Okay," Parker said. "Then what?"

"Wait for them to open the gate," Hughes said.

"And if they don't?" Parker said.

"We've already been over this," Annie said.

"We'll figure it out," Hughes said. "Can't make any more of a plan until we see what we're dealing with." He took the radio out of his lap and handed it to Parker. "Maybe check in with Roy. See how he's doing."

"I'm not driving his RV if he's tired," Parker said.

"Course not," Hughes said.

Parker fiddled with the radio for a moment, then pressed the *talk* button. Hughes heard a squawk sound. "Roy, it's Parker. How you holding up? Over." The radio squawked again.

"All good," Roy said. His voice sounded scratchy. "You?"

"Good on our end," Parker said. "We're thinking of hitting a police station on the way down. Pick up a bullhorn so we can talk to Atlanta when we reach the wall. Over."

"Roger that," Roy said. "I'll keep my eyes out."

The forest finally thinned, and the road passed through what was once a lightly populated area on the outskirts of a place Hughes had never heard of named Dahlonega.

"Careful here," Annie said. "This isn't a wide spot on the road."

"How big is it?" Hughes said.

"I'm not sure," Annie said, "but the University of North Georgia is here."

"Talk to Roy," Hughes said.

Parker reached out on the radio. "Hey, it's Parker. Over."

"We're good here," Roy said. "Town's abandoned."

"You sure?" Parker said. "Over."

"It was evacuated," Roy said.

That seemed about right, Hughes thought. There was no traffic jam coming or going. The road was clear. And they were in the town proper now, no longer on the outskirts, with a Walmart Supercenter on the left and, just past it, a chicken franchise on the right. Hughes saw no signs of any kind of disturbance, now or in the past. No wrecked cars, no bodies in the street, no broken windows, no nothing. The town was empty but intact.

"Ask him where everyone went," Hughes said.

"Where'd everyone go?" Parker said. "Over."

"Told you," Roy said. "Florida. Mass exodus to the Caribbean."

"Then why isn't Atlanta empty?" Parker said. "You said it was overrun. Over."

"Six million people in Atlanta," Roy said.

Hughes swallowed hard and imagined a mega-horde of six million infected.

"Not everybody left," Roy said. "Some thought they could ride it out."

Which logically meant, Hughes thought, that some people in Dahlonega must have stayed behind to ride it out too.

"Police station ahead," Parker said from the passenger seat.

Hughes saw it now. A medium-sized building on Main just off the highway with a few cruisers out front. Not the municipal cops but the Sheriff's department. Breaking in wouldn't be any kind of a challenge. No telling if there was a bullhorn inside, though.

"Pulling into the station," Roy said and slowed his RV to a stop in the parking lot in front of the door.

Hughes pulled up behind him and killed the engine. "Sit tight a minute," he said and took the monocle off his head.

The world went black, and he felt a bit dizzy. His right eye had adjusted to the darkness long ago, but the pupil in his left eye was still dilated from the night vision, creating a splotchy visual field that seemed to tilt to the left. It made no sense, but he'd swear he could breathe better now even though he couldn't see.

Nobody moved or said anything. They just sat there a minute with the windows rolled down and listened.

Hughes heard nothing. No vehicles, no footsteps, no rustling, no crickets, no wind, no nothing. This small Georgia city couldn't be quieter. He wasn't sure when he'd last hear silence so absolute. There was usually something—a little breeze if nothing else—but here there was nothing at all.

He considered swapping the Suburban for a police car, thinking that Atlanta might be more likely to open up if they arrived in one of those, but whoever manned that gate would have to know there were no more cops patrolling anywhere in America. There weren't even cops in Lander, Wyoming. A police car's engine would no doubt be better than the Suburban's, and police cruisers had push grill guards mounted on front. There wouldn't be enough room in the back, though. Not in a sedan. And Hughes didn't see any police trucks in the lot.

"I don't see or hear anything," Parker said. Neither did Hughes. "I think we're good."

"You and Annie stay here," Hughes said and got out.

∽

Parker removed the night vision monocle strapped to his forehead and held it up to his eye with his hand. Using it like a telescope felt better. He hadn't noticed until now, but his neck muscles had to strain slightly to hold his head up with the added weight.

He watched Hughes move toward the police station with Roy, a crowbar in one hand and a pistol in the other. "I'll keep watch on the right," he said to Annie. "You keep watch on the left."

"Yes, sir," Annie said.

"It's not an order, Annie," Parker said. "Just making sure we're covering everything."

"Sorry," she said.

Parker wasn't trying to be bossy. He was taking the harder job. He couldn't see shit in his sector. Just the road curving around to the right through some trees. If anyone was lurking back there, he wouldn't see them unless they moved, and he might not see them even then. He wished he had thermal vision. Not even a squirrel would be able to hide in the trees if he had thermal vision.

Annie's sector was more visible and easier to keep tabs on. Across the street on her side was a gigantic empty parking lot in front of an L-shaped strip mall housing a furniture shop, a Fresh N' Frugal grocery store, a fitness place, and a Chinese buffet restaurant. God, what Parker would give for some King Pao shrimp and sticky rice with a side of pot stickers and a fortune cookie chaser.

Hughes popped open the station door with the crowbar, the sound as loud as a gunshot. Parker scrutinized the trees off to the right, listened hard . . . and heard no reaction. No movement of any kind. They seemed to be alone.

"There's nobody here," Annie whispered.

"I don't see or hear anything either," Parker said quietly.

But then, maybe he did. Something moved at the edge of the trees. He had no idea what it was. It was just a flicker of green light across a black canvass. Perhaps a branch had moved in the wind, but there was no wind. He saw it again, closer to the truck this time.

The little city they'd stopped in might not be empty after all. He didn't want to say anything, though, until he was sure.

"You seeing anything?" Parker said.

"Still nothing," Annie said.

Parker turned around to check Annie's sector, made a quick scan of the parking lot, then focused for a moment on the Chinese buffet place to see if his image was stable. The scene was grainy and dim, but he saw no flashes of green that could be mistaken for movement.

He returned to scanning the trees on his own side. Barely a second later, he thought he saw something again, right there at the edge of the vegetation line.

Then Hughes and Roy emerged from the station, Hughes with what looked like a bullhorn in his hand. "Found one," he said and handed it to Annie in back and got in the driver's seat.

"Does it use batteries?" Annie said.

"Yeah," Hughes said, "but it's loud, so don't test it. I turned it on inside and tapped on it. Seems to work."

"Let's get out of here," Parker said, alert and watching the trees again.

"What's going on?" Hughes said.

"Can't tell," Parker said. "Just go."

Hughes put his keys in his lap instead of the ignition. "You still willing to drive?"

Parker felt a pinprick of adrenaline. This was not the time to get out of the truck and switch seats. Not if someone or something was out there. But how could anything be watching them? Parker could see because he had night vision. Anyone or anything else out there would be blind. He lowered the monocle away from his eye and saw nothing but the silhouettes of the treetops against a gray background of sky. There weren't even stars overhead. Just a cloud slab. The night concealed them and made them safe.

"Fine, I'll drive," Parker said. "Let's just get out of here."

"I'll sit in back and let Annie up front," Hughes said. "She should navigate. She knows the area. I've never even been here before."

"Okay," Parker whispered. "Quietly." They all got out of the truck and switched places. Parker took the driver's seat, Annie the passenger seat, and Hughes climbed in the back.

Parker reattached the monocle to his head so he could use it hands-free, turned the ignition key, and followed Roy back to the road leading south to Atlanta.

∽

Parker had wanted, in a casual sort of way, to sit behind the wheel since they'd left Iowa, but he wasn't so sure now that he was actually doing it. Driving in total darkness with night vision in one eye was nobody's idea of a road trip.

At least they were out of the forest. Though the road was still lined with trees in most places, the rural highway became a wide and empty four-lane, not quite an Interstate freeway but a major artery feeding traffic down from rural Tennessee into the great southern metropolis.

"How much farther?" Parker said.

"Twenty miles maybe," Annie said.

Almost an hour then at this speed, Parker thought. "We still don't have a map."

Hughes radioed Roy. "Hey, man, we still need a map, over."

"Interchange with 53 coming up," Roy said through the speaker. "Outlet mall there. Plenty of gas stations and restaurants."

They reached the interchange not five minutes later, and Parker followed Roy onto the exit ramp. They pulled into a Chevron station to get out and stretch and fill up the fuel tanks. An attached minimart had been stripped of everything edible, but there were still magazines and maps on the racks near the cash register. Annie snatched one and they piled back into the vehicles and returned to the road.

A few minutes later, just past the turnoff to Mary Alice Beach Park on the shore of Lake Lanier, Parker saw something he never thought he'd see again in his life: the bright glow of civilization lighting up the underside of the clouds. It was faint but unmistakably there, like a dingy dome of light on the horizon.

"My God," Hughes said from the back.

"So it's real," Annie said from the passenger seat. "Atlanta's still standing."

Parker couldn't believe it. Roy hadn't told them the power was on. Not in a thousand years would he have expected this. There was a downside, however—and it was a big one.

"This complicates things," Annie said.

"It sure does," Hughes said.

"Get Roy on the radio," Parker said. It was the first time he'd given an order to Hughes instead of the other way around. It's what happened, he figured, when a man sat behind the wheel of a truck.

"Roy," Hughes said amid radio squawks. "We're seeing city lights. Over."

The radio crackled and Roy answered. "Course. Grid's still up."

"How are we supposed to sneak in at night if the place is lit like a stadium?" Hughes said. "Over."

"Only downtown and Midtown are lit," Roy said. "Everything else is out."

Parker relaxed a little.

"Ask him about the CDC," Annie said.

"What about the CDC?" Hughes said into the radio. "They have power there? Over."

"Dunno," Roy said. "Maybe it's lit and maybe it ain't. My guess is it's lit. Would have to be if they're in there."

"Alright," Hughes said. "Let's take it slow. Over."

"Roger that," Roy said.

Parker and Roy kept their speed below thirty miles an hour, less than half the posted limit. He did his best to watch the road, but his eyes were drawn to the shining arc on the horizon.

"Wow," Annie said.

Parker tapped the brake and slowed a bit. "What?" He scanned the road ahead of him, but he didn't see anything other than asphalt and trees.

"I took the night vision off," Annie said, "and the lights are gone."

Parker could still see it.

"The light's really dim," Annie said. "City's darker than it looks. Only we can see it from here."

Parker nodded. Of course. They had only just now noticed the lights, and they were using night vision. The radiance was barely perceptible, so dim that he wondered if they'd see it at all, even with night vision, if there weren't clouds in the sky to reflect it back down toward earth. The city center was still far away. Atlanta's suburbs sprawled an incredible distance. And besides, the skyscrapers were probably dark at night. While fragments of the city might still be holding on, life couldn't be normal there. Downtown wouldn't be bustling with office workers and traffic. Wouldn't make any sense to light everything up even if the buildings were packed to the top floors with refugees. People needed darkness to sleep, and blazing towers of light would attract infected from everywhere.

An exit ramp appeared on the right leading to a cluster of gas stations and chain restaurants.

"Anybody seeing anything?" Parker said. "Any movement, anywhere at all?"

"Nothing," Hughes said.

"No people," Annie said, "no infected, no cars, no nothing."

"Roy said the army's inside Atlanta," Annie said. "Maybe they've come out and cleared the area."

Parker shook his head. "No bodies. It all looks undisturbed." The buildings weren't even boarded up. "Nothing much happened here." Nothing but a mass exodus. He wondered how many infected could actually be in this city if so many people had left.

If Roy hadn't warned them that the suburbs were overrun, Parker might have thought Atlanta was a much safer place than it actually was. All along he'd assumed the eastern United States might have fared better than the West Coast since people out here had more time to prepare for what was coming, and in some ways, that seemed to be true. The outskirts of Seattle and Portland looked nothing like this. Even cities as far east as Omaha looked nothing like this.

Of course, they weren't actually in Atlanta yet or even its suburbs.

"How much farther?" Parker said.

"Ten minutes," Annie said. "We'll be in Alpharetta in ten minutes."

She was wrong. They got there in less than five.

But it wasn't what they expected. The four-lane highway mushroomed into an eight-lane freeway, and it was still devoid of people, infected, and cars—an astonishing fact of apocalyptic geography. Wherever the people of the eastern seaboard had run off to once they knew what was coming, they had all the time they had needed to get there.

And yet, according to Roy, Atlanta's suburbs had been overrun not even two weeks ago.

"Something's wrong," Hughes said. "This is too easy."

Or Roy is full of shit, Parker thought. They were still cruising along at a comfortable thirty miles an hour, but Parker didn't like it either. Unless Roy was lying, they couldn't possibly glide all the way into the city like this.

"Get Roy on the radio," Parker said.

The radio squawked. "Talk to us, Roy," Hughes said. "What's going on?"

"We get off soon," Roy said. "Roadblocks coming up."

Roadblocks? Parker thought. The hell for?

"Army cut the main highways," Roy said.

"Why?" Hughes said. "Over."

"No idea," Roy said. "Seemed they had something in mind but retreated behind the walls before they could finish. No point uncutting the roads."

Parker kept his eyes on Roy's RV, about two hundred feet in front of him.

"Czech hedgehogs ahead," Roy said into the radio. "This is where we get off."

"Czech hedgehogs?" Annie said.

"Anti-tank obstacles," Hughes said. "Like huge iron jacks."

"They expecting a Canadian ground invasion down here?" Parker said.

"Czech hedgehogs stop cars and trucks even better than tanks," Hughes said.

"Why bother?" Parker said.

"God knows," Hughes said.

"Maybe they hoped they could wall off the suburbs as well as the city," Annie said. "But they ran out of time."

Perhaps, Parker thought. Either way, the easy driving on the eight-lane was over.

The RV's brake lights came on, and Roy indicated a turn onto Exit Ramp 9 toward Hayes Bridge Road into Alpharetta. Parker followed him onto the offramp, made left turns where signs pointed to Alpharetta and DeVry University, and—just like that—they were properly in the suburbs, with a wide thoroughfare fronted by a low-rise Marriott Hotel and a series of office parks.

Infected milled about in the road, not a horde or even a pack but stray individuals, two of them standing there in the street, one sitting cross-legged on a patch of grass where a sidewalk would be in an older part of the city, and three or four others, spaced far apart in the parking lot in front of the Marriott, apparently asleep on the pavement.

Parker and Roy each slowed their vehicles to ten miles an hour. The first infected was bang in the center of the road, standing there motionless but turning toward the RV and the Suburban with its head cocked sideways as if it didn't know what to make of the sound coming toward it.

Roy drove around it.

Parker slowed the Suburban to less than walking speed as he neared.

"Don't stop," Annie said.

Parker could clearly see now that the infected was a middle-aged woman. Everything was rendered with green pixels, but he knew she was black. She had distinctly African-American features and looked strangely undangerous bathed in night-vision green, more curious and perplexed than hostile, her eyes trying and failing to pinpoint the Suburban's exact location.

"She can't see us," Parker said. "Not even a little bit."

Neither Annie nor Hughes replied, as if they were just as transfixed as he was. The infected woman was recognizably human. She had parents. Children, perhaps. A home once, and a job. A life down here in suburban Atlanta. Maybe she commuted every day into the city to an office in one of the towers. Whatever she'd done and whomever she'd loved before the virus struck her down, she couldn't remember.

"You ever seen one of them like this?" Parker said.

"How could we?" Annie said.

Not even behind glass in some kind of a zoo would the infected look like this, Parker thought. Only with night vision could they be observed in a nonaggressive state so up close and personal. The infected woman groped toward the Suburban in the darkness like an eyeless creature.

Parker turned the wheel and drove past her. He did not want to hit her, did not want her making any kind of contact at all with the truck. No telling what she'd do. She probably wasn't intelligent enough anymore in her diseased condition to realize she was so close to her prey or to even realize she was facing a vehicle, but he didn't want to take a chance and give her an excuse to scream, to cry out, to alert the others that she'd found something. The others wouldn't be able to find Parker or his friends either if she did scream, but he didn't want whatever was around all riled up. Easier, and safer, to keep them docile so he could drive around them as easily as if they were orange cones in his path.

He and Roy took things painfully, agonizingly slow. It wasn't any kind of a problem. Not at first, anyway. They only had to swerve around an infected every once in a while. Those that moved, moved slowly. Those that stood around did little more than turn their heads at the approaching sound with a dim bovine wonder. Some that were lying on the ground stirred and sat up, but some of them didn't. None of them charged. None of them screamed.

"Imagine trying this during the day," Annie said.

Parker shuddered. Trying this during the day would be a drastically different experience. That was for damn sure. The infected would scream, cohere into mobs, packs—even hordes—and they'd charge. Parker wouldn't be able to poke along at ten miles an hour, and he wouldn't be able to dodge them. He'd have to run them down and pray not to get stuck.

The lights on the horizon glowed brighter now.

"Annie," Parker said. "Can you see the city lights without night vision now?"

"Yeah," Annie said after a moment. "We're getting closer. And hey. There's more off to the east."

Parker couldn't see anything at all to the east without turning his head. He had no peripheral vision. None of them did. He sneaked a quick head swivel, though, and saw what Annie was talking about: another dome of light on the eastern horizon.

"I see it too," Hughes said. "What's over there?"

"Nothing," Annie said. "Farmland."

"Can't be nothing," Hughes said.

"You sure that way's east?" Parker said. He heard Annie rustle the map while he kept his eyes on the road ahead of him.

"Positive," Annie said. "Athens is that way, but it's far."

"Shit," Hughes said. "There's stars in the sky that direction."

Uh oh, Parker thought. The weather was clearing. He was pretty sure now what the glow was. Clouds had covered the sky for days, but they were shifting.

"The moon's coming up," Annie said. "Isn't it."

"We need to stop," Parker said. "Get Roy on the radio. The

infected are going to see us."

Hughes radioed Roy and told him the bad news. Without peripheral vision, the guy might have no idea the moon was about to rise in the east if nobody told him.

They were on a major suburban traffic artery now, with three lanes in each direction divided by a curbed grassy median. Strip malls, gas stations, and chain restaurants filled the void between the countryside and the city.

"Pulling over," Roy said into the radio and took his RV off the main drag into a parking lot. Parker followed and stopped in front of a franchise he'd never heard of before called Captain D's Seafood Kitchen. Not until he got out of the truck and met Roy in the lot did he notice that Captain D's was all boarded up, the first time he'd seen such a place on a streetscape that otherwise looked intact. Atlanta's mass exodus had been a hell of a lot more orderly than Seattle's.

"Plenty of clouds still overhead," Roy said, looking up.

"Shh," Parker said. He didn't see or hear anyone else, infected or otherwise, but they'd already made plenty of noise just pulling in and parking. He constantly had to remind himself, though, that while he could see, any of those *things* in the area couldn't. Night vision was unnatural. He had to *trust* it. The deeper parts of his brain, the subconscious and primitive threat-detection regions, automatically assumed that if he could see, everyone and everything else should be able to also.

Hughes and Annie got out of the Suburban and huddled on each side of Parker, the four of them all gadgeted up and looking like a cyborg gathering in apocalyptic suburbia.

Parker scrutinized the eastern horizon. He could see stars in that direction but only low in the sky, no higher than a visible inch or two above the strip mall across the street. The moon was going to rise any second, but most of the sky was still cloud-covered.

"I think we'll be okay," he said.

"Mmm," Hughes said.

Parker licked his index finger and held it still in the air for a moment. He felt nothing. The atmosphere couldn't be calmer. "There's no wind," he said. "The clouds aren't moving."

"No wind down here," Hughes said and looked straight up, "doesn't mean there's no wind up there."

"Clouds don't look like they're moving," Roy said.

"No, they don't," Annie said.

"We should wait until tomorrow," Hughes said. "I hate to piss on everybody's parade, but somebody has to."

"You want to hole up in this fish shack?" Parker said and gestured with his head toward Captain D's. "We wait until tomorrow, the sky could clear up for a week. We can always retreat if we have to."

"That's a hell of a risk," Hughes said.

"We wouldn't have come here at all if we weren't willing to risk it," Annie said.

"Doesn't mean we should be stupid," Hughes said.

"We aren't being stupid," Parker said. "We'll keep an eye on the clouds. If the sky starts opening up any more than it already has, we'll have plenty of time to bug out before the moon's overhead and lighting everything up."

Nobody argued, but nobody agreed with him either.

"Okay?" Parker said.

Still, nobody said anything.

"We didn't come this far only to get this far," Parker said.

Hughes looked at the sky one more time. The clouds had not moved at all, and they didn't look like they were going to. "Fine," he said.

"Agreed," Annie said. "Let's go."

Nobody bothered asking Roy his opinion, nor did he volunteer one.

∽

ANNIE DIDN'T WORRY about the moonlight. Parker was right—they'd have all the time they needed to backtrack out of the suburbs or even the city if they had to, as long as they didn't wait until the sky cleared entirely and the moon was right overhead.

She enjoyed riding in the front seat for a change and felt slightly peeved that neither Parker nor Hughes had been gentlemanly enough to offer it to her before. She understood why: they were both large men who required more leg room, but still. The back seat of the Suburban wasn't exactly cramped.

A fire station appeared on the left side, and on the other side of the road, incongruously out in the sprawl, was a classical two-story nineteenth century building that nobody had ever demolished. It had pillars in front of the main entrance and a spindle-lined balcony on the second floor.

Bright green light washed over the roof and the cityscape to the west. The moon was up now.

"Here we go," Hughes said.

Annie hunched over in the passenger seat so she could check the sky to the east through the driver-side window. The cloud cover held. The moon would be obscured again after rising a few more degrees.

She removed the night vision from her eye to check her surroundings naturally. She could see a little bit better unaided now than before, but not much, just the vague shape of things against a gray background—and only the tops of things, really—where they created silhouettes against the sky. No actual details were visible. The road was but a strip of heavy gray unspooling in front of her, and she couldn't tell where the asphalt ended and the sidewalk began. She and her friends were still more or less safe, at least for the moment, and they'd probably stay that way as long as the sky didn't light up more than it already had.

Then she saw it. An infected, dead ahead in the road, shambling toward the Suburban. And she wasn't using her night vision. She saw it with her naked eye.

Roy swerved around it without any trouble.

Annie put the night vision back on as the Suburban approached. The infected was a young man, perhaps a teenager, with a horrific gash on the side of his face. As Parker drove around it to the left,

Annie turned her head to keep her eyes locked on to its face. The infected likewise turned its head to keep its eyes locked on her as the Suburban passed, its mouth agape as if something as large as a dinosaur were lumbering by in the dark.

"It saw us," Annie said.

"It saw the truck," Parker said, "but it didn't see us."

She supposed Parker was right. To an unaided infected eye in the night, vehicles would be dark blobs moving across an inscrutable landscape. A healthy person would recognize them, of course, and not just by the sounds they made. Annie could see well enough now without her night vision to discern cars and trucks from, say, boulders and bushes. She wouldn't be able to see inside any vehicles, though, at least not well enough to see faces behind glass. The infected, therefore, wouldn't know their prey was on the other side of the windshield. Not in this gloom.

She saw more of them ahead, eight or nine milling about in the road in a disorganized pack. The low moonlight provided enough illumination to activate them but not yet enough that they could navigate without stumbling aimlessly.

Parker and Roy slowed the vehicles. The infected ahead were too spread out to drive around. They were a safe enough distance away, almost a full city block, but they were shambling ahead.

"They see us," Annie said and scanned the area with her night vision. On her right was a bank with a parking lagoon around it, empty except for an armored car, and beyond that, a grocery store with a whole lake of parking.

"Pull into that bank lot," Annie said.

"On it," Parker said.

Hughes radioed Roy and told him.

Roy made the turn first, then Parker. Easy enough. They cruised from the parking lot at the bank, passed the armored car, headed into the grocery store's lot, then reconnected to the main road. The pack of infected followed but were left behind at once.

Annie removed the night vision again and surveyed the cityscape with her bare eyes. She could see a little bit better than she could even a couple of minutes ago. The moon was higher in the sky now and illuminating the surface, including the sides of the buildings. It would ascend above the cloud cover soon enough, but they had another problem to worry about: the city lights were closer, and brighter, and made worse by cloud cover. The light was coming from below, bouncing off the ceiling above, and radiating down into the suburbs. The clouds were going help obscure the moonlight but amplify the city lights.

"Brighter now," Parker said. "Get us on a different road."

Annie consulted the map. "Head west on Dogwood Road toward Morgan Falls Overlook Park."

"Why that way?" Hughes said.

"Looks quieter," Annie said. "Spread out. More residential."

Hughes huffed, as if he didn't like sitting helplessly in the back seat with no sense of control or even a map. He had a job to do too, though, so he radioed Roy and relayed Annie's directions.

Parker followed the RV onto Dogwood Road, exiting the suburban sprawlscape and plunging them into a forest on what looked like a rural two-lane highway.

"The hell are we?" Hughes said.

"We're still going the right way," Annie said. "Heading south from Alpharetta to Sandy Springs. This isn't unusual. Atlanta is huge, but it's a city in a forest like Seattle and Portland."

There weren't even any houses on the side of the road here, nor were they any infected. If Annie didn't know better, she'd think they were in the wilds of Kentucky again.

"Good job, Annie," Parker said.

"Take it slow, Roy," Hughes said into the radio.

So Annie was navigating now, and she was doing a heck of a job of it. They truly didn't need Roy anymore. She could whack him right there in the suburbs and never look back, never regret it. He had entirely outlived his usefulness. They could find a nice quiet place, radio for him to stop for a moment, and plug him right in the face.

"Darker here," Parker said.

And it was. Most of the trees were leafless this time of year, but they still made long, dark shadows on the road that blocked much of the light from above.

Parker took the Suburban across the Chattahoochee River on Johnson Ferry Road, turned right onto Riverside Drive, and emerged in a lightly wooded area where long driveways winded up to mansions on hills. The streets were quiet and clear.

Annie checked her map. "I think we're coming up on the Perimeter."

"What's that?" Parker said. "Freeway," Annie said. "I-285." A ring road, and the midpoint between downtown and the countryside.

They went straight through a traffic circle, across an overpass wrapped with a hurricane fence above the dark and silent Perimeter road, and into more trees. Halfway there now.

Annie bit her knuckle. "Roy said there were infected all over the suburbs."

"We've seen 'em," Parker said.

"Not really," Annie said. "We saw more of them the night we left Lander than we've seen here."

"Don't get cocky," Hughes said. "Hordes move around."

"I'm not getting cocky," Annie said. "I'm not convinced Roy was actually here. We've hardly even seen any damage."

"Most people left," Parker said.

"Exactly," Annie said. "So how many infected could there be?"

"Six million people lived here," Hughes said. "Less than ten thousand lived in Lander. And you said it yourself. We saw more there than we've seen here. So, whatever is here, we haven't seen yet."

Annie consulted the map again and checked the street signs to ensure she knew where they were.

"Bunch of malls off to the right," she said. "Don't go that way. Head east."

"Which way's east?" Parker said. The suburban roads weren't laid out on anything resembling a grid.

"Make a left on Powers Ferry Road," Annie said. "There's a golf course. Plenty of open space. Coming up in a minute or so."

Hughes radioed the directions to Roy.

Annie stewed. No point following the sonofabitch, especially now that she was leading him from behind. But she marveled at her surroundings. They were in a bonafide forest with stately old homes set back from the road. And this was after crossing the Perimeter to the inner half of the metro area. Whoever had lived here lived well. The area was effectively rural yet barely a half hour's drive from downtown. The best of both city and country. And there were no infected here, even after the end of the world.

"Stay on this road," Annie said. "Up ahead we'll take Old Ivy to Roxboro, which will take us right to North Druid Hills."

North Druid Hills. That's where they'd find the wall.

"How far is that from here?" Hughes said.

"Three of four miles maybe," Annie said.

"Brace yourselves," Hughes said. "We're getting close to the city center."

"Don't worry," Annie said. "We're skirting it."

The RV suddenly loomed larger ahead. For a brief moment, it appeared to be moving in reverse toward the Suburban. Parker slammed on the brakes. Annie lurched forward and strained against her seatbelt. The RV was not moving backwards. It had come to a sudden stop in the road. With its tail and brake lights off, Parker hadn't realized what had happened until he'd damn near driven up Roy's ass.

Annie squinted into her night vision and saw nothing beyond the RV except the road and more trees. A church with a magnificent steeple rose above a steep hill to the left. To the right, a driveway led into the woods.

The sky above blazed with so much light that downtown could be on fire.

"What's going on, Roy?" Hughes said into the radio.

Roy's voice crackled through static. "Pack of 'em ahead."

"How many?" Hughes said.

"Back up, Parker," Annie said.

"Wait," Hughes said.

"Twenty or thirty of 'em," Roy said.

"They see you?" Hughes said.

"They hear us," Roy said. "They hear our engines. But I don't think they can see us back here in the trees."

Annie switched to naked-eye vision again so that she could see what the infected would see. She saw almost nothing at all, even with her right eye adjusted to the darkness already. The light reflecting off the clouds above had little effect on the ground. She did see a pale light at ground level straight ahead past the trees, though. She checked the map and saw that they were near a major intersection and presumably some kind of business district. Nothing major like a mall, but an end to the woods they'd been driving through.

"What else do you see, Roy?" Hughes said into the radio.

"Parking lot," Roy said. "The infected are coming out of a parking lot and onto the road. And there's an electrical station behind a fence off to the right."

Annie couldn't see any of it.

"There's a big intersection on the other side of this pack," Roy said.

"And?" Hughes said.

"Looks like it's clear," Roy said.

"What do you think?" Hughes said, not to Roy but to Annie and Parker.

"We could run 'em over," Parker said.

"Are you kidding?" Annie said.

"Not even a little bit," Parker said. "Figure we'll have to do that at some point before we get to the wall."

"Why don't we back up?" Annie said.

"They'll just follow us," Parker said.

"Roy," Hughes said into the radio. "How far away are they?"

"Hundred feet, maybe," Roy said. "They've stopped now."

"Back up," Annie said.

She realized with a jolt that nobody was keeping an eye out behind them.

"Hughes," she said, "Check behind us." It was the first time in her life she'd ever told Hughes to do anything.

"Clear," Hughes said.

Parker backed up the Suburban. He took it slow, slower even than walking speed. Driving forward with one eye and no side vision was hard enough. Driving in reverse for even a couple of feet was as much a leap of faith as anything else.

"You're good," Hughes said. "Just hold the wheel straight."

Parker sped up a bit and Roy followed him backwards in his RV.

They only made it a short distance when Annie noticed that Roy wasn't following anymore. He couldn't see out the back. He'd hardly see anything in his mirrors with night vision.

"Roy," Hughes said. "You okay?"

He didn't answer. Instead, the RV surged forward, slowly at first and then faster. Much faster.

My God, Annie thought. He's going to ram them.

Parker was still driving backwards, craning his head over his shoulder to look out the rear window.

"Stop!" Annie shouted.

Parker brought the Suburban to a halt. "The hell is he doing?" he said after turning his attention back to what was in front of him.

Annie heard what sounded like sacks of potatoes hurled at the side of a car, followed by screams of shock, pain, and alarm.

"Running them over," Annie said.

Parker sat up at full attention and leaned forward at the wheel.

Annie could see the infected now, first as flickers of movement on each side of the RV, then more clearly as those that weren't hit chased the vehicle in the dark.

Parker stepped on the gas.

"Wait," Annie said. "Hold back a second." There could be hundreds more up there for all anyone knew, and they'd be drawn by the screams of those that had just been run down.

Parker hit the brakes.

Annie didn't hear any more screaming. She thought she heard some moans of pain up ahead, but she couldn't be sure.

"Kill the engine," Annie said.

"Hang on," Hughes said.

"Just do it," Annie said. "We'll be able to hear better. And they won't hear us."

Parker nodded and killed the engine. It would only take a second to turn it back on again.

Annie listened hard. She clearly heard moaning now. Roy hadn't killed everything he'd just hit. She could see the wounded infected now too, lying on the ground, clutching their bruised and bleeding abdomens and limbs.

Roy had cruised on ahead, clear into the intersection, and she could barely make out his RV at this distance. She could, however, hear slapping, shouting, and grunting. The survivors surrounded his vehicle. There was just enough light now that they'd be able to see it. Then more sounds: a revving engine, a loud and hard smack, and more screams of pain. Roy was being mobbed.

"We need to move," Hughes said.

"Let them finish him off," Annie said.

"Not yet," Hughes said.

"It will save us the trouble later," Annie said. "And what good is he now? He doesn't know where we're going any better than you do."

"We help him," Hughes said, "he helps us."

"When has he helped us?" Annie said.

"He got us this far," Parker said. "And he just cleared a path forward."

Let his last act be a sacrifice for good then, Annie thought. The perfect ending for a terrible man whose mother should have had an abortion.

Parker started up the Suburban and drove toward Roy.

"Goddammit," Annie said.

Seconds later, they left the trees behind and entered a huge six-lane intersection, with Roy's RV caught in the middle of it, surrounded by infected, midrise towers looming ahead in the distance.

"Shit," Parker said. "We're downtown. Annie!"

"This isn't downtown," Annie said. "This is Buckhead."

"Buckhead?" Parker said.

"Northern Atlanta," Annie said. "Downtown is still miles away."

Two dozen infected swarmed the RV. They seemed more curious than hostile, not quite sure who or what was inside. Roy hit the gas and lurched forward toward a lamp post, then slammed into reverse and did the same thing backward.

"Why doesn't he just turn and drive straight?" Annie said.

"He can't see," Parker said.

"So, what are we doing?" Annie said.

Hughes got on the radio. "Roy, we're right behind you."

"Can't see shit," Roy said.

"I know," Hughes said. "There's a lamp post in front of you. Don't hit it. Turn the wheel thirty degrees to the right, then drive straight."

"I can't see shit!" Roy shouted.

"I know," Hughes said. "Just... Parker, lay on the horn."

"Are you crazy?" Annie said.

"Roy took out half of 'em already," Hughes said, "and there aren't any more."

Annie swept the scene with her night vision. Hughes was right. The roads were clear in every direction.

Parker leaned on the horn, the sound beyond blaring, effectively a siren and louder than anything shy of a gunshot.

It got the infected's attention. That was for damn sure. They stopped struggling to get inside Roy's RV and turned their full attention to the Suburban instead.

"I don't think they see us," Parker said.

Annie didn't think so either. They moved toward the sound, though. And they weren't far away, barely fifty feet at the most.

Roy, now free, turned his RV to the right and exited the intersection.

"Go," Annie said.

Parker let up off the horn and followed Roy away from the melee.

"We need to turn left on Old Ivy Road," Annie said. "It's coming up right away."

"Roy," Hughes said into the radio. "Make the next left."

Roy made the left and Parker followed.

"You see?" Hughes said.

"See what?" Annie said.

"We still need him," Hughes said.

"More like he needs us, actually," Annie said.

"We needed two vehicles to get through that," Parker said.

Annie huffed but said nothing.

16

Atlanta looked a lot more urban all of a sudden, with midrise apartment buildings lining the side of the road and high-rise towers puncturing the sky in the near distance. If Annie hadn't told him otherwise, Parker would have sworn they were arriving downtown. Buckhead alone was larger than most American cities, yet it was a single neighborhood of Atlanta that he'd never even heard of before.

They'd made it all the way through the suburbs unscathed—not at all what Parker had expected. None of them had expected it. Roy had said the suburbs were overrun, yet here they were, deep now into the city. The infected hadn't died off or been killed off. The sidewalks and streets weren't littered with bodies. They were strangely empty.

Had Roy even been there a few weeks earlier, like he'd said, or was he lying?

Parker wondered if Annie was right about Roy. He was not adding value. Not anymore. Sure, he'd helped clear a pack of infected out of an intersection, and they'd helped him in return, so in theory it made sense to tag team. But it made a lot less sense when Parker played the tape back in his mind and imagined what he would have done if Roy hadn't been there, if the Suburban had been the only vehicle on the road when the infected appeared. Parker would have had options. For one thing, they had a hundred pounds of ammunition in the back of the Suburban. They could shoot their way through just about anything. More easily, though, Parker could have turned around and taken a different road. There were hundreds of different routes to get from A to B in a place the size of Atlanta.

Roy's intel was bad, and he was tactically useless. He wasn't even a guide anymore, with no real idea how to get where they were going. Annie was directing them now, leading from behind with a map. Roy should be following in his RV, not out front and taking Annie's directions over the radio. Then again, Parker reasoned, with Roy out front he was effectively their human shield. Anything that came at them head-on would slam into him first.

That still left the problem of what to do with him.

∽

AFTER DIAGONALLY TRAVERSING THE CONTINENT, from the Pacific Northwest to the southern Atlantic seaboard, clearing the last gap should have been easy. Annie, squinting at the map, calculated the distance from Buckhead to North Druid Hills along Roxboro Road at only four miles, five miles tops. They could have made it in less than fifteen minutes poking along at a measly twenty miles an hour, but nothing prepared them for what they encountered.

The sky grew brighter as they neared downtown, and after crossing Interstate 85, the clouds overhead buzzed with reflected electricity. Annie removed her night vision and saw everything—a shopping mall on the left, a low-rise bank branch on the right, six empty lanes dead ahead—with near perfect clarity, as if the landscape blazed under full moonlight. She could almost make out colors.

By the time they reached the upscale Druid Forest neighborhood, Annie *could* make out colors, and could do so perfectly: gray asphalt, tan winter grass, prickly Georgia evergreens towering above beige-yellow homes.

Annie heard the horde long before she could see it. The sound was faint at first. She thought the engine might be emitting some kind of screech or hiss, but it grew louder after a quarter mile and even louder than that after a half, finally congealing into a low and unmistakable roar.

Now she understood why the suburbs and even the city so far had appeared to be empty, why she'd hardly seen any infected, why the vast cityscape had been abandoned even by them. They were drawn to the light in downtown Atlanta. They might wander around more or less aimlessly during the day, but at night they hurtled toward the bright urban core like insects to candles and lamps. There could be tens or even hundreds of thousands ahead.

No way could they drive through it.

"Stop the truck," she said and sank low in her seat, trying to make herself smaller.

Parker clenched his fingers around the steering wheel and slowed the Suburban to jogging speed. Roy, still out ahead, slowed his RV.

"Stop!" Annie said.

Parker floored the brake pedal. Annie lurched forward against her seatbelt.

"Hughes," she said. "Hand me that radio. Please." Dammit, she had to talk to Roy.

Hughes passed the radio forward, and Annie pressed the *talk* button. "I'm sure you can hear that," she said. "Over."

Roy's voice came back to her, crackling through static. "Even the dead hear it." He stopped his RV, a block or so in front of the Suburban.

"Where's the wall?" she said.

"Told you," he said. "North Druid Hills."

"Where is it, *exactly*?"

"Just south of there," Roy said. "Midway between North Druid Hills and Emory University."

Annie looked again at the map. "That's two miles away!" she shouted.

She killed the radio and dropped it on the floor at her feet.

The roar ahead was incredible. It wasn't the loudest thing she'd ever heard. It wasn't much louder than freeway traffic from a moderate distance, but it sounded nothing at all like the whoosh of tires on pavement. This was the purely organic sound of menace boiled down to its essence, of species-wide anguish and pain, the sound of the end of the world.

Annie understood now why Roy believed the universe was committing suicide. He'd been to Atlanta. He'd heard this before. The sound itself could have driven him mad. For the first time, she wondered if he might have been a normal, functioning person before he came here and heard this, when he still installed home security systems for a living. Was that even possible?

Annie, too, had heard the same sound before—in her own mind back in Washington state, when she spent three days as a *hungry hungry predator*, as if a force backed by the whole weight of the universe compelled her to destroy and devour every human being she could find.

"What do we do?" Parker said.

The horde must have been a mile thick on the ground. Annie and her friends could not make it through. Surely, Parker must know that. He had to be asking where else they should go or if there was even a point going anywhere.

Nobody said anything for a while.

Hughes finally broke the silence. "We need—" he said and coughed. "We need to know what we're dealing with."

Annie turned around in her seat and stared at Hughes in the back. She could see his face in the light.

"What we're dealing with," she said, "is the biggest horde in the world."

She imagined a drone's-eye view of the landscape ahead. A mile-wide swath of infected and, beyond that, a thirty-foot wall. On the other side of the wall, weak and terrified humans, hunkering down, half starving and more than half panicked, waiting for the inevitable end.

Roy had been right all along. Everyone left alive in Atlanta had been kidding themselves. The people who had fled on boats to the

Caribbean had been kidding themselves. Annie, too, had been kidding herself when she'd fantasized about fleeing to Canada. This was the flinch response, the instinctive regret of a suicide halfway to the sidewalk from the top of a building. It wasn't rational. It was biology.

And yet. And yet. Roy had agreed to lead her and her friends to Atlanta, knowing in advance what they'd find once they got there.

She shook her head back and forth as if something were stuck in her hair. Think, Annie. Get it together.

"Are there any hills around?" Parker said.

"None that are high enough where we could see much," Annie said. "This isn't Seattle."

"Not hills," Hughes said. "But skyscrapers. We can drive back to Buckhead. Climb the stairs to the top of one of those towers and see what we're dealing with from the roof."

Annie didn't like it. "We'd be walking up into a deathtrap." There'd be no way out if a bunch of those things surrounded the building. "You want to get cornered again like we did in the warehouse?"

Hughes blew out his breath.

"We can't drive through whatever's ahead," Annie said.

"Sure as hell can't walk through it," Hughes said. "But we might be able to drive around it."

"They're surrounding downtown," Annie said.

"You don't know that," Hughes said.

"They're drawn by the light," Annie said.

Parker needed to turn the Suburban around. If the horde surged their way, they'd be swallowed by a tsunami of teeth.

"We need to get out of here," Annie said.

"We at least need to know where the edge of the horde is," Hughes said.

"What difference does it make?" Parker said. "We're going to have to go through it whether it's a mile deep or two hundred feet deep."

"It's not two hundred feet deep," Annie said. "The wall is on the south side of the North Druid Hills. That's two miles away."

"Are we sure that's where it is?" Parker said.

"That's what Roy said," Annie said. "And there's no one else we can ask."

She wasn't going to ask Roy about it again. No point. She never wanted to ask him again about anything, but she pressed the *call* button on the radio anyway.

"Any ideas, Roy?" she said. "Over."

"I'm sorry, ma'am, no," Roy said.

Of course not. There were no options. They didn't have a helicopter or plane, and no one knew how to fly anyway. They couldn't float down a river. There weren't any nearby. They couldn't sneak in under the cover of darkness. There was enough light in the sky now that Annie could read a magazine without a flashlight or night vision. They couldn't call ahead and ask for a rescue or even get close enough to the walls to signal for help. They might be able to get someone on the handheld radios, but not from this far away from the wall. They might try using a flashlight to send a message in Morse Code from the top of one of the towers, but again, those towers were deathtraps. They might be able to find a flare gun and shoot it into the sky, but the odds that anyone inside the walls would come outside and save them were miniscule. Why would they?

"We need a bigger truck," Hughes said.

"We need a tank," Parker said.

They weren't getting a tank, but Annie remembered something. "A few miles back," she said, "when it was still dark, when we drove around a pack in the street, we went through a parking lot at a bank."

"I remember," Parker said.

"There was an armored car in the lot!" Hughes said.

"Yes," Annie said. "There was."

Nobody said anything for a moment. Annie refused to get excited, but she had to admit there was a tiny chance that it might work. They might get stuck in the horde, but the infected couldn't break in. That was the whole point of armored cars. No one, and nothing, could get inside. Survival was possible.

"Can we find that bank again?" Parker said.

"I know where it is," Annie said.

"We need keys," Parker said.

No, they didn't, Annie thought. They had the next best thing.

"Remember that diner in Iowa?" Annie said. "Where we met Roy?"

Nobody said anything. Of course they remembered.

"Lucas gave me his set of lockpicks."

17

Hughes took a deep breath as Parker turned the Suburban around and headed north again toward Buckhead. His body felt like an overinflated tire that had just sprung an air leak; only now did he realize how tired he'd been. He and his friends weren't going to be okay, exactly, inside an armored bank car, but they couldn't easily be killed inside one either.

What about Roy? He wasn't going to follow in his RV anymore. He'd have to ride with everyone else. Annie was going to hate it, and she would be right. It was going to be a problem.

Hughes wouldn't be able to keep an eye on the guy, because he was going to drive. Break time was over. His eyes weren't fatigued any longer, and he didn't even crave sleep. Most of all, he missed being in front where he felt in control of the vehicle and the mission.

"You sure this is going to work?" Parker said.

Hughes chuckled. "Which part?"

"The lockpicks," Parker said.

"They'll work," Hughes said. "We have door picks and auto picks. I checked." He only vaguely knew how to use them, but he understood the theory well enough. There would be a learning curve. It would take a while, but he'd work it out.

"What do we do when we get stuck?" Annie said.

"Easy," Hughes said. "Don't get stuck."

"We can't drive through a hundred thousand infected," Annie said. "The tires'll spin in blood, brains, and ground-up limbs before we can run over even a hundred of them. You want to get out and push?"

Oh, she of little faith. "That's not going to happen."

Annie snorted. "I'm not going to sit there and wait to die of hunger and thirst while diseased maniacs scream at us through the windows. I'll blow my brains out."

"You will do no such thing," Hughes said.

"We have plenty of suicide pills in the first-aid box," Annie said.

Hughes flinched. She sounded like Roy. "We're not going to get stuck."

"You know something the rest of us don't?" Parker said.

It wasn't that complicated. If Hughes had learned anything about the infected, it was this: they only attacked if they saw you or heard you. "We can paint the windows," he said, "so they can't see us, and we'll drive one mile an hour. They'll move out of our way. They won't even know we're inside."

"You want to drive blind?" Annie said.

"We can leave an unpainted slit so we can see out," Hughes said.

"Not bad," Parker said and nodded.

But they could do even better. "We can also pull them away from the walls," Hughes said.

"Pull a million infected away from the walls," Annie said.

"There aren't a million of them," Hughes said.

"Close enough," Annie said. "What, get them all to chase us to Tennessee, then turn around and come back?"

"We don't want them to chase us," Hughes said.

Annie laughed.

"We want them to chase something else," Hughes said.

"Sic them on Roy," Annie said.

This time Parker laughed.

"Not Roy," Hughes said. "Buckhead."

"Buckhead?" Parker said.

"The neighborhood with the skyscrapers." Hughes said. "We drove through it fifteen minutes ago."

"You and your skyscrapers," Annie said.

"We could set them on fire," Hughes said.

Nobody said anything. Hughes smiled in the dark and leaned back in his seat.

He knew what his friends were thinking. They were considering what could go wrong, and the answer was: plenty. They could get attacked while sloshing gas cans around. They could get trapped inside one of the buildings. The fire could spread and burn down the city.

"Brilliant," Parker said.

"Hardly," Annie said. "Remember Seattle?"

How could Hughes forget? Seattle was his hometown. When they'd sailed past it on the Puget Sound on their way to the San Juan Islands, they saw that the entire city had been incinerated to blackened foundations. It might as well have been nuked. Hughes had assumed a rare Northwestern lightning storm had started a blaze, but now he wondered if someone had set a fire on purpose while fighting or distracting a horde.

He didn't want to do the same to Atlanta, but Atlanta wasn't Seattle. Downtown Seattle hadn't walled itself off. It had no functioning urban core. Atlanta did. There had to be at least one fire station up and running somewhere downtown. The wall builders would have made sure of it. They might not be able to prevent flames from leaping over the wall, but they should be able to douse any that did.

Besides, a fire in Buckhead would probably stay in Buckhead as long as it didn't burn during a windstorm, especially if Hughes and his friends only lit one building on fire, whichever was the tallest and most easily seen from downtown. The horde would almost certainly be drawn to the flames during the day when a tower of billowing smoke wouldn't compete with the nighttime glow from downtown.

"We could end up setting the entire state of Georgia on fire," Annie said.

"Impossible," Hughes said. "Forests caught fire here for millions of years before firefighters even existed."

"Okay," Annie said. "But cities have always had firefighters. Until Seattle."

"It's a risk," Hughes said. "But would that be any more dangerous than what's out here right now? What would you rather be dealing with if you were inside the walls? A fire that will burn itself out in a couple of days or a million infected?"

"We could wait for the infected to starve to death," Parker said. "Things that can't continue forever, won't."

"Things that can't continue forever," Hughes said, "can continue for a lot longer than you think they can. And we're racing against a clock here. Those things will eventually starve to death, yes, but so will everyone in the CDC. They can't go outside the walls to get food. Not while they're surrounded. For all we know, they're down to their last rations already. We might be doing them a favor by setting the city on fire."

"Okay," Annie said. "So, we torch a skyscraper. Then what?"

"I don't know," Hughes said.

"You don't *know*?" Annie said.

"Depends on what happens next," Hughes said. "Does anyone or anything see us? Do we end up attracted a horde from the countryside instead of downtown? Does a helicopter swoop in with fire retardant?"

Nobody said anything.

"We navigate the path as it unfolds," Hughes said.

∼

Full darkness descended again as they returned to the north and away from the well-lit downtown.

"Where am I going, Annie?" Parker said.

Annie leaned forward in the passenger seat so she could see Roy's RV in the side mirror. He drove without headlights, but she saw his rig perfectly with her night vision. "Keep going straight for a while."

She didn't need to look at the map for the return trip to the bank. There were only a handful of turns, the next still a few miles ahead.

"We need to take care of Roy," she said.

"Later," Hughes said.

"He's not coming with us."

"We've been over this."

"Not since we decided to switch vehicles, we haven't. You can't expect him to follow in his RV."

Hughes said nothing.

"I'm not riding with him," Annie said.

Hughes still said nothing. Annie knew what he wanted to say. Roy was an extra set of eyes and hands. He was a capable fighter. He hadn't hurt anyone since Iowa. But Hughes didn't say any of those things. He had to know she was right, that this was the end of the line.

"We have to deal with him at some point," she said.

"We don't, actually," Parker said. "We can turn him in after we get through the gate."

After we get through the gate? Annie marveled at Parker's optimism. She couldn't decide if she should laugh at him or scoff.

"He won't see it coming," Parker said. "He has no idea that we know the truth about him."

"I'm not riding with him," she said.

"You—" Hughes said and turned around in his seat so he could look at her.

"Annie," Parker said. "We need to be careful."

"I am being careful," she said.

"You're being emotional," Parker said.

Right. She was being "emotional"—a rich observation coming from a man who'd reacted and behaved more emotionally in the time she had known him than anyone she'd ever met.

"I've been dealing with a lot of shit," Parker said. "You know. You've been with me through all of it."

At least the man was self-aware.

"I—," Parker said. He couldn't continue, but he didn't have to.

The next and final turn was coming up.

"Make a right," Annie said.

Parker turned right. They were getting close to the bank now.

"I . . . ," Parker said, "reacted impulsively. Back on those islands. And I don't want to see the same thing happen to you."

"I'm not you!" Annie said. "You attacked Kyle for no goddamn reason. Roy is a serial killer. He can't be allowed to run wild."

"He's not running wild!" Parker said. "He's under our control whether he knows it or not. And we need to deal with him coldly and rationally, not because he deserves it but because it is necessary. Until then, he's useful. He doesn't know we have Lucas's cell phone."

Annie took a deep breath. Parker was far too complacent, and he wasn't even close to convincing her. Any number of things could go wrong, including things no one had thought of.

"We're here," Parker said.

The bank was straight ahead on the left, the armored car still in the lot. Parker cranked the wheel, pulled off the main road, and came to a stop a few parking spots down.

Annie turned around in her seat. Roy was still coming up the main road.

"Don't do anything stupid," Hughes said.

She wasn't going to do anything stupid. She was going to do what was necessary, as Parker had put it. Her friends would be mad at her, but once it was done, it would be done, and they wouldn't hold it against her for long. They'd know she was right, in the end.

She held the Glock in her right hand near her feet.

Hughes turned around in his seat and stared at her through his night vision monocle. He looked like a robot. "Give me your gun."

Annie lay the Glock at her feet and raised both hands in the air.

"I don't have it," she said.

"Give it to me!" Hughes said.

"You can see that I don't have it."

Hughes opened the front passenger door and got out in a flourish without checking his surroundings or to even trying to be quiet. Then he opened her own door and at once saw the gun at her feet. She leaned back and let him snatch it. He grabbed her crowbar as well for good measure as Roy pulled into the lot and parked his RV two spaces down.

Parker stepped out of the Suburban wielding a hammer. Hughes took a step back and made room for Annie to exit the vehicle. He had a crowbar in each hand, and he stuffed Annie's Glock in his jacket pocket. Roy climbed out of his RV with his sword in one hand and a pistol in the other.

"I need a weapon," Annie whispered to Hughes.

"Hold on," Hughes said, eyes on Roy.

"Seriously," Annie said, a little too loudly.

Hughes made a downward motion with the flat of his hand.

"Give me one of those crowbars," she whispered, more quietly this time.

Hughes eyeballed the rear of the Suburban. The lockpicks were buried somewhere back there in a box.

"I won't do anything," Annie whispered and glanced at Roy. He was standing there with his feet apart and wielding his blade like he couldn't wait to start chopping heads. "None of us can be out here unarmed."

Hughes scrutinized Roy. The guy had a gun as well as a sword. Hughes went ahead and handed one of the crowbars to Annie, then popped open the Suburban's hatch and fished around in the back for Lucas's lockpicks.

Annie kept her distance from Roy and scanned the area with her night vision. The building in front of her was a one-story bank branch. Beyond it, a wasteland of parking surrounded the husk of a grocery store.

The suburbs seemed a bit darker than when she had been there earlier. The moon was higher up in the sky yet more fully obscured by clouds than before. The only way to be sure she and her friends were sufficiently cloaked in darkness, though, was to take off her night vision and see what everyone and everything else would see.

She removed her monocle, and the world seemed to tilt sideways. She couldn't see anything at all except a black horizon, a faint gray slab of pavement below, another gauzy haze of gray up above, and purple plasmatic afterimages. She couldn't make out the bank building, the grocery store, the vehicles, or even her friends. The darkness hid them completely. No one and nothing would be able to see them. As long as they kept quiet, they were not even there.

A pack of infected was somewhere in the area, though. A whole gaggle of them had been right there in the road less than an hour earlier, forcing Parker to drive around them through the bank's parking lot. Annie wouldn't have noticed the armored car otherwise. Which meant she was standing outside in the one part of suburban Atlanta she knew for a fact wasn't safe.

Annie didn't see or hear anything or anyone moving, but she could faintly hear the roar of the horde now in the distance. The sound was barely there, little more than a tiny disturbance in the atmosphere, and she hadn't even noticed it at first, but it was unmistakable now that she knew what it was.

She heard nothing at all in the immediate area except Hughes rummaging around in the Suburban. There was nothing else to hear in an ocean of parking. There were no leaves to rustle, no twigs to snap underfoot. An infected ambling slowly along wouldn't make much, if any, sound unless it dragged its feet.

Parker sidled up to Roy. Annie kept her distance. In the absolute stillness, she could hear them perfectly.

"New plan," Parker whispered to Roy. "Thinking of setting an apartment tower in Buckhead on fire."

Roy snapped his head back.

"Draw them away from the walls," Parker said.

Roy paused a moment, then grinned. "I like it." Annie bet he did. "Just need a couple of gas cans."

"Then we're going to paint over the windows and drive one mile an hour," Parker said. "Those things won't know we're inside."

Roy pursed his lips.

Hughes eased shut the Suburban's hatch door. "Got 'em," he whispered and waved the set of lockpicks in his hand.

"You know what to do with those?" Roy whispered.

"Sort of," Hughes said. "Might take me a while."

"Give them to me," Roy said.

"You some kind of expert?" Hughes said.

"I've done it before," Roy said.

"You picked an armored car?"

"Picked a regular car. Picked a couple of trucks."

"Fine," Hughes said and handed over the lockpicks.

"You all will have to watch my back while I work," Roy said.

"I'll watch the front," Hughes said. "Parker, stand behind me. Annie, you stand at the rear of the car."

Annie sighed. Roy was safe for the time being. She hated that Hughes kept finding uses for him.

She moved into position while Roy fiddled with the lockpicks. She imagined riding in the back of the armored car with him, his rank smell cloying at her, his weapons in reach, thoughts of murder and rape poisoning his mind, and a feeling of hope in his belly that he might soon be cured so he could keep on raping and killing indefinitely.

She kept her eyes on her sector, toward the street and away from the bank. Roy made a lot of noise fussing with the lockpicks: metal sliding and scraping against metal punctuated with his own huffs and grunts. The sound really carried, surely to the grocery store and beyond. She didn't see anything moving or stirring, though, as if she and her companions had all of suburban Atlanta to themselves.

She considered sneaking around and whacking Roy in the back of the head with her crowbar. The night monocle blocked his peripheral vision. He would not see her coming, nor would he hear her if she stepped quietly.

Roy paused a moment in his work, and then Annie heard a *thunk*.

"Got it," Roy said and opened the door.

Annie only now realized she'd been partially holding her breath.

"Nice job," Parker whispered. "Will those work on the ignition?"

"Sure, they will," Roy said and climbed inside the armored car.

Annie gripped her crowbar with both hands. If she didn't move against him soon, she'd have to get in the back with him. But she'd have to wait for him to get the engine started first.

After Roy jiggered the lockpicks for a few more minutes, the green night-vision landscape exploded with bright white light. Annie yanked the monocle off her face, wondering for a moment if it had shorted out, then saw with her naked eyes what had happened: the armored car's headlights were on.

"Shit," Roy said and grunted.

Annie heard a snap and a clink. Darkness returned to the world.

"The hell was that?" Parker said.

"Headlights came on," Hughes said. They must have blinded him since he was standing right in front of the car.

"Lockpicks work," Roy said. "I only turned the ignition halfway, but some asshole left the light switch in the on position."

At least no car alarm had gone off.

"Maybe they come on automatically," Parker said.

"Shh," Annie said. "Just find the switch so they stay off."

"Hang on," Roy said. "Found it." Annie heard a faint *flick*. "They're off now. I think."

"We need to load up before you turn the ignition again," Parker said. "In case the lights come on again."

Hughes nodded.

"Not yet," Annie said. "Shh."

Nobody moved. Nobody breathed.

The headlights had only been on for a couple of seconds, but they had provided a momentary beacon for any and every infected in every direction. Roy may as well have fired up a searchlight onto the clouds announcing *prey in the parking lot*.

Annie heard nothing but blood rushing in her ears.

"I think we're okay," Parker whispered.

"Let's just wait here a minute," Annie said.

They waited and listened.

Annie didn't expect to hear much. The infected would be drawn to the light if they saw it, but they wouldn't know it meant *prey* unless they actually saw her and her friends. That hadn't happened, but it didn't mean Roy hadn't inadvertently baited a trap. Yet nothing seemed to be coming. No movement registered in the glowing, green suburban expanse.

"Let's load up our stuff," Hughes whispered.

He got into the car, climbed over the front seats into the back, and opened the rear swinging doors from the inside.

The car's cargo hold was spacious and empty, but there was nowhere to sit. It was built for transporting money and valuables, not people. Either Hughes or Parker would drive—most likely Hughes. Which meant that either Annie or Parker would end up riding in back. Whoever it was could sit on one of the boxes from the back of the Suburban. It would be fine, especially since the plan was to drive through the horde slower than walking speed.

"One of us is going to have to ride back there," she said, not realizing she gave the game away until after she'd said it.

"One of us?" Roy said.

Shit, she thought.

"You planning on sitting on my lap in the front, darlin'?" He was barely fifteen feet in front her with a sword in his hands, but he had a cocksure grin on his face and leered at her like he was toying with a child or even a kitten.

Until now, Annie had suppressed her shadow self so completely that she had almost forgotten it existed. Yet it had always been there, buried deep within, an integral part of her being even before the virus unlocked it. This was the region of her mind and body programmed to strangle a cougar, to snap the jaw of an attack dog, to gouge out the eyes of a rapist, to shoot a home intruder through the center of mass.

To cave in the skull of a serial killer using a crowbar.

It took less than two seconds for a human being to lunge fifteen feet, and it could take more than that for the human mind to register that another person was lunging if it wasn't expected. And for Roy, it wasn't expected. He did not know that she knew the truth about him. And he failed to understand what it meant that she'd been infected, that'd she'd pursued prey with the relentless rage of a *hungry hungry predator*, that she'd been in beast mode for days, and that neither her mind nor her body would ever forget how to get there.

Annie took the first of three long strides from the balls of both feet, an apex predator launching from its hind legs forward and up, the crowbar behind her like an extension of her own arm and primed for the widest arc and maximal scything power.

Hughes took a step back and away, registering what was happening before Roy did. Hughes must have known an attack was imminent the instant she'd said *one of us will have to ride in the back*. Her meaning must have been obvious to him and to Parker: only one person would have to ride in the back because Roy would be dead.

Three things happened during Annie's second and faster long stride toward Roy. First, his face changed, his smirk vanishing as his head tilted slightly to the side like that of a confounded dog. Second, Parker took his own startled step back. Third, Annie twisted her arm so that the hand gripping her weapon was now facing upward, allowing the crowbar to extend even farther backward for the greatest possible reach.

Three more things happened as Annie completed her third and final stride toward her enemy: she bared her teeth like a wolf; she used her core, shoulder, and arm muscles to deliver a catastrophic blow with her weapon; and Roy flinched, leaned back, and raised his sword—awkwardly but instinctively—and parried what otherwise would have been a cataclysmic impact to his face that would have instantly killed him.

Metal struck metal. Annie's swing was much stronger than Roy's. He barely managed to deflect it; the power of her blow forced Roy's sword so far back that he nearly slit his own throat with it. He gasped. Annie grunted like a bear. Someone—either Parker or Hughes—grabbed her from behind and pulled her back and away.

"Jesus Christ!" Roy shouted. No attempt at all to be quiet.

"You sonofabitch!" she shouted and struggled against whoever restrained her.

"Annie!" Parker's voice, right there in her ear. "Stop it!" He managed to wrench the crowbar out of her hand without loosening his grip on her.

Hughes placed himself squarely between her and Roy.

"He's not coming with us!" she shouted.

"Ma'am, I'm sorry," Roy said. "It was a joke. Jesus Christ."

She twisted in an attempt to free herself from Parker's restraint. "He's not coming with us," she said, more quietly this time and a lot more confidently than anyone should have expected. It was not an opinion or wish on her part. It was a fact, stated coldly. She couldn't break free from Parker's grip—he was easily three times stronger—so she couldn't kill Roy herself right then and there, but she didn't have to. She could doom him with five words: *we know what you did*.

She need only speak, and Parker and Hughes would dispatch Roy at once. They wouldn't have any choice. Because Roy wouldn't cooperate anymore if he knew that his secret was no longer secret. In an instant he'd know he had everything to lose and nothing to gain.

"We're all on the same side here," Roy said. "We're all human."

A scream rang out across the empty lot and echoed off the front of the grocery store. It came from a medium distance away, two or three suburban blocks perhaps, followed by a pregnant silence.

The war between Annie and Roy vaporized. She stopped struggling against Parker, and Parker responded by relaxing his grip. Hughes and Roy turned together toward the sound as if their bodies were controlled by the same mind. All held perfectly still.

Annie spotted the infected at the far edge of her night vision's range, a couple of football fields away and well beyond the grocery store. As many as ten slinked blindly toward the bank in the darkness. She had a hard time convincing herself that they couldn't see her. She saw them perfectly, after all, and she was standing right out in the open. The rational part of her mind understood how night vision worked, but the primitive threat-detection system in her brainstem shouted, *if you can see a predator, it can see you*, and it flooded her body with cortisol and adrenaline. The infected were effectively eyeless, though, and she knew that, so she inhaled and exhaled as slowly as she could.

Those things could not mount a formidable offense as long as nobody turned the headlights back on. They could be neutralized cleanly and stealthily in the darkness.

Annie was unarmed, though. Parker still had her weapon.

"Give me my crowbar," she whispered.

"Shh," Parker whispered.

Hughes and Roy nodded at each other and stepped forward together toward the infected, Roy with his sword out in front of him and Hughes with his crowbar at his side.

"Let them handle it," Parker said.

Annie struggled against Parker for a moment, not in a serious attempt to break free but as a silent protest. Roy was making himself useful again while she stood around like a post.

Roy and Hughes moved toward the infected, smoothly, quietly, deliberately. Annie couldn't hear them. She couldn't hear the approaching infected either, even though they were coming straight toward her without even attempting to be quiet. Night vision was truly a super weapon. Annie marveled that she and her friends hadn't made better use of it until now.

The approaching infected did not run. They must have been too far away to be entirely sure what they'd heard and didn't know they'd find prey once they got where they were going. All they knew was that they'd heard something coming from a general direction.

The gap between Hughes, Roy, and the infected narrowed as they converged near the center of the grocery store's parking lot. The infected were far enough that they posed no threat whatsoever to Annie but close enough now that she could count them. There were exactly nine ambling and shuffling along, and they were spaced far enough apart that they didn't quite constitute a pack. They were more of a scattered line, queueing up like sheep to get their idiot throats slit one at a time.

Hughes raised a hand and signaled for Roy to stop and let the infected close the distance under their own steam. He stepped a healthy distance from Roy and stood there, crowbar in hand, cocked and ready to swing like a crocodile beneath the water, its eyes peeking just over the surface and waiting for its prey to swim toward its mouth.

When the first of nine stepped into killing range, Hughes swung his crowbar with the power of a bodybuilder at bat over the home plate, all but removing the infected's head from its neck. The blow sounded like a pumpkin falling from the top of a parking garage and splatting onto the pavement below. Annie had heard this sound so many times that it no longer sickened her, but in a world gone utterly quiet, it sounded louder than it usually did.

The eight remaining infected screamed at the same time and charged. They did it blindly and stupidly but with a startling ferociousness. Hughes and Roy both took a step back.

Roy slashed one across the midsection with his sword. Hughes caved in another's skull. Hughes had barely a second to take a breath before striking the next one, and Roy seemed to relish stabbing a fourth in the face.

There was a slight delay before the final four reached the killing ground. Roy and Hughes stretched out the delay a little bit longer by taking a few more steps backward to give themselves another moment to breathe, to recover their balance, and to regain their bearings before for the next and last onslaught. An unnecessary response, and a disastrous one. Without peripheral vision, they botched it and crashed into each other.

Something happened to Hughes. He keeled over, as if someone or something had blinded him. It took Annie a moment to figure out had happened: Hughes's collision with Roy must have knocked off his night vision. He was only out of commission for a couple of seconds, but that was enough.

Roy sliced the first of the four remaining infected across the throat with a savage right-to-left swipe, flipped the sword around, then slashed the next one's face on the backswing. The third ran straight into Hughes and knocked him to the ground. Annie couldn't tell from a distance whether Hughes had enough time to reattach the monocle to his face, but it didn't matter. He was a football field away with a rabid infected on top of him, and not even Roy, who was standing right there, had enough time to stop what came next.

Hughes raised his hands to protect his face, and the infected bit one of his fingers. Roy ran his sword through its head and finished off the last one with an impalement strike through its chest, but he was too late.

Hughes had already been bit. He screamed twice, first from the pain and the shock and again when Roy—out of nowhere—sliced off Hughes's arm between the wrist and the elbow.

18

Roy stood like an executioner over a screaming and now-mutilated Hughes, his head high, his shoulders back, and blood dripping from his sword. Before Parker could fully process what had just happened—had the fucker actually cut off Hughes's arm?—Annie charged into the grocery store's parking lot like a berserker. Parker ran after her faster and harder than he'd ever run in his life.

"Stop!" he shouted. She was going to get herself killed.

Roy would run his sword through her next if she didn't stop, but Parker caught her by the back of her coat and swiped the night vision monocle clean off her head, sending it clattering to the pavement.

Annie shrieked. Parker seized her upper arms with both hands and forced her onto her knees. "Not now, Annie. We can't do it now."

"You son of a bitch!" Annie screamed.

"Settle her down and help me!" Roy shouted.

"With *what*?" Parker said, straining to keep a thrashing Annie from elbowing him.

"Get a tourniquet on him!" Roy said. "He might live. If we hurry."

Goddammit. Parker let Annie go and kicked her night vision monocle hard enough to send it skidding so far across the pavement that she might never find it in the dark. He half hoped he broke it so that she'd be blind as long as he needed her blind. He left her and made his way to where Roy stood over his doomed friend writhing on the ground.

Parker ignored what he saw and knew, let his instincts take over, and removed his coat and the T-shirt he wore underneath. Roy held Hughes in place while Parker wrapped his shirt as hard as he could around Hughes's left biceps and tied off the ends. Hughes gritted his teeth and strained with all his might not to yell out. Parker wished he could place something in his friend's mouth to bite down on.

There was a hell of a lot of blood, Hughes's arm still gushing as if he'd sliced his own forearm with a razorblade in a bathtub. The makeshift tourniquet above the elbow barely slowed down the bleeding.

"We need to put pressure on the wound," Roy said. "Hell, we need to cauterize it."

Hughes groaned and kicked.

"How are we supposed to do that?" Parker said.

"I've got a blowtorch in my RV," Roy said.

Jesus Christ, Parker thought.

"I'll get it," Annie said.

Parker turned around. She was right there behind him now and wearing her night vision again.

"Where is it?" Annie said. As if Roy were no longer her enemy.

"Cardboard box under the bed," Roy said.

Annie headed back toward the vehicles.

Parker wondered what else she might find in Roy's creepmobile and if he'd ever used that blowtorch on some of his victims.

He returned his attention to Hughes. His friend was dying and would almost certainly turn. Far better to put him out of his misery than ramp it up all over again with a blowtorch. He shuddered at the very idea. He wouldn't be able to do it. He doubted Annie could either. Roy would have to do it. Roy or nobody.

He heard the RV door open and slam shut.

"This isn't going to work," Parker said.

"It might," Roy said.

The theory was clear enough. Roy had hoped to sever Hughes's arm before the virus had time to spread to his heart and then throughout the rest of his body. It wouldn't work, though, because Roy's sword was smeared with infected blood and virus when he made the cut.

"Your sword wasn't sterile," Parker said.

"Don't know if that matters," Roy said. "Hughes's blood washed the infected's away."

"Mmm," Parker said. "Maybe." He doubted it. "You ever done this before?"

"No," Roy said.

"What made you think of it now?"

Roy looked up and toward something unseen in the distance. "Dunno. I just did it. The way you catch yourself when you fall."

Parker nodded. Hughes would be out of his misery in a few more minutes anyway, and he'd be in heaps of pain anyway, so . . . why not try?

There was no logical reason why not, but Parker wouldn't have done it. Such a brutal act wouldn't have even occurred to him. And he realized, at that moment, that something inside him had changed. Not long ago, he had thought of nothing but murder. It had given him panic attacks. The virus had done terrible things to his mind, but the damage seemed to have finally worn off. Annie had been right all along—Parker wasn't a monster. He'd be okay. He was already okay. Only a pitiless psychopath like Roy would have sliced off Hughes's arm without flinching.

Hughes was fading now and no longer struggling much. His face was contorted in agony, but his breathing was slower. He was losing a lot of blood. More likely than not, the virus was having its way with him.

Annie returned with the blowtorch.

"I'll do it," Roy said. Annie handed it to him, the war between them forgotten for now.

Parker couldn't watch, which was just as well because he

shouldn't. He needed to stand guard, to hold their ground against any other infected in the area that might bear down on their position after all the racket they'd made.

Roy flicked the blowtorch on, and an explosion of light in Parker's night vision nearly blinded him in one eye. He removed him monocle and blinked several times as his eyes adjusted.

Ghostly blue light washed over the parking lot as boiling hot vapor jetted out of the blowtorch's nozzle. Parker shuddered. He knew Roy was getting to work when the acrid stench of copper wire and barbecued hamburger reached his nose. He braced himself for more screaming from Hughes, but it never came.

"He's gone," Annie said. "Isn't he?"

"I don't rightly know, ma'am," Roy said.

Was Hughes about to turn? Had he bled to death? Passed out from blood loss? Nobody had any idea.

"It's done," Roy finally said and shut off the blowtorch. "The bleeding stopped."

Darkness returned to the world, and Parker placed the monocle over his eye again. He exhaled hard as yet another gruesome science experiment unfolded before his eyes. Hughes would either turn or he wouldn't, he'd either get up or he wouldn't. Parker, Annie, and Roy all instinctively took a few steps back in case the worst was about to happen.

Parker had an inkling now how his friends must have felt after they'd infected him on the island. That experiment had worked; he had recovered. They knew now that Annie's immunity could be transferred to somebody who shared her blood type. But they'd never know the results of Roy's brutal experiment if Hughes bled out and didn't get up. They'd never know if the amputation stopped the virus or not if he didn't live long enough to turn or to not turn.

Parker couldn't quite believe that his friend was about to die, but he hadn't really believed Kyle would die either. This wasn't a movie where the heroes had to survive to the end. Hardly anybody survived in this pitiless world.

The three of them stood around Hughes in a circle. Parker

couldn't tear his eyes away from Hughes's mutilated arm, at the frightening pond of congealing blood underneath him, at the shocked and anguished expression still on his face. Even by the Hobbesian standards of the world they lived in now, this was a bad way to go.

Parker wondered where to bury his friend. In somebody's yard, he supposed. They couldn't just leave him out there in the parking lot.

"How much time should we give him?" Annie said.

"An hour," Parker said. Hughes would turn in twenty minutes or less if he was going to turn. A half hour should be enough time, but unless they doubled it, Parker would spend the rest of his life wondering if they had given Hughes enough of a chance.

In the meantime, they didn't dare pick him up and load him into the car. Hughes was a big man. If he turned in that car, he'd likely kill all of them.

"We can leave right now," Roy said, "if we tie him up."

"We're not tying him up!" Annie insisted.

"Shh," Parker said.

Hughes coughed. Not the wracking cough of the flu or even a cold. It was barely more than throat-clearing.

Parker watched intently. Was this a death spasm? The first twitch of a diseased resurrection? It didn't mean Hughes was okay. The infected had lungs. They coughed as much as the healthy did.

"I'm going to get some pain meds out of the truck," Annie said and walked off.

Parker nodded. They had a whole miniature pharmacy in the back of the Suburban, including opioids. Parker doubted that any number of pills could soothe a scorched and severed limb, but they wouldn't make it hurt worse.

Hughes coughed again and opened his eyes.

Parker took a knee a safe distance away. It still wasn't clear what was happening. "Hey," he said. "Is that still you in there?"

Hughes grunted, nodded, and winced. He hadn't turned. Not yet, anyway. For the first time, Parker gave himself permission to hope.

"Annie's getting some Oxy out of the truck," Parker said.

Hughes closed his eyes and nodded. He couldn't see anything anyway without night vision.

Annie hustled back with a small bottle of pills and a large bottle of water.

"Hey," she said and smiled at Hughes. "Can you talk?" She kept her distance, still unsure if it was safe to approach.

Hughes propped himself on his good elbow, disturbing the thickening pool of blood underneath him.

"Take it easy," Parker said.

Hughes managed to sit all the way up with considerable effort. "We have to go," he managed to say.

Parker didn't trust his own sense of time well enough to gauge how much had elapsed since Hughes had been bit. Long enough to trust that he wouldn't turn?

"I'm okay," Hughes said.

"No," Annie said, her voice cracking. "You're not okay."

"I'm not going to turn," Hughes said.

"How can you tell?" Parker said.

"I just can," Hughes said. "I'm not on my way down. I'm on my way up. Give me some of those pills."

"Give him one," Parker said.

"Give me four," Hughes said and coughed again.

"You've lost a lot of blood," Roy said. "Four will probably kill you."

Hughes exhaled and nodded. "Two."

"One," Parker said. "That arm is going to scream like a mother no matter how many you take."

∼

Hughes didn't turn. Annie didn't think he'd die, either. He appeared to stabilize after she and the others let him rest on the pavement for a half hour or so. At least it was long enough to let the painkillers kick in. They gave him a little more time to be sure, then heaved him off the ground and loaded him into the back of the armored car.

"You got any antibiotics?" Roy said, eyeballing the ghastly wound on what was left of Hughes's arm. "He's gonna need 'em."

"We do, actually," Parker said.

"I'll get them," Annie said and set off again for the portable pharmacy in the back of the Suburban.

She was going to miss that truck. It had proven itself over thousands of miles. In addition to being comfortable for four people, it had room for all their weapons, gear, and supplies. They wouldn't need half of that stuff anymore. They had no further use for tents, backpacks, pots and pans, or even sleeping bags. If all went well, they'd only be in the armored car for a couple of hours. And if it went badly, well, they wouldn't need anything for very much longer. As she'd already told Hughes, Annie wouldn't let herself starve to death. She'd end it long before it came to that. She'd end it for all of them, starting with Roy.

She found a bottle of Amoxicillin, returned to the parking lot, placed a pill on Hughes's tongue, and tilted a bottle of water into his mouth so he could swallow it. Her friend had been reduced to a giant baby bird. He couldn't protect her anymore. It was her job now to look after him. She ran a hand across his forehead and through his hair. "We're going to make it," she told him, though she didn't quite half believe it. "The doctors will take care of both of us."

Hughes smiled at her.

"You're a good woman, Annie," Hughes said and coughed. "Truly, you are."

"You ride in front, ma'am," Roy said. "I'll ride in back with your friend here."

Annie nodded without looking at Roy.

"I'm sorry for everything," Roy said.

No you aren't, Annie thought.

"You have every right to despise my guts," Roy said.

Annie didn't trust herself enough to even respond. Like it or not, she had no choice now but to deal with Roy later.

They loaded all the essentials from the Suburban and the RV into the armored car and set off with Parker behind the wheel, Annie in the passenger seat, and Roy in back with Hughes. They headed out slowly at first while Parker got used to driving a vehicle he wasn't familiar with. It was a lot heavier than the Suburban, even more so than Annie had expected. The damn thing felt like a tank.

She realized now that Parker was right, about so many things but especially Roy. She was no longer even annoyed that Roy kept finding ways to make himself useful. She needed him to make himself useful now that they were effectively down a man. At this point, he was merely a tool, both for good and for ill.

But for Roy, Kyle would still be alive. At the same time, also but for Roy, Hughes would be dead. For the briefest of moments, Annie wondered if he just might be on the road to redemption. But no, that wasn't possible. She might believe he was coming around if she didn't know the truth about him, but nothing Roy could ever do in this world would balance what he was already guilty of. No judge or jury would ever let him go free just because he had saved Hughes. He did a good thing, yes, but for his own reasons. He only cared about getting inside the walls so he might later get himself vaccinated.

Parker, on the other hand, had already walked his road of redemption. She was proud of him. There he was, taking charge, making decisions, and braving danger and risks with aplomb. She could hardly imagine a more decent person. She almost didn't recognize him, but at the same time she wasn't surprised. Part of her had always believed in Parker. Not from the very beginning, of course. He was an insufferable ass when she met him. But she'd never seen anyone sorrier than Parker after he recovered from that terrible virus. Even before then, Annie could see that he was struggling to overcome his worst instincts, and look at him now. Parker was more than recovered. He was a brand-new person, better than he had been before.

It made her wonder if perhaps she was wrong about everyone else left in the world. Not Roy, surely. Roy needed to go. Everyone else, though—what about them? If Parker could be redeemed, others could be as well. She must have believed that instinctively or she wouldn't have gone to Atlanta.

She understood something now that Parker and Hughes had

seemed to know all along. Only the ruthless could survive in this world, but ruthlessness had to be mastered. It was a constant struggle. Annie had failed to keep her shadow self on a leash back there in the parking lot. The wise ruthless person knows when to fight and when to wait.

Parker and Hughes weren't naïve about Roy. On the contrary. He was their collective shadow self, pointed outward and weaponized against the infected.

∼

Parker was hoping the armored car would be one of the newer models with the newer features—cameras, two-way radios, tiny "gun doors" cut into the sides so that those on the inside could safely shoot at whoever was outside. He didn't know if armored cars actually had any of the features. All he knew for sure was that this one did not.

He pulled into the parking lot of a big box home improvement store. He wasn't sure if they'd find any gas cans in there, but surely they'd find paint to cover the windshield. No one would bother looting paint after the end of the world.

He barely stopped himself from killing the engine. Parker had no idea how to use lockpicks to turn the engine back on again. Better to leave it running even though the noise attracted violence like a magnet.

"I'll go inside," Roy said. "You two wait here."

"You sure?" Parker said, just to be polite.

"You need to stay at the wheel," Roy said, "in case more of those things show up. If they do, just drive around the block and come back and get me."

Roy hopped out of the back with his sword in one hand and his pistol in the other. He kicked in one of the sliding front doors. Parker half expected an alarm to go off.

"Hughes," Annie said. "How you doing back there?"

Hughes grunted. "Unfortunately still alive."

"Hey," Parker said.

"I am so sorry," Annie said.

"Don't be," Hughes said weakly.

"How can I not be?" Annie said.

"It's not your fault," Hughes said.

"It is, actually," she said. "If I hadn't gone after Roy, this wouldn't have happened. I was wrong and you two were right."

"Save it," Hughes said. "You weren't entirely wrong."

Annie didn't reply.

"When you went for Roy," Hughes said, "I did not try to stop you. I didn't expect you to lunge at him like that, but—" He coughed a couple of times and groaned in pain. "I felt relieved that what needed to happen was finally happening. I thought you were going to take his head off. I stepped in to protect you, not him."

Annie didn't reply to that either.

"I need to sleep," Hughes said.

"Don't die on us," Parker said.

"I'm not dying," Hughes said.

"Don't *turn* on us," Parker said.

"I'm not turning either," Hughes said. "Enough time has passed now. I think."

Annie and Parker kept quiet so that Hughes could either sleep or die. He'd make it or he wouldn't. There was nothing else they could do for him now.

Parker imagined himself in Hughes's place. Which was only natural, he supposed. It was what everyone did at funerals and at the scenes of car accidents. They imagined themselves lying there in the road or in the coffin. He wondered how he would feel if Roy had saved him. Would he be grateful? Would he feel like he owed Roy his life?

∾

Hughes drowned in the agony of an exploding star destroying a planet. On a scale of one to ten, he was at twenty. Holding down a conversation was impossible. The pain was so all-consuming that the universe consisted of nothing else. He was amazed that his friends couldn't feel it.

He'd lied when he told them he wanted to sleep. He just wanted to suffer in silence as a volcano erupted from what was left of his arm. There was no other option. He had to welcome it, make room for it, embrace it, even lean into it. Go into a pain trance and meditate on it. Struggling just made it worse.

He inhaled and let the pain in. He exhaled and let the pain in. He relaxed and let it consume him.

Pain was more than a sensation. It was an emotion, and Hughes channeled it into hatred. He wished to destroy Roy now more than ever. Roy was the only reason Hughes was lying in the back of an armored car with his arm turned into mincemeat. Roy was the only reason he'd been attacked in that parking lot in the first place. Roy—and Lucas—were the reasons Kyle was gone.

If Roy hadn't saved him, Hughes would be dead. Hardly ideal, but he wouldn't know he was dead. He wouldn't be suffering. He wouldn't know the world had ended. The entire human race would have extinguished itself as far as he knew, and he'd finally join his wife and son in the blackness.

~

PARKER ONLY NEEDED a couple of minutes to get used to the armored car. It was heavy, sure, but it wasn't a pig to drive. He scanned each side of the road for a gas station.

"So, Roy," he said. "What does the world look like to you now?"

Roy didn't answer.

"You've changed since we met you," Parker said.

"Have I?" Roy said.

"The universe is committing suicide," Annie said. "That's what you told us."

"And yet," Parker said, "here you are."

Roy said nothing.

"Have you changed your mind about that?" Parker said.

"I'm human," Roy said.

"What's that supposed to mean?" Annie said.

"Nobody wants to live forever," Roy said. "Nobody wants to retire to a little house for a thousand years and another thousand years after that. But everybody wants to survive."

"There's something you need to know," Parker said. "Annie and I haven't been the same since we turned and recovered." He shuddered at what that virus would do to a person like Roy even after it had vacated his system.

"Annie handled it better than I did," Parker said. "I was a disaster. For a while there, I wasn't even sure I recovered."

Parker didn't know why he was telling him this. Roy would never turn and recover. Parker and Annie would make sure of that. Roy wouldn't live long enough to see a vaccine created.

"Did you run around biting people?" Roy said.

"Afterward, you mean?"

"Yeah."

"I thought about it." Even without peripheral vision, Parker knew Annie turned in the passenger to look at him. "I thought about it all the time. And not just biting people either. I thought about stabbing people, slitting their throats, and bashing their heads into walls. I didn't actually do it, but I was terrified that I would."

Nobody said anything for a long couple of moments.

"He's better now," Annie said.

Parker knew he shouldn't push it, but he went ahead anyway. "I barked myself up a tree and couldn't come down until after I talked to a therapist. You okay with that?"

"Am I okay with that?" Roy said. "And where in Sam hell did you find a therapist?"

"Wyoming," Parker said. "And I mean, it could happen to you if you turned and recovered. A vaccine might not prevent it."

For a long time, Roy didn't answer. Parker wondered if he'd pushed things too far, if Roy suspected now that the others knew his secret. Parker had some plausible deniability—he was talking about himself, after all—but Roy might still be suspicious. It would explain to him why Annie had attacked him in the parking lot. He didn't need psychic powers to figure it out.

"I wouldn't get my panties in a wad over it," Roy finally said.

A gas station appeared on the right. Parker pulled in and came to a stop behind a pickup truck parked near the air hose since the pumps wouldn't work. He questioned now why he looked for a gas station in the first place since they'd have to siphon fuel from another vehicle anyway.

"I got it," Roy said and climbed out the back with two empty gas cans in his hands and the siphon hose between his teeth.

"Let's talk about something else," Annie said, "when he comes back."

"Roger that," Parker said.

"Hughes," Annie said. "You okay back there?"

Hughes grunted. Still alive, at least.

Parker stepped out of the car to provide security as Roy inserted the hose into the pickup truck's tank. The sky to the east glowed faintly. The sun would be up soon.

"We should paint the windows too," Parker said, "while we're stopped."

Roy, hunched over a gas can while fuel poured out of the hose, craned his head to look at the sky. "Won't be invisible much longer."

Parker felt beyond tired. Sleep was a basic human drive. It could not be resisted forever, not even in times of danger and stress. He wanted to suggest everyone grab a quick nap, but that would be folly. He'd sleep for hours, not minutes. He had no choice but to gut it out for a while. Once the sun came up, his metabolism would switch into waking mode and rev up again.

He wouldn't have to wait long. The sun would be up in less than an hour, and the infected would see them.

The infected would see everything.

19

They torched the tallest building in Buckhead. Smashed through the windows, sloshed two cans of gasoline onto the floors and walls in the lobby, and set the whole thing ablaze with a match.

Parker felt like a terrorist. He'd grown accustomed to breaking into and looting stores, raiding cabinets in private homes, and siphoning fuel out of other people's gas tanks, but destroying a steel and glass condominium tower—shops, restaurants, penthouses, and all—was something else. Parker was no real estate expert, but he was certain that building must have been worth north of a hundred million dollars. He hoped no one was living in it, but there was no way to be sure. He and his friends were not going to climb all the stairs and kick in every door. Not if they wanted to get out alive.

They drove away in silence as the flames licked the first floor's ceiling.

The early rays of dawn warmed the skies. Parker no longer needed his night vision. And thank goodness for that because he could barely see anything; the entire windshield save for a two-inch wide slit was now covered with porch paint. His rear- and side-view mirrors were useless. He hoped it wouldn't rain any time soon because the windshield wipers were painted stuck to the glass.

Parker drove a mile, then two, toward North Druid Hills, marveling at how different the cityscape looked in natural light after he had finally grown accustomed to night-vision green. For the first time Atlanta looked real. It wasn't a dream. He was really there. He was really doing this.

And he knew where he was now. The Druid Forest neighborhood was coming up. That's where they'd stopped earlier and heard the horde from a distance. He pulled the car to the side of the road and stopped.

"We should wait here," he said.

"Agreed," Annie said.

The infected were somewhere up ahead, but Parker didn't know how far up ahead. And he had no idea, really, if the infected would truly be drawn to a burning skyscraper or not.

Parker still wanted sleep, especially now that he was no longer driving and his mind had nothing to do.

"Actually," Annie said. "We should get off this street. Park on one of the side streets. Those things will be coming straight up this road."

"They'll walk right on past us," Parker said. "We're just another parked car out of thousands."

"You want them surrounding us?" Annie said.

"Unavoidable," Parker said. "The damn things will be everywhere, not just on this road."

"Lady's right," Roy said. "And reckon we ought to cover the windows with blankets or something, even the slits we left, case one of them puts an eyeball up to the glass."

"It'll be dark in here," Parker said, "even with the sun up. They won't see shit."

"Better hope not," Roy said.

Was Roy scared? Parker doubted it. He remembered something Annie had told him the first time he had a panic attack, back in the Oregon desert when he still feared that he might snap at any moment and kill somebody. *You know who doesn't feel anxiety*, Annie had asked. *Psychopaths*.

"You nervous, Roy?" Parker said.

"No," Roy said, "but not stupid either. Best park on one of the side streets."

"Just do it," Annie said.

Parker relented, put the car into gear, drove to the next cross street, and saw that Roy and Annie were right. A sign along the curb read No Outlet. With only one way in and out, the infected wouldn't come up behind them. They wouldn't bother wandering down the side street at all.

So, Parker made a K-turn and parked next to the curb, pointing the front of the vehicle in the direction of Roxboro Road. He almost killed the engine again before remembering, *no*, he did not have a key. He'd have to sit there with the engine idling just as he had at the home improvement store.

They sat there for a long time. Parker struggled against his body's nearly overwhelming drive to sleep and stared intently through the unpainted slit in the windshield for movement ahead.

"Do you think it would be okay if we napped?" he finally said.

Nobody said anything. He realized, only after checking, that Annie, Roy, and Hughes were all asleep—assuming Hughes hadn't finally keeled over.

Annie didn't slump against the window to sleep as she usually did. She just tilted her head back. Roy, however, was sprawled across the floor in the cargo area as if he'd been shot.

Parker couldn't resist: he scrutinized Roy as if the man was some kind of cross-breed, with one parent a human being, the other an alien from a distant, brutal galaxy. Roy was missing parts that the rest of them had.

Parker let Roy be and returned his attention to the front of the car and the streetscape before him. Still nothing happening.

The clouds from the night before cleared. The sun was all the way up now and bathing the urban landscape in warm yellow hues. Parker listened hard but couldn't hear anything but the idling engine.

As quietly as he could, he popped open the driver's side door just a crack and paused before pushing it all the way open. He didn't see or hear anything moving, so he opened the door all the way, stepped out, and marveled at the feel of the sun on his face. The sunlight was brighter and warmer down south, much warmer than in Seattle this time of year. It felt more like the middle of spring than late winter.

He could hear the horde in the city center now. The sounds of moaning and yelling and jostling were sharp—and near. To the north, toward Buckhead, a column of black smoke rose in the sky. It looked like a tire factory was on fire.

"Hey." Annie's voice.

Parker slipped back inside and gently closed the door. Darkness and relative silence returned.

"They're coming," he said. "They're louder, and closer, and I can see the fire."

Hughes groaned from the floor in the back. "Don't . . ."

"Hey, man," Parker said. "You want some water?"

"Don't go . . . out there again," Hughes said.

Roy was still splayed out on the floor in the exact position he was in before.

"Roy," Parker said.

Roy didn't move.

"Roy!"

Roy bolted upright and turned his head from side to side, unsure where he was or what was happening.

"Give Hughes some water, will you?" Parker said. "The fire's lit, the infected are coming, and we're going to have to be as quiet and still as the dead before long."

They came just a few minutes later, surging up the Roxboro Road like a flood after a dam breach, grunting, moaning, sputtering, shifting, spitting and coughing, moving across Parker's field of vision from right to left barely a hundred feet from the car, oblivious that they were observed through a slit in a painted-on windshield.

They smelled like a hog farm, even with the windows rolled up. And they were covered in dirt and muck and blood and gore. What on earth were they eating? Each other, perhaps. No—almost certainly. What else was there? There were no human victims left on this side of the wall.

They'd die then, eventually, given time. Things that can't continue forever, won't. The city would be safe soon enough, even beyond the wall. Parker might have a much easier time getting Annie and Hughes inside if he waited a month or even a couple of weeks.

Hughes was right, though, that they couldn't wait. Everyone inside the walls might starve first. They weren't going to eat each other. If things were that bad on the inside, the CDC would be in no condition to help Annie or make a vaccine.

Besides, Hughes needed doctors now too. He might survive in the wild without medical attention, but Parker wouldn't bet on it. He sure as shit didn't want to hole up with Roy for two months.

The horde moved lemming-like up Roxboro Road for five minutes, then ten, then twenty.

"Unbelievable," Annie finally said.

"We couldn't possibly drive through that," Parker said.

"No, we couldn't," Annie said.

"Hughes," Parker said. "How you doing back there?"

"He's out," Roy said.

Parker exchanged glances with Annie.

"Don't worry; he's breathing," Roy said.

The horde didn't stop. It kept moving, boundless as the ocean, drawn to the burning tower in Buckhead. Finally, after more than half an hour, it began thinning. Gaps appeared here and there, with the stragglers bringing up the rear spaced farther and farther apart. After a few more minutes, the way ahead cleared.

Parker and Annie leaned forward to get a better look through the slit on the glass.

"I think we're good," Parker said and reclined again in his seat.

"Wait!" Annie said.

Another one, solitary and limping, ambled up Roxboro as if it didn't care whether or not it actually got anywhere.

Parker gave it a couple of minutes. The road seemed to be clear, for real this time. "We go?"

Annie nodded, okay.

Parker checked the dashboard. Still half a tank of gas left.

He rolled his shoulders, cranked his head to each side to release the tension in his neck, took a deep breath, put the car into gear, and stepped on the gas. He gingerly approached the intersection, found the road clear in both directions, and made a right toward the wall.

His nighttime advantage, where he could see everything and the infected couldn't see anything, was completely inverted now. It was his turn to be blind. He could hardly see anything ahead of him—and nothing at all to the side or the rear—so he didn't dare drive faster than five miles an hour.

Stately row houses lined the right side of the road, and a vast green park sprawled to the left. The way forward headed generally southwest, temporarily changing direction once in a while around gentle s-curves. If Parker hadn't known better, he'd have no idea a horde had been through here. The infected left nothing in their wake.

A business district appeared after another s-curve with a donut chain on the left and a corporate pharmacy on the left, both boarded up.

"North Druid Hills," Annie said.

"This is it?" Parker said. "Really?" He'd expected hills overlooking downtown, not a suburban-looking strip packed with big-box stores, fast-food joints, lube shops, and drive-thru banks. In the distance, though, a tall church spire rose into the sky above the commercial detritus.

"Take the next right," Annie said. "Do it slowly."

Parker was already driving as slowly as he reasonably could, not even bothering to shift into second gear. He made a right at the light onto Lavista Road. "Now what?"

"Take the next left at Houston Mill Road," Annie said. "Believe it or not, the CDC is only one more mile, and it's a nearly straight shot."

~

ANNIE ALWAYS KNEW the last mile was going to be the hardest. Even so, when Parker made a left onto Houston Mill Road, just a single mile north of the Centers for Disease Control, she briefly let herself believe they had made it.

The road was a two-lane, an almost rural corridor through deciduous and evergreen trees and sporadically punctuated by one-story ranch houses. Another s-curve lay ahead; nothing in Atlanta they'd seen so far was laid out on a typical urban grid.

What she saw after rounding the first s-curve should not have surprised her, but it did. The entire landscape was covered in gore. Not just the asphalt but front lawns were smeared with blood, guts, bones, tattered clothing, and shit. Not an inch of ground appeared clean. She gagged on the stench.

Parker stopped the car.

She and Parker leaned forward to get a better view through the unpainted slit on the glass, the gruesome scene before her as if thousands of people had swallowed live hand grenades after pulling the pins.

"Mother of pearl!" Roy said from the back, sounding like he was going to retch. "The hell's going on?" He couldn't see anything at all from the cargo compartment.

"Blood and guts everywhere," Annie said. "Like an organic bomb exploded. They were here less than an hour ago."

Parker placed a hand on his stomach.

"You okay?" Annie said. She felt her own gorge rising.

"I don't know," Parker said.

"You want me to drive?" Roy said from the back.

"No," Parker said. "Just give me a minute." He leaned back in the driver's seat and wiped his hands on his pants.

"They eating each other or what?" Roy said.

"Seems so," Annie said.

"What are they drinking?" Roy said.

"There's water all over the place," Annie said. "Rivers, creeks, lakes, even in this part of the city."

Parker exhaled slowly, sat up straight, and put his hand on the gear shift.

"Take it real slow," Annie said. "One mile an hour."

Parker put the car in gear and crept forward as slowly as the vehicle would go without stalling. Annie could have crawled faster. The CDC was still a mile away, so at this speed it would take them a full hour to get there.

But the wall, she assumed, would be closer than that. Surely the engineers who had constructed it would have added a buffer zone, some patch of ground between the medical complex and the barrier itself. For all she knew, there were actually two walls, two concentric rings around the campus in case the outer one was breached with enough room between them for military trucks, guard towers, supply lines, and so forth.

She studied the map. If she were tasked with surrounded this CDC with a wall, where would she put it?

South Fork Peachtree Creek formed a natural east-to-west barrier a quarter mile or so north of there. A creek wouldn't stop a horde unless it roared through a slot canyon, but it would be an engineering obstacle. There were only a handful of bridges over that creek. It must have created traffic bottlenecks during normal times. The wall builders would have wanted to keep it outside their enclave. They didn't need it as a water source because another creek ran right alongside the CDC and Emory University immediately to the south. Candler Lake was most likely inside the wall, so South Fork Peachtree Creek would be on the outside. The longer Annie looked at the map, the more she was sure of it. That creek—and therefore most likely the wall—was less than three-quarters of a mile from their current location.

Parker kept the armored car moving at an excruciatingly slow speed. Annie was tempted to tell Parker to hurry it up, to move things along, but she knew better.

"This feels too easy," Parker said.

"Don't get cocky," Annie said.

"How close are we?" Roy said from the back.

"A little more than a half mile," Annie said.

"How fast are we moving?" Roy said.

"A mile an hour, maybe," Parker said. "We'll get there."

"Like the lady said," Roy said. "Don't get cocky."

Annie squinted through the slit on the glass and saw movement around the next s-curve. The car was moving so slowly that what lay ahead came into view just a sliver at at time: diseased post-humans, matted with gore, shifting about and pressing themselves against even more infected in front of them, trying and failing to move forward.

Annie saw only the bleeding edge of what she knew was a much larger mass that would come into a full view as soon as Parker finished making the turn. Instead, Parker stopped the car.

"What's happening?" Roy said from the back.

"Whole city of them dead ahead," Parker said.

Annie had to force herself to breathe even though she knew nothing outside the car would be able to hear her.

"They haven't spotted us yet," Parker said.

"How many?" Roy said.

"Hundreds," Annie said. "Thousands. Probably hundreds of thousands." The wall—or at least where she assumed the wall would be—was still a half mile away.

"Keep going," Roy said. "Drive through them. Do it slowly. They'll move out of our way."

Annie felt like her organs were turning to liquid. Roy was right—she knew he was—but there would be no turning back once they were surrounded.

"Annie," Parker said. "You need to get down. If one of them presses their face to the glass, they might see you."

"And they might see you," Roy said.

"I can't drive if I can't see out."

"Hang on," Roy said. Annie heard him rummaging around in a supply box. "Here," he finally said and handed Annie a black fleece hat and a plaid scarf. "Put these on. Cover your face. Everything but your eyes."

Annie handed the gear to Parker. He put the hat over his head, wrapped the scarf around his neck and over his face, and tucked the ends into his jacket collar. It ought to work. Annie couldn't see anything but his eyes.

"Do we have any sunglasses back there?" Annie said.

"I had a pair," Roy said, "but I left them in the RV."

"This will have to do then," Annie said. "Parker, you're going to have to sit perfectly straight. Don't move in your seat. Don't even breathe any more than you have to."

Parker nodded and pressed his foot to the gas pedal.

20

Leap, and a net will appear. That's what Parker's father once told him when he was nervous about starting a cabinetry business instead of going to college. A successful merchant and businessman, his father insisted that Parker should trust that things would work out, that the universe would meet him halfway, that if he ignored the butterflies in his belly and hurled himself into the void, the very fact that he'd acted would transform the world—and the transformed world would include a net that would catch him. It wasn't a leap of faith. It wasn't about trusting the universe. Parker couldn't control the universe. Nobody could. It was about trusting himself—the only person in the world he could control or direct.

That's what he told himself as he pressed his foot to the gas pedal and moved the armored car toward the horde. *Leap, and a net will appear.*

He had to trust himself and his friends. Trust that their plan was a good one. Trust that they truly were invisible inside the car. Trust that those things could not get inside. And trust that if anyone still lived on the other side of that wall, they'd do everything in their power to help if they knew that he and Annie were immune to the virus.

The edge of the horde was three hundred yards away. At first, the infected didn't notice or hear the car coming. As Parker inched along, though, and narrowed the gap to two hundred yards, some of them turned around, cocked their heads to the side, peeled themselves away from the others, and slowly made their way forward.

"They see us now," Parker said. "Two blocks away. They're coming toward us."

"Our diversion in Buckhead failed," Annie said, slumping in the passenger seat with her head down. "Didn't it."

"Didn't fail, ma'am," Roy said, still on the floor in the back next to Hughes. "It just wasn't enough to clear all of them out."

"They can't see the fire in Buckhead from here," Parker said. "We're too far away now, and there are trees everywhere blocking the view."

"At least we got rid of half of them," Roy said. "Just take it real slow. Take it real easy."

The horde was enormous. Parker saw hundreds of infected occupying the road ahead and spilling off to the side and into the trees. If they were this thick on the ground all the way to the wall, he'd be driving through them for almost a half mile.

Parker took it as slowly as he could, so slowly that he had a hard time keeping the car in gear. If he couldn't balance the clutch and the brake precisely, the engine would stall. For the first time since he was a teenager, he wished he was driving with an automatic transmission instead of a manual.

A dozen infected shambled toward the car, more out of curiosity than anything else. They didn't attack cars. Cars weren't food. Cars were objects, moving along for mysterious reasons. Interesting enough to approach, but nothing to get too excited about.

Parker found it amazing that they couldn't remember that people drove cars. The infected seemed to regard them the way squirrels and birds did—big metal objects with no intent, will, or purpose of their own.

More saw him coming when he narrowed the gap to less than a hundred yards. Whole batches of them were turning around now. By the time Parker closed the distance, more than a hundred faced him directly.

Parker held his breath and pressed forward. Driving into the edge of the horde was like launching a boat from the beach into the sea. The infected stepped aside, half of them to the left and half of them to the right, like water parting at the prow of a ship.

Parker gagged on the smell: spoiled meat, rotten eggs, and unclean toilets tinged with vomit. The sound was panoramic now: grunts, moans, wheezes, and even something that sounded like mooing. He distinctly heard screams farther ahead.

The car was surrounded within seconds and yet—astonishingly—Parker hadn't hit or even touched one of them. The infected had plenty of time to move out of the way. He imagined that the scene from above must look like creek water swirling around a boulder.

The infected eyeballed the truck intently, so Parker held his body perfectly still. It didn't seem to occur to them that they might try to peer inside through the unpainted slit on the windshield, but every couple of seconds Parker could swear he made fleeting eye contact with one of them.

They couldn't see him, though. There would be glare on the glass now that the sun was up. Still, he didn't dare move. Even a hint of perceived motion inside the car might make them curious. They might attempt to get closer for a better look. If they got close enough to the glass to block sunlight, there wouldn't be any glare. If even one of them sensed prey was inside and screamed, it would be over.

"What's going on?" Annie said. "What do you see?"

"They're getting out of the way," Parker said. "They don't seem to think the car's dangerous. It's more like an annoyance."

Then he hit one of them. Not hard. Just a tap, really. But then he ran over its foot. It yelped in pain and slapped the hood.

Parker panicked and hit the brake, and he was too slow on the clutch. The engine stalled out and died.

The infected he'd injured freed itself but not before agitating the crowd.

The armored car was high off the ground. It wasn't really even a car. It was more of a truck. The infected couldn't easily hop onto the hood like they could on a sedan. But they could climb onto it, and two of them did. There weren't curious anymore either, nor did they see the vehicle as an annoyance. They were angry. They just weren't sure why or what they should do about it. So they stomped on the hood. Several on the street kicked the grill. A few of them slapped the doors.

Annie cowered and moaned. Neither Hughes nor Roy made a sound in the back.

One of the infected on the hood noticed the slit on the windshield. It crouched down and peered in as its comrades assaulted the vehicle.

Parker froze, still as a mountain during a storm. He did not breathe. He did not even blink.

"What's happening?" Annie said.

Parker shushed her without moving.

The infected was staring right at him. It had long purple hair and a suppurating wound on its cheek. Parker was pretty sure it was a teenage girl. It stared right into his eyes, squinting, tilting its head, and pressing its nose to the glass.

Don't blink, Parker thought. You blink, you die.

His eyes burned. He desperately wanted to close them, but he didn't dare. The diseased girl would scream, and that would be that.

"Turn the engine back on," Roy said.

Parker shushed him too. "One of them is looking at me through the glass."

Thank God he'd covered his face with a scarf, or that thing would have seen his lips move. It was still looking right at him.

He wouldn't be able to keep his eyes open much longer. It was not a question of willpower. Blinking was a reflex. He could override it for a short time but not forever.

Several infected were still pawing the vehicle, but a little less enthusiastically than before. They apparently weren't sure what to make of it. But that *thing* on the hood wouldn't stop staring at him. He willed it to go away or at least turn away, but it kept staring at him.

"Kick the floorboards," he said to Annie.

"What?" Annie said.

"Kick the floorboards. Do it now. It's looking right at my face."

Annie kicked the floorboards. The teenage thing with the hair gasped and looked away.

Parker closed his eyes. He could sense the diseased girl moving across the hood toward Annie's side like a shark through water. It didn't seem to know what to make of the sound, though. Annie was too low in her seat to be seen, and there was no indication that her kick meant *prey*. Parker waited a couple of moments, then slowly opened his eyes a mere fraction so he could see through the watery slit between his lids.

The teenage infected wasn't looking at him anymore. It was standing up on the hood now. Parker went ahead and opened his eyes all the way.

The infected girl stomped the windshield with the flat of her foot.

Annie gasped.

"Shh," Parker said. "It can't break the glass." Not if the glass really was bulletproof.

It stomped the windshield again.

"We need to move," Annie said, crouching even lower now.

"Wait it out," Parker said. "Don't move and they'll forget anything ever happened."

Another infected slapped the passenger side door right next to Annie.

"Shh," Parker said.

The infected girl on the hood bent down to peer into the windshield again, and this time she screamed.

PART IV

END OF THE ROAD

21

Parker thought he had a pretty good idea how the infected behaved after observing them, up close and from a distance, for so many months. They were drawn toward any and all stimuli, whether movement or sound. A gunshot, a passing vehicle, a hopping rabbit, a flashlight at night, a fire—anything that would capture the attention of other living organisms whose senses were functioning properly. The infected would walk, not run, toward the stimulus to investigate . . . unless they saw something they could consume. In that case, the infected screamed, ran, and attacked.

No one knew for sure exactly why the infected screamed. Almost certainly not to warn. Dogs growled to alert an enemy of potential violence. Cats and snakes hissed for the same reason. This was not that. It would make no logical sense for an infected to deliberately tell its prey that it should run. Nor would it make any logical sense if the infected screamed to alert others that it had found food so that it could share. As far as Parker knew, no predatory animals in the wild willingly shared meals with other predatory animals that were not its kin. Cats large and small dragged their prey to a safe location where they could eat in relative peace without having their meal stolen by scavengers or competitors. Even domesticated house cats instinctively dragged a captured chicken leg under a table.

Parker thought he might have the answer: the infected screamed to alert others so that they could hunt together in packs. That was what primitive humans did. A solitary human with a spear in his hand had little chance against a saber-toothed tiger and no chance at all against a mammoth. Such animals could only be felled by a pack. Sharing had nothing to do with it. Humans were among the slowest and weakest predators of their size in the world. They had a stark choice: work together or starve.

Whatever else the infected were now, they were still biologically human. They did not have superhuman strength or superhuman endurance. If they wanted to eat, they'd have to hunt in packs, especially since their prey were armed with far more sophisticated weapons than teeth, claws, or spears.

That was Parker's theory anyway, and it had helped him and his friends figure out how to manipulate the infected and escape from them more than once. If, while trapped, they could hunker down out of sight until the infected were distracted by something else, he and his friends could leave.

It didn't always work, though. The infected had to forget prey was hiding nearby, and this was all but impossible while any of them were screaming. One scream inevitably triggered another. Besides, waiting for a horde to wander off could only work if the horde had somewhere else to wander off *to*.

And once the infected girl on the hood of the car screamed when she thought she saw prey moving inside, it was as if the entire universe were attempting to smash Parker and his friends.

The infected outside would never stop assaulting the vehicle. There was nothing else around to distract them, and they had nowhere else they could go. They pressed in on all sides as if the armored car were a gravitational sink sucking in teeth, hands, eyeballs, and feet from every direction. The roar was incredible. If Hell had a sound, this was it.

At least the car's engine was running again. Roy had to climb into the front and spend a few minutes fiddling with the lockpicks, but he'd gotten things moving.

Parker kept his foot on the gas pedal. There was no point driving one mile an hour anymore—far better to crush the bastards—but the sheer weight and density of diseased bodies jammed shoulder to shoulder in front of him slowed the car's advance much more than he had thought it would. Driving into this shrieking throng was much more difficult than running down a handful of stragglers in the street. It was more like driving through twelve-inch-deep mud.

And Parker could barely even see where he was going. In front of him, through the slit on the glass, he couldn't see anything but the frenzied mob. He could only see up at a 45-degree angle over their heads. Because they were in another rural-like part of the city, he could only navigate by steering between the tops of the trees since he couldn't see anything else. If there was something in front of him—an abandoned car, a tank trap, a ditch, a hole, or anything else—he would have no idea until he hit it.

Parker finally saw it: the wall. It seemed to rear up suddenly in a mixed forest of deciduous and evergreen trees. It appeared distinctly military and vaguely Middle Eastern, with consecutive concrete slabs nearly twenty feet high, creating the kind of hard and impenetrable barrier designed to repel suicide bombers and car bombers.

Parker saw no one standing on the top of the wall: no guards, no watch towers, no would-be rescuers, not even an electronic surveillance system.

The scene wasn't at all what he had expected. He had imagined coming upon the wall in an urban environment—the Centers for Disease Control was a moderate walking distance from downtown Atlanta, after all—and yet, aside from the wall itself, there seemed to be no structures of any kind in any direction. He and his friends had reached a dead end in a forest. There were no side roads. He could not turn left or right. There was nowhere to go but back.

Hills rose up on each side of the road. The infected were thinner on those hillsides, as if they didn't want to wander off sideways and would rather surge forward toward the wall. There were corpses on the ground in the trees with living infected hunched over their bodies like demons, gnawing on limbs and consuming entrails.

"Where on earth *are* we?" Parker said.

"We're there," Annie said. "This is it."

"We're in a forest!"

"The CDC is just up ahead," Annie said. "Just in front of the wall should be South Fork Peachtree Creek."

If anyone was watching from above, they'd see the car. Parker was pushing through the horde slowly, no faster than walking speed, but it created an extraordinary disturbance. Any observer would be able to hear it as well as see it. But for all Parker knew, the city had been empty of the living for months, the wall a mere legacy of the dead.

Two of the infected on the hood stomped the windshield with the heels of their feet. The first wore a black dress shoe on one foot and a bloody sock on the other, but the second wore what looked like steel-toed boots. Parker didn't know much about armored cars or bullet-proof glass, but he knew that if enough bullets struck the same location repeatedly, the armor would eventually fail.

He wondered if he and his friends would really be safe in this car indefinitely. With the stash of food and water in the cargo area, they might be able to hold out until the horde finally starved to death, but could the armor withstand being relentlessly kicked for days? For a week? Armored cars were designed for something else and had never been subjected to this kind of stress test.

Parker stopped the car, shifted into neutral, and kept his foot on the brake. "The hell do we do?" he shouted over the din. He couldn't drive around and look for a gate or a guard tower. He could only turn around and go back. According to Annie's map, there was a creek up ahead somewhere, and he risked driving right into it if he kept going.

Even if he could find a gate somewhere along the perimeter, no one on the other side of the wall would dare open it. The infected would pour inside like a flood after a dam breach. And he couldn't think of a way that anyone inside the wall could come out and rescue him and his friends even if they wanted to.

"Get us as close as you can to the wall!" Annie shouted. "Then we'll yell through the bullhorn."

"Roy!" Parker shouted. "We're close enough now that we might be able to get someone on the handheld radios!"

"On it!" Roy shouted.

With so much noise outside the car, Parker doubted Roy would be able to hear if anyone answered the radio, but if anyone answered, they'd be able to hear Roy.

Parker stepped on the gas again and pressed forward against the surging mass in front of him. The concrete bulwark ahead loomed ever higher until Parker sensed he was less than a hundred feet from it. Then he put the gear into neutral, let the engine idle, and set the parking brake.

Roy shouted into the radio. "We're immune! Come out and get us! We're just outside the wall on Houston Mill Road!"

The car violently rocked from side to side and from forward to back as the infected warred against it.

Parker blew out his breath and turned around in his seat, relieved to finally be able to look at something—anything at all—other than those things scrambling around in front of the windshield and trying to kick in the glass.

Roy fished the bullhorn out of a cardboard box in the back and passed it forward to Annie. She was about to lower the passenger window on her side but froze at the last moment. Parker understood why. Nobody wanted that window lowered by even an inch. But she'd have to lower it at least three inches, if not five or six, so that the sound of her voice could carry toward the wall rather than reverberate inside the car.

Parker swallowed hard. "Don't lower it more than two inches!" he shouted. "In case we can't raise it back up!"

He knew what would happen the moment she lowered that window: the infected outside would place their hands on top of the glass and attempt to pull it all the way down. He doubted they could do it, but he had no idea if Annie would be able to roll the window back up again.

She lowered it two inches, and the roar of the horde doubled in volume. Several sets of fingers gripped the top of the glass. Parker recoiled against the driver's side door.

"Roll it up!" Parker shouted.

It seemed she couldn't hear him and instead placed the bullhorn to her lips.

Parker reached over and shook her shoulder.

She turned to look at him. Real fear on her face.

"Roll it up!" Parker shouted again. "See if you can roll the window back up!"

He glanced down and saw that he could control all the windows in the vehicle from the driver's seat, so he pressed and held the *up* button himself. The machinery was stronger than the infected—the window slowly rose and mashed two sets of fingers into the top of the door. Parker lowered the window again a half inch to let the infected retract their hands, then sealed it up.

Relative silence returned for a moment until Roy shouted into the handheld radio again. "We're immune! Come out and get us on Houston Mill Road!"

"Okay!" Parker shouted. "We can open and close the window again. Lower it four inches and yell out the bullhorn."

"Six inches!" Annie yelled.

Parker held up four fingers. Just to be safe.

Annie nodded and rolled down the window using the button on her side.

Unspeakable noise rushed in again like water pouring through a sluice gate. Annie raised the bullhorn to the open air and shouted: "We are immune!"

No one answered back. No gate opened up in the wall. Not even those *things* outside reacted in any discernable way. They were already attacking the car with maximum ferocity anyway.

"We are immune!" Annie shouted again.

The bullhorn worked. It sounded like her voice was being blasted out over a loudspeaker. Parker couldn't be sure how well her voice carried over the wall, but anybody listening must have heard something.

"We are immune!" she shouted again. "We can transfer our immunity to other people!"

Which was not strictly true. Annie was immune, and she had transferred her immunity to Parker and maybe to Lucas. But Parker didn't know if *he* could inoculate somebody else.

He watched the top of the wall . . . and saw nothing at all. No evidence that there was anyone up there listening.

"Can they even hear us?" Annie said.

"I don't know," Parker said. "Probably?" The real question was, was anyone still alive on the other side of the wall to hear anything?

Annie rolled up the window, and a relative hush seemed to fall over the world. Now that she had drawn attention to herself, the infected concentrated nearly all their attacks on her side of the vehicle. If there had been any question before whether or not prey was inside the car, there was not anymore. They slapped the glass, jiggered the handle, and kicked and pounded the door. Annie leaned away from it as if it were on fire.

"What now?" Annie said.

"Wait until dark," Roy said, leaning forward and appearing between Parker and Annie like a summoned apparition. Parker had almost forgotten about Roy and Hughes in the back.

"They'll settle down at night," Roy said.

Parker doubted that. A total absence of light might settle a horde down, but they were parked right next to the wall. The city lights from the other side would be blazing as soon as the sun went down.

"They must have heard me," Annie said.

"They heard you," Roy said.

"If there's anyone listening," Parker said. "I'm seriously beginning to wonder."

"When these things, as you call them, quiet down at night," Roy said, "we can try again. It'll stir 'em up some, but they can't get in."

"What now?" Annie asked again.

"Nothing," Hughes said from the back. Thanks goodness. He was still alive and aware of what was happening. "We wait."

"I can keep trying the radio," Roy said.

Parker doubted very much that the radio would work. It would be stupid not to at least try, though.

He closed his eyes and slowed down his breathing so he could slow down his heart rate and his mind. He inhaled, counted slowly to five, exhaled, counted slowly to five, then started again. He tried to think about nothing at all but his breath. Even with the howling mob outside the car, he might be able to get himself into a relaxed state if he kept at it long enough.

The infected kept pounding and screaming, kept rocking the car back and forth, kept doing their damnedest to get inside and destroy the last person who might be able to save whoever was left in the world.

Parker eventually managed to calm himself, not by slowing his breathing and his heart rate but by accepting that he didn't need to do anything. His only option was backing up and driving away from the wall, but what would be the point? They'd driven three thousand miles to get to there, and they'd finally made it. Drive away? To where? He wouldn't be able to find some peaceful section of wall to park next to instead. Atlanta's entire enclave was no doubt surrounded. And the longer they stayed in one place, the more likely they'd get the attention of anyone still alive on the inside. Parker realized, now that he thought of it, that they should have painted WE ARE IMMUNE on the top of the car when they still had a chance. He could, he supposed, drive away to a safe place, paint the top of the car, and come back. But he doubted it would be worth all the trouble, and the last thing he wanted was for anyone watching to think he and his friends had given up and were leaving. Annie could always yell through the bullhorn again if the horde settled down.

But the horde did not settle down, not even after night fell. A solitary infected or a smaller pack might get distracted by something else and forget there was prey in the car, but *the horde remembered*. And there was nothing around to distract them. The only stimulus in the middle of a gigantic mass such as this was the other members of the horde. And the other members of the horde kept attacking and screaming. If even one of them kept at it, the others would do so as well. All the infected would have to stop and forget at the same time, and the chances of that happening were effectively nil.

~

ANNIE SLEPT FITFULLY THAT NIGHT. They all did. The relentless and remorseless *things* outside the car did not stop, did not even let up, and she knew they never would until they breached the car or starved trying. She and her friends would have to evacuate in the morning.

She doubted she slept more than thirty consecutive minutes and gave up even trying at first light. Parker stirred in his seat, too, and Annie sensed movement from either Roy or Hughes in the cargo area.

"We should try the bullhorn again," she said. "Even though those things aren't any quieter."

"Let's wait a bit," Parker said. "Give anyone on the other side a chance to wake up."

"That wall," Roy said, "is being manned twenty-four hours a day. I guarantee it."

"If it's manned at all," Parker said.

"Hughes," Annie said. "You okay back there?"

Annie heard nothing but the barrage of noise outside the car.

"He's fine," Roy said. "He just waved at y'all from the floor."

Annie wasn't asking for a status update from Roy. She turned around in her seat. Hughes was lying on his back with a jacket under his head for a pillow. He waved at Annie.

Roy squinted at her when she briefly made eye contact with him.

She rolled down her window partway and shouted through the bullhorn again. "We are immune! Our immunity can be transferred!" She repeated that message every thirty seconds or so for more than an hour and finally rolled the window back up.

"I don't think anyone's there," she said.

"There has to be," Roy said.

"No, there doesn't," Parker said.

"Somebody's keeping the lights on," Roy said.

"The lights aren't on a hand crank," Parker said. "They can stay on for weeks by themselves."

"What if," Annie said, "they can see us but can't hear us? There might be a CCTV camera somewhere."

"Hang on," Roy said. He fished around for something in back.

Annie realized she wasn't hungry. She hadn't eaten anything at all for twenty-four hours, but still she didn't want food. Her body was officially in a fasting state now, and yet . . . she wouldn't be able to swallow anything if she tried. Unlike those *things* outside the window. God only knew how long it had been since they'd had a meal. She could partake of granola bars, cereal with reconstituted milk, peanut butter, or beef jerky, but the infected would have to feast on each other if they couldn't break into the car. Which meant she could last longer than they could, or at least longer than most of them.

Roy was still doing something in the back—she could sense his movement and hear something just below the threshold of identifiable sound. She stared at the top of the wall and wished she could miracle herself over it.

"What do you think?" she said to Parker.

"Should we back up and find a better spot?" Parker said. "Might be easier to see us in some places than in other places."

"They have to be watching every part of the wall. If they're watching."

"Maybe they don't care about us."

"Even if they know we're immune?"

"Even if they know we're immune."

"They're the CDC. They'd have to care."

"This is a bust. There's no one here and nothing happening."

"Maybe they're telling us to go somewhere else and we just can't hear them."

"They should hold up a damn sign then."

"Great minds think alike," Roy said and appeared over Annie's shoulder. She smelled his wretched breath even over the stench coming in through the air vents. She wanted to tell him to brush his damn teeth, but she realized she hadn't brushed her own yet. She had a bottle of water but nowhere to spit. The best she could do was suck on a small bit of toothpaste.

"Here's a sign for *us* to hold up," Roy said and handed her a large square of cardboard with the words WE ARE IMMUNE painted on it.

Annie took it from him gingerly, careful not to brush her hand against his. "What am I supposed to do with this?" She couldn't hold it up to the windshield—the glass was covered in paint and blocked by the infected. Nor could she stick her arm out the passenger-side window and hoist the sign in the air.

"Here," Roy said and handed her a crowbar and a roll of duct tape. "Tape it to the wrecking bar and stick that out the window."

Annie nodded and took the items from him, her fingers just grazing his. She set the gear in her lap and wiped her hands on her pants.

She spent the next two minutes taping the sign to the crowbar, winding the tape around as tightly as she could. Then she rolled down the window a couple of inches, slid the cardboard sign through the gap, and jammed it as high in the air as she could.

The mob outside howled and ripped the sign to pieces in a matter of seconds.

She rolled up the window.

"I think we need to get out of here," Parker said.

Annie wasn't sure, but she was inclined to agree. Nothing was happening here. They'd made it, but they hadn't made it.

"And go where?" Roy said.

"Anywhere but here," Parker said.

"Not anywhere," Annie said. "Somewhere along the wall that's more open and visible."

"Where?" Roy said.

"Hang on," Annie said and fished around at her feet for the map. She unfolded it and saw a better option at once, a wide-open space where she and her friends could be seen far more easily than they could in this cramped, remote, and practically rural dead end. "There's a golf course just south of Emory University. Go back to North Druid Hills, head south on Clairmont Road, then swing through Chelsea Heights."

A fat infected's face leered at her through the passenger window with its teeth bared.

"And once we get out of here, we can take a break from this shit," she said.

"We can paint the word *immune* on the roof of the car," Roy said, "when we get to a safe place."

Of course, Annie thought. They should have done that already. Damn Roy for making himself useful again.

"Hughes?" Annie said.

"Go!" Hughes cried from the back.

Annie watched as Parker nodded, released the parking brake, slammed the gear stick into reverse, and stepped on the gas. Annie hadn't realized he'd left the engine running all night. The car began moving backward at once, and Parker cranked the steering wheel hard to the right.

The infected outside doubled down on their attacks the moment the car began moving, and the vehicle had barely backed up five feet before meeting some kind of resistance and stopping.

Parker slammed the gear stick into neutral.

"What?" Annie said. Had they backed up onto a curb? No. Something else. There was no curb here. Nothing but trees on each side of the road.

"Ran over something," Parker said. "Or onto something."

An infected in the road. Either a dead one or a live one. Probably a dead one if Parker had run over it. He shifted into first gear, pressed the gas pedal with his foot, and . . . nothing happened.

Annie heard the high-pitched whine of spinning tires.

Parker revved the engine hard. The tires only spun faster, and the car slid slightly from side to side as if on ice.

"Turn the wheel the other way," Roy said, "and back up again."

Parker did what Roy told him to do, and the wheels spun out again.

Annie gulped. They were stuck. Either in mud or in the blood and guts of one of those things.

The infected behaved differently now. Most of them were busy inspecting the front of the vehicle rather than punching and kicking the windshield and the doors. The sounds some of them made were different now, too, as if they were curious, almost investigatory, rather than angry. They had something to think about other than the fact that prey was inside the car.

But that didn't last. It was but a momentary lapse of aggression. The infected, having satisfied their need for new stimuli by checking out the grill and the tires, resumed their assault on the vehicle. They slapped the windows, hurled themselves feet- and shoulders-first at the doors, and screamed like they were boiling alive in pitch.

Parker tried the gas pedal again and got nowhere. He shifted into reverse again and got nowhere. He cranked the wheel as far as he could to the left and the right and got nowhere.

Annie picked up the bullhorn, rolled down the window a couple of inches, and shouted her heart out. "Help us! We are immune! We can save everyone!"

But nobody answered. Nobody seemed to even hear her.

"You bastards!" she shouted through the bullhorn. And then she rolled up the window.

They were dead in the water. They couldn't escape. And no one was coming to rescue them.

22

Parker tried his best to be optimistic. Just wait, he told himself. Something was bound to happen eventually. But nothing kept happening, and when the sun went down again, he knew they were going to die there next to the wall. If anyone was going to come to their rescue, it would have happened by now. If anyone had heard Annie's pleas, they would have come. If anyone on earth would take the trouble to rescue their fellow human beings from a horde of infected, it would be whoever protected the CDC when potential saviors came knocking.

Nobody came.

So, Parker leaned back in his seat and turned off the engine. He realized as he did it that it was his way of telling the others that he'd given up without having to say it out loud.

Nobody else said anything either, but Annie covered her face with her hands.

Parker felt better now that he had accepted what was going to happen. It would be okay. He didn't have to struggle anymore, and he and his friends did not have to die violently. They had an entire pharmacy back there in the first-aid box. Each of them could swallow a bottle of pain pills and wash them down with some water. They could ease themselves out of the world and deny those *things* the grotesque satisfaction of ripping them to pieces alive.

At least they'd tried. Hell, they even made it. There was nothing left, though—not even here—but the vestigial remains of a dead civilization. Atlanta was the last city. It had held on longer than anywhere else on the continent. Good job, Atlanta. The human spirit, defiant to the end. But it wasn't enough. No city could stand alone with this kind of storm encircling the world.

Parker could die peacefully, and he could die at peace. He remembered how he had felt in Lander, Wyoming. How he had *yearned* to be on his deathbed so that he'd finally be able to relax knowing he'd made it to the end of his life without killing someone.

He had just one regret: Holly. His wife. Whom he'd punched in the face, so long ago now, in a moment of anger. He only hit her once, and he *knew* he'd never do it again as long as he lived, but she left him anyway, and he couldn't blame her. She had done the right thing even though it was the wrong thing. He never would have hit her again, but she couldn't know that. He had no right to expect her to know that or to believe it. If she were the kind of women who could believe something like that, he wouldn't have married her in the first place. He was not, after all, the type of man who hit women.

Except that he was. For a brief and terrible moment, he was. And now he was that man forever. And if he could hit Holly, and if he could try to kick Kyle over a cliff, what on earth could stop him from killing someone after his mind had been poisoned by that unspeakable virus?

There was only one thing that could stop him: himself. And he'd done it. He made it all the way to the end of his life without committing an atrocity.

He was finally proud of himself. He only wished he could have come this far while he was still with Holly. He could have died with her in Seattle or brought her to Atlanta to die here with him instead.

Was she looking down on him from the afterlife? Did she know where he was? What he had done? That he'd traveled with Annie Starling, the most precious person alive, on a journey across the wasteland to save everyone? He hoped so. Because then she could finally be proud of him.

∽

Hughes could hardly believe he was still alive. He should have turned into one of things and been put out of his misery and rage by his friends. Or he should have bled out. Or he should have died from shock or from a festering wound.

None of those things had happened because he'd been saved by a psychopath.

And for what? So he could suffer in agony for another forty-eight hours? To hell with this, he thought. *Let's just get on with it.*

∽

Annie couldn't sleep. Not because she wasn't tired, but because she did not want to.

She was going to die soon, most likely tomorrow, and she wanted to think, to remain conscious, to simply continue existing while she still had some time.

At least she had a couple of options. She could slit her wrists. Shoot herself in the head. Eat a meal's worth of prescription pain meds. All of the above were better than starving or dehydrating and certainly better than being eaten. She should count herself among the lucky ones, but she still couldn't believe it and couldn't accept it.

She and her friends had made it all the way to Atlanta. For at least the last thousand miles, she wasn't convinced that the effort was worth it, but now she could see where she had been wrong. Roy wasn't worth saving, and neither was Lucas. But Hughes was worth saving. Kyle was worth saving. What was left of the human race may have been reduced to little better than a barbarian horde like the infected attacking the car, but Parker had redeemed himself. He was a more admirable person now than he had been before. If he could become a better man after the end of everything, others could as well.

She was not going to succeed, but she was glad that she'd tried. It had given her life meaning. Her earlier wish to flee to the far north of Canada was as petulant as it was selfish, and a life lived in perpetual survival mode would have brought her no happiness. She wasn't sure if God existed or if the universe had a plan for its creatures, but in a way it didn't matter: people infused their own lives with purpose. They pursued careers, raised children, cherished friends and family, and worked to better their communities. Some dedicated their entire lives to helping others. Annie imagined they must have been the happiest people around.

Had she not been immune, had she not survived Seattle, and had she not accepted this mission, she wouldn't have bonded with Kyle, Parker, and Hughes. She loved those people more than she had ever loved anybody.

She checked her watch. Almost three o'clock in the morning.

The infected outside relentlessly assaulted the car, but they were just background noise now.

A light came on in the cargo area behind her. Someone, probably Roy, was awake and rummaging around. Hughes, as far as she could tell, still didn't have enough energy to even sit up, let alone rifle through boxes.

She turned around to see what was happening and was astonished by what she saw.

Roy sat on the floor with Hughes's head in his lap. He tipped a water bottle into Hughes's mouth and placed two different pills on his tongue—a painkiller and an antibiotic. Roy was almost gentle about it, as if Hughes were a wounded animal.

She would give just about anything to replace Roy with Kyle. How much better she'd feel dying with her head in Kyle's lap while he petted her and told her it would be okay. Instead she had to breathe the same rancid air as the man who had effectively killed him.

When the sun came up, she was not going quietly, and neither was Roy.

When dawn finally broke after an interminable night, Annie was ready.

This time her friends wouldn't stop her. She would happily execute Roy just as she would have happily executed Joseph Steele on the outskirts of Lander, Wyoming. Perhaps that meant there was something wrong with her, but she didn't think so. Somebody had to administer justice. Did juries feel remorse after condemning the guilty? Why should they? It was their job. And while nobody had appointed Annie an administrator of justice, nobody else was around to do it instead.

"Hey, Roy," she said and turned around in her seat.

Roy was slouching against a backpack on the floor.

"What's up?" he said and raised his eyebrows.

She pointed her Glock at his face.

Roy's left eye twitched ever so slightly. That was his entire initial reaction. Then he raised his hands with a shrug.

Parker was still asleep and leaning his head against the driver's side window, oblivious to the hysterical infected wailing and pounding on the glass a mere inch from his cheek. Hughes was on his back, either dead out or dead outright, with his mutilated arm resting on his chest.

Roy hardly seemed fazed by the gun in his face. Annie supposed he had prepared himself to die today like the others had, so what real difference did it make if Annie shot him? Better than being eaten alive.

Annie wouldn't just cold shoot him dead, though. It wouldn't feel enough like justice. Roy had to know why.

"I'm sorry again, ma'am," Roy said.

Annie forced herself not to scoff. "Tell me what you're sorry for," she said. "Tell me exactly."

"I was reckless."

"And?"

"Kyle and Lucas are dead."

"And?"

This time Roy did react. He narrowed his eyes and pushed his head forward. "You angry about Hughes?"

"This isn't about Hughes."

Bewilderment on his face now.

"Tell me the rest," she said.

Parker stirred in the driver's seat. Hughes opened his eyes and strained to sit up. He flinched when he saw what Annie was doing, then scootched himself out of the way with a resigned look on his face. He and Parker had to know this was coming if they'd bothered to consider it for even a second.

Roy seemed to search his mind for what Annie wanted to hear. After a couple of moments, his face changed. She wasn't sure what she saw there, but it looked something like fear. He must be thinking that she couldn't possibly know. She wasn't a mind reader. How could she know?

"Come on," she said. "Let's hear it."

Roy's face went ashen. Annie wasn't a mind reader, but she was a pretty good face reader. Roy realized that she knew. He just couldn't figure out how.

"Take it easy, Annie," Parker said. She ignored him and did not even look at him. He might try to talk her down, but he wouldn't stop her. That would be dangerous. Roy could reach for his own weapon if Parker disarmed her, and God only knew what he would do with it.

Roy looked around the floor of the cargo area as if he might find something useful. His sword wasn't quite within reach, and every gun but hers was in a box all the way in the back. He licked his lips and swallowed.

Annie wasn't sure what to make of this. Psychopaths supposedly did not feel any fear or anxiety, but perhaps they just felt less of it than everyone else.

"You think a lot of yourself," Roy said. "Don't you."

"Tell me why I'm pointing a gun at you," she said.

"You think you're so special. Little Princess Annie, off to save the world."

"You believed it yourself, man," Parker said. "Or you wouldn't be here. None of us would be here."

"I was right all along," Roy said, shaking his head and chuckling darkly to himself.

"About what?" Annie said.

"About the universe killing itself," Roy said. "You're going to eat that gun."

"Beats eating a rat."

Roy snapped his head back. He looked around the cargo area one more time, then trained his eyes on her again. She could practically see him scrolling through his memory to figure out how on earth she possibly could have said this. There was only one answer, but it took him a couple of moments to find it. "You hacked Lucas's cell phone."

The entire car rocked hard to the right as one of the infected hurled itself against the outside.

"Didn't need to hack it," Hughes said. "I just found it and turned it on."

Roy pursed his lips and nodded. "So you all know."

"We know," Parker said.

"Since when?" Roy said.

"Since Arkansas," Annie said. "Since the night Kyle died."

Roy didn't seem to know what to say. Not that it would make any difference. Nothing he said could change what happened next.

"Tell me something," Annie said. "Because I'm honestly curious."

Roy raised his eyebrows.

The car heaved to the right again as if it were a boat jostled by waves.

"What do you get out of it?" she said.

Roy shook his head and snorted. "You wouldn't understand.,"

"You'd be surprised," Annie said, "how much I'd understand."

Roy seemed to have forgotten the most salient fact about Annie: she had spent three full days roaming the countryside as a *hungry hungry predator* and killing anything living as though it was her job. Compared to what she had once been, Roy was a pacifist Quaker.

"I was one of those *things*," she said.

The tension in Roy's shoulders seemed to relax. He was more at ease now, as if he and Annie were just two fucked up people about to die at the end of the world who might as well share a few war stories first. "What was that *like*?"

"You wouldn't understand," Annie said.

Roy laughed. It was a genuine laugh, too, from deep in the belly. Annie could not help but smile. Roy seemed supremely unbothered now by the fact that Annie held a gun to his face and would certainly shoot him. "I'll show you mine if you show me yours."

Annie nodded. "You first."

She sensed a new disturbance outside, some strange new vibration, but she wasn't sure what it was.

"Something's happening out there," Parker said.

Nobody said anything. Everybody just listened. Something, somewhere, was pulsing.

"That's a helicopter!" Parker said. "Somebody's coming!"

Roy dropped his hands to his lap. Annie inched the gun forward. "Hands up!"

He didn't comply. "Or what?"

"Or I'll shoot you."

"You're going to shoot me anyway."

"You want to die now or later?"

Roy sighed and put his hands up. Then he cocked his head to the side as if he might be able to hear better that way. He looked agitated now, no longer taking his imminent demise in anything remotely like stride.

In her peripheral vision, Annie saw Parker peer through the slit on the window. "See anything?" She dared not take her eyes off Roy.

"Nothing," Parker said. "Wait. There it is. Definitely a helicopter! It's coming this way and carrying a shipping container."

A shipping container? "Like for a boat?" Annie said.

"Or a railroad car," Parker said. "I can't tell. But it's coming right toward us."

"Dropping supplies for us," Roy said. "Thoughtful."

The human subconscious was a peculiar thing. It was faster and smarter in some ways than the conscious mind. Touch a hot stove, and you'll move your hand away before you even feel any pain. Get a sudden bad feeling about something, pay attention: your subconscious has detected danger even if you aren't sure yet what it is. Yet our subconscious minds often betrayed us when one instinct overrode another. That's what happened to Annie.

She knew she had to keep her eyes locked on Roy, but she couldn't resist the instinctive response to possible rescue: she turned around in her seat, just for the briefest of moments, to steal a quick glance through the unpainted slit on the windshield, hoping to glimpse for herself what was happening outside the car.

She saw exactly what Parker had described: a military-style helicopter hovering low over the horde between the armored car and the wall, a rust-colored shipping container hanging below from some kind of cable. Then she sensed something behind her. Movement in the back of the car. She turned around and in a hot flash of panic saw Roy holding a hunting knife—black handle, backward hook near the blade tip—to Hughes's throat.

Annie didn't know where the knife came from. From Roy's jacket pocket, perhaps, or from the floor behind him. She had never even seen it before. But there it was, jammed against Hughes's trachea as he lay on the floor. Roy slowly scooted himself over so that he was behind Hughes and had better leverage.

Annie trained her weapon on him. She could shoot him, no problem. She might even kill him before he could stab Hughes in the neck. She wasn't sure she'd pull it off, but she had other options.

"Hurt him," she said, "and I'll shoot your balls off."

Roy didn't react the way she'd wished he would react. Rather than move the knife away from her friend, Roy lifted Hughes's head and rested it in his lap. He looked more comfortable that way, and now his groin was protected. He was settling in for a long standoff.

Outside the car, the helicopter descended. The roar was incredible, drowning out even the screams of the infected, as the car shuddered in the rotary's downdraft.

"Don't do it, man!" Parker shouted to Roy.

"Don't worry about him!" Annie said. No matter what happened out there, Annie would not turn away from Roy again as long as he continued to breathe. Parker could tell her what was happening. "What's going on out there?"

"It's dropping the shipping container!" Parker said. "Dropping it right onto the heads of the infected."

Annie heard no more screams from outside, but she faintly heard the sounds of hands slapping on metal as the helicopter receded. The infected were attacking the container now instead of the car. The hell was going on out there? Were soldiers going to spring out of it with guns blazing?

"Where did they drop it?" she said. "Why did they drop it?"

"They dropped it next to the car!" Parker shouted.

Annie did not understand. "Are we supposed to climb on top of it?"

"Beats me!" Parker said.

Annie squinted at Roy. "Let him go," she said, no longer bothering to shout over the racket. She could barely hear her own voice, but Roy knew what she said.

"And why should I do that?" Roy shouted.

This time she did shout. "Because I'll shoot your balls off if you don't!"

Roy didn't move. She didn't want to break eye contact, but she flicked her eyes toward Hughes. His head was in Roy's lap. She couldn't shoot Roy's balls off without first shooting Hughes through the face.

Roy smiled.

The look on Hughes's face almost killed her. He was stoic, resigned, as if he no longer even cared if he made it out of this.

"I'll blow your kneecaps off!" Annie shouted.

"Go ahead," Roy said and shrugged.

Roy couldn't stop her. He'd kill Hughes, though, for sure. Which might have been fine five minutes ago, but not now. She couldn't for the life of her figure why a helicopter had dropped a shipping container next to the car, but she'd understand soon enough. Hughes's life mattered now more than ever.

The infected were a little bit quieter now than before, their attention diverted by the helicopter and the shipping container randomly dropped onto the road.

"How can we end this?" Roy said.

Annie jabbed the barrel of her weapon toward his face. "You have two options." He wasn't stupid. She did not have to tell him. He could die instantly or he could die painfully. The good news for him was that he got to decide.

"I want a third," Roy said.

"There is no third," Annie said.

"There has to be," Roy said.

Annie shook her head. "There doesn't. And there isn't."

"You want to shoot me in the head or shoot me in the balls," Roy said. "I respect that. I do. But I want to go with you."

"Impossible," Annie said.

"Your whole mission's impossible," Roy said. "Yet here y'are. About to be rescued. You can drop that gun and take me with you. Just tell me what you want."

"I want Kyle back," Annie said. "And that woman on Lucas's phone with the rat in her mouth. Can you do that for me?"

Roy didn't answer.

"No?" Annie said. "Head or balls then."

"I won't hurt anyone else," Roy said.

"And I'm supposed to believe that," Annie said.

"Think of it from my side," Roy said. "Better to be good and live than to die if those are my options."

"Too bad those aren't your options," Annie said.

"They could be."

"You might even mean it, sitting there with a gun in your face. But you'll change your mind the minute you're loose again with no one to stop you."

"I never hurt anybody before this," Roy said.

"Before what?" Annie said.

"All of this." Roy gestured with his free hand toward the mayhem outside the car. "It messed me up. Messed Lucas up too. Until we met you and could finally hope again."

Annie wanted to believe him. Wanted desperately to believe him. Everything would be so much easier if she believed him. She could let him go and trust that she'd been doing the right thing all along, that she could save the world *and* human nature at the same time. But she didn't believe that.

She didn't know much about psychopathic killers, but she knew this much at least: they felt very little emotion. Some of them could hardly feel anything. They might appear perfectly normal and even charming from the outside, but inside they were nothing but ashes. A healthy person would practically die from stress after slitting an innocent woman's throat, but a psychopath could finally feel *something*.

"You and Lucas were going to kill us in Iowa," Annie said.

Roy said nothing.

"Go on," she said. "Deny it."

"I won't insult your intelligence," Roy said. "But we didn't. We helped you. And I saved Hughes."

"You're holding a knife to his throat."

"You're holding a gun in my face."

Annie couldn't blame Roy for trying to talk his way out of this. He never wanted to kill himself. He wanted to live and to kill other people.

"Head or balls," Annie said.

"You take my balls," Roy said, "and I take his head."

"For what? One last thrill before you bleed out in agony?"

"I don't want to kill him."

"Then don't."

"I want to go with you."

Annie cocked her head to the side. "How do you think that would work, exactly? We're supposed to pretend we don't know what you did? We're supposed to let it go because you didn't slit our friend's throat? You know that's impossible."

"You don't care more about strangers I *might* hurt in the future than you care about your friend here. You won't sacrifice Hughes to save the lives of people you've never met."

Annie felt a chill. The minute Roy said it, she knew it was true.

He'd checkmated her. She couldn't let Roy murder Hughes so that she could save the lives of random strangers in Georgia. Not when she'd risked her own life, and the lives of her friends, to make it this far so that she could save *everybody*.

Roy was right. But he didn't know he was right. He seemed to understand empathy even though it was alien to him, but he only understood it intellectually. He had no idea what empathy felt like. That was his blind spot.

Annie thought hard. Whatever she said next could determine if Hughes lived or died. How could she use Roy's blind spot against him? What could she say that he would believe?

She almost gave up but then found the answer.

"You're wrong," she said and shook her head. "This is not about saving strangers. This is revenge. It's about Kyle. I'll shoot your balls off *because I want to*. More than anything else in this world, I want to watch you die screaming."

She knew that she convinced him because she realized, as soon as the words came out of her mouth, that those words were true. Roy knew exactly what that felt like, so he had no trouble believing that Annie could feel that way too.

Roy swallowed hard.

"But I'll let it go if you let him go," she said.

Roy raised his eyebrows.

"I won't even shoot you. I'll let you swallow that entire bottle of Oxy if you let him go and stay out of our way."

Roy flexed his fingers around the knife handle.

Annie sensed another disturbance outside.

"Chopper's coming back," Parker said. "Carrying another shipping container."

Roy tensed, but he didn't move or say anything.

Annie felt the pulse of the rotors chopping the air.

Parker had to shout to be heard over the machine noise. "It's setting the container down on the other side of the car this time!"

Annie understood now what was happening. "They're boxing us in!" she yelled. "If they drop one in front of us and another behind us, we'll be surrounded on all sides and sealed off from the horde."

"Goddammit, woman!" Roy said. He pressed the blade more tightly against Hughes's throat as the helicopter receded again. He was thinking about stabbing Hughes in the throat just to spite her. That was clear.

She aimed her Glock right in the center of his face and looked down the sights. She could take him out right now. He'd probably die instantly, too quickly to hurt Hughes, and it would be over. But she could be wrong. Roy might not go instantly limp the moment the bullet entered his head. He could murder Hughes in his last nanosecond.

"Take the Oxy, Roy," Annie said. "It's your best bet."

Roy was sweating now. He was getting desperate. "Me taking the Oxy is *your* best bet. I'll cut his throat. I'll fucking do it. I don't mind a little pain. I won't care anymore after I'm dead."

"Bleeding out through your balls isn't a little pain," Annie said. "I'll also blowtorch your face, and I'll start with your eyes." Her hand shook the Glock.

Roy's left eye twitched. "You're bluffing."

"I killed people with my teeth," she said. "Ripped their jugulars right out of their throats."

"When you were infected," Roy said.

"Yeah, when I was infected. But it was still me. It was me doing it."

She wasn't bluffing. Not anymore. If Roy murdered Hughes, Annie would torture him to death.

"I'll cut you up into cubes," she said.

She took a deep breath and held the gun steady. One of them was going to yield to the other, and it wouldn't be her.

"You are a bitch," Roy said.

23

Two more helicopters came with two more shipping containers, just as Annie had predicted. They dropped one in front of the car and another behind it, walling off a near-perfect box around the car. The containers were too high to scale. The infected might eventually climb on top of each other and get themselves up and over, but it would take them some time. They still swarmed around and on top of the vehicle, but the pandemonium outside was quieter now, hushed by the blockade and reduced nearly by half.

Annie could almost relax. Roy had finally given up, as she knew he would, and he let Parker climb into the back and hog-tie his wrists to his ankles. Hughes dragged himself to the very back of the cargo hold and pointed Annie's Glock at Roy's knees.

Now that she could finally take her eyes off Roy, she had something equally unsettling to look at: the faces of the infected peering into the armored car through the slit on the windshield, maniacal, ravenous, delirious with rage, a force as seemingly unstoppable as a tsunami.

And yet it had been stopped, dammed by metal containers. The infected contained inside the box weren't going to last very much longer. Surely the men in the helicopter didn't expect her and her friends to climb out of the car and clear the area with hammers and crowbars.

"Hughes," Annie said. "You okay back there?"

"Peachy," Hughes said.

"So what are you gonna do," Roy said to no one in particular, "after this?"

"What do you care?" Annie said.

"Just making conversation," Roy said and shrugged.

Annie turned away from him in disgust. She couldn't answer that question anyway. She didn't expect to be a free agent once she got inside the walls. The authorities might not chain her to a hospital bed, but she didn't expect that whoever governed Atlanta would be any more interested in letting her wander around freely than the mayor of Lander, Wyoming, had been. But why would she even want to? The center of Atlanta was one of the safest places in the world. That was obvious now. Whatever else was going on in there, they had electricity and helicopters. They had some kind of surveillance and a competent security force willing and able to rescue her and her friends after all. Life might be dismal inside, but it wouldn't have to be dismal forever, especially if they could make a vaccine and open the gates to the outside.

Nothing had happened, though, since the shipping containers were dropped.

"Where are they?" she said.

"Just sit tight," Hughes said. "They'll be back."

Annie knew they'd be back. They weren't going to barricade the car from the horde and leave it at that. She was just antsy to get on with it, antsy to finally get away from Roy as she was to reach safety.

A fifth helicopter came a few minutes later. This time, with the roar of the horde greatly diminished, Annie heard the *whop whop whop* of the blades from a farther distance than she had heard it before. She couldn't be sure, but this helicopter sounded beefier than the others.

Something was about to happen. Hopefully it would not involve fire.

"Brace yourselves," Hughes said.

Annie preemptively winced just seconds before a rifle shot split the air from above and the infected spun up into an even more furious frenzy.

"Are armored cars bulletproof from the air?" Parker said.

"I hope so," Hughes said.

Roy laughed.

Annie heard a second rifle crack, and this time she saw an infected drop to the pavement as if its marionette strings had been cut, the bullet apparently piercing the top of its skull.

"How many are inside the box with us?" Hughes said, unable to see anything at all from the back.

"Hard to say," Annie said. "Maybe sixty?"

The rifleman dropped them one at a time from above. Annie couldn't be sure, but it seemed like he never missed. The chopper was fifty feet in the air at the most and shooting at targets that couldn't shoot back. Like spearing fish in an aquarium. One after another, the infected fell to the ground until Annie could see only five of them, all of them on the hood of the car, pawing and kicking at the glass.

Annie couldn't see the helicopter above, but she sensed it moving a bit toward the east.

"They leaving?" Parker said.

"Changing the angle," Annie said. To shoot the rest from the side in case the car's armor didn't hold up from the air.

A gunshot dropped the infected on the left. The bullet pierced the left side of its abdomen, exploded out the right side, ricocheted at an angle off the hood of the vehicle, and smacked into the windshield with a cracking *plink*.

"Glass holds up," Parker said.

"Didn't take a direct hit," Annie said.

"It's okay if it does," Hughes said from the back. "It's built to stop incoming rounds."

A second and third infected collapsed onto the hood, one shot through the head, the other through the thigh. The latter thrashed so hard that it knocked a fourth clean off the car and onto the pavement. A second shot into its chest cavity quieted it, and blood spattered the windshield.

Only two remained now: one on the ground where Annie could only hear it, the other on the hood bellowing at the helicopter. Both were felled from the sky.

The smell of gun smoke wafted in through the vents.

It was over.

"Nobody move," Hughes said. "We don't know what they're going to do next."

Hughes was right. For all Annie knew, the angels from Atlanta were about to torch the scene with a flamethrower.

Instead a man shouted "Clear!" into a bullhorn. "You can come out now."

∼

THE HELICOPTER HOVERED, without quite landing, just above the shipping container to the right of the car. Its appearance was distinctly military: grayish-green exterior, missile racks, a pilot wearing a bug-head helmet, doors wide open with a gunner strapped in and hanging out the side.

"How many are you?" the gunner shouted into the bullhorn.

"Three!" Annie answered. She almost slipped up and said four. Then she held up three fingers. The guy almost certainly couldn't hear her over the rotor wash. She had to turn her face to the side to keep blowing grit out of her eyes. She couldn't even hear the horde on the other side of the shipping containers, though she knew the infected must be clamoring to get over them.

The gunner unspooled a rope ladder. Annie would only have to climb twenty or so feet. Hughes wouldn't be able to make it, though. Not without help. And she couldn't have the gunner climb down to help him or he might see Roy. And he would ask questions.

Annie held up her index finger, the universal sign for *one moment*, and returned to the car.

"Hughes will need to go first," she said to Parker. "You and I have to help him."

She had two more things to do first, though. She stuck one of the Glocks in her jacket pocket and warned Roy. "Step out of this car," she said, "and I'll shoot you."

"Yes, ma'am," Roy said.

"Don't think I won't."

Then she picked up the other firearms and flung them one at a time over the shipping container to the left of the car and into the horde on the other side. The guys in the helicopter must have thought she was mad, but if she didn't do it, Roy could come out shooting. He could still hobble out even though he was hog-tied, but he'd be unarmed, and she'd shoot him as promised. Her rescuers would understand once she showed them the pictures on Lucas's cell phone.

Hughes was doing better. Nobody needed to carry him out of the car. He managed to hop out and walk to the rope ladder without any trouble. Climbing up was trickier, but he managed. He only had one hand, but he held himself in place as he climbed by using the elbow of his mutilated arm. The pain must have been out of this world.

Annie mostly kept her eyes on the car in case Roy came out, but he never came out. She climbed the ladder after Hughes. Parker went last.

From her elevated perch inside the helicopter, Annie could see the horde swirling around the shipping containers. It spread as far as she could see in every direction, even into the trees, until it abutted the wall, which she was still too near to see over.

"You folks really immune?" the gunner asked Parker. He wore military fatigues with a green forest camouflage pattern and a stitched nametag identifying him as Martinez.

"I am," Parker said. "And she is."

"You'd better be!" Martinez shouted.

The implication was clear: if Annie and Parker weren't immune, they'd have been left to die at the hands and the teeth of the horde. No one would have bothered to save them. Atlanta either didn't have the resources to feed and protect any more people or its authorities didn't care enough about regular people outside the wall to even bother attempting a rescue. For all Annie knew, life could be grimmer in there than it had been in Lander, Wyoming, with more people, less space, and less food.

"Ma'am!" Martinez shouted. She could barely hear him over the machine screech. He gestured toward one of the seats. "Strap yourself in!"

She and Parker sat down. Rather than help her, Martinez tended to Hughes, who wouldn't be able to belt himself in on his own with only one hand. The seatbelt was complicated. It had four straps instead of just one or two, and Annie had to snap them into a circular fastener designed to rest in the middle of her chest.

She sat on the left side of the helicopter next to the wide-open door. She was safe now. At last. She considered saying she'd forgotten something, climbing back down, and blowing out one or both of Roy's kneecaps. Her rescuers would never know. They wouldn't hear the gunshot over the shrieking whine of the engine.

But she supposed it was fitting that Roy die by suicide. It fit with his ludicrous philosophy anyway. Even though a painkiller overdose was one of the easiest ways out, it would still take a hell of a lot of nerve to swallow a fatal dose for a person who didn't actually want to die. Roy's ever-popular flinch response might stay his hand. He could end up dying of thirst or at least suffering the effects of extreme dehydration before finding his courage.

As it turned out, Roy's flinch response manifested itself in a different way. He emerged from the armored car with his hands in the air, his rope restraints somehow removed.

Annie felt a coldness in the core of her body followed by a flood of adrenaline.

Martinez saw Roy out of the corner of his eye and did a double take. "Hey!"

Parker and Hughes were strapped in on the right side of the helicopter and couldn't see what was happening below.

Annie reached for her Glock, but she was secured so tightly with four diagonal straps that she couldn't free it from her jacket pocket.

"There's a fourth survivor down there!" Martinez shouted.

Parker surged forward against his own restraints and shouted at Annie. "Roy's coming out?"

Martinez shouted at her as well. "I thought you said there were three of you!"

Annie nodded. "We can't take him!"

Martinez snapped his head back. "Is he bit?"

"He's a murderer!" Annie said.

Martinez went rigid.

"He's a serial killer!" Parker yelled.

Martinez turned his head from side to side. "He's what?"

"He's a serial killer!" Annie shouted. "We have to leave him."

Martinez flexed his arm muscles and flared his nostrils.

Annie unfastened her restraints and stood. "We have to stop him!" she shouted and removed the Glock from her jacket.

Only now did she realize that Martinez was furious not at Roy but at her. He grabbed her gun with his right hand, straightened his elbow, pushed her forward into her seat, grabbed the butt of her gun with his left, used both hands to snap it into an upside down position, then yanked it away from her. He did all this in a fluid motion that took less than half a second, as if he'd already done it ten thousand times. If her finger had been inside the trigger guard, it would have broken between the first and second knuckles.

Roy stood barely twenty feet below her with his hands in the air like a supplicant.

"Leave him!" she screamed.

"We're not leaving anybody!" Martinez shouted. She could barely hear him at all and relied on lip-reading as much as her ears to understand what he said.

"You don't understand!" Annie shouted.

She turned to her friends. Parker had unhooked his restraints, but he remained seated. Hughes shook his head from side to side, telling her it was over.

Martinez forced Annie back into her seat and belted her in. She struggled, but he overpowered her as easily as if she were a child.

"He's a serial killer!" she shouted.

Martinez leaned forward and spoke directly into her ear to make damn sure that she heard him. "Ma'am," he said. "I don't know him, and I don't know you. We're not leaving anybody."

Annie curled her lip and recoiled as Martinez dropped the rope ladder and helped Roy ascend into safety. Martinez helped Roy secure himself in his seat and held both him and Annie at gunpoint as the pilot took the helicopter into the air toward the wall over the screaming heads of the horde.

24

The perimeter around Atlanta's intact urban core stretched in an oblong shape for roughly two miles, from the Centers for Disease Control and Emory University on the northeastern edge to the skyscrapering city center to the southwest. The wall itself was clearly defined, not only because the structure was plainly visible but because it was surrounded on all sides by a sea of infected larger than the safe zone itself. From the air, Annie could see the burning skyscraper in Buckhead now, too, besieged by a secondary horde peeled off from the main one.

Martinez kept his service pistol trained on Annie and Roy, though Annie knew he wasn't going to shoot anybody after taking so much trouble to rescue them.

She thought they'd head directly to the CDC, which would have been a five-minute walk from their starting point without a wall in the way, but the pilot turned right and nosed toward the city center instead. Hundreds of people milled about down below, all of them on foot.

The pilot landed just shy of downtown on a helipad marked by a giant white cross at a complex called the Atlanta Medical Center that appeared to have been built in the 1980s.

A dozen civilians approached as the pilot shut off the engine. They were clean, well dressed, and flanked on each side by pairs of uniformed soldiers carrying rifles. Two men, apparently doctors, wore lab coats. At the head of this phalanx was a bespectacled black woman who appeared to be in her forties wearing a dark blue blazer. She carried herself like she was the boss of something, either the medical complex or possibly even the city.

Martinez holstered his pistol and gestured with his head for everyone to get out.

Annie unhooked herself and disembarked ahead of Roy without making eye contact with him. She needed to make damn sure she spoke to whoever was in charge here before Roy could get in a word.

The bespectacled black woman looked concerned, even anxious. She stood closer to the helicopter than anyone else. Annie knew she would be the first to say something.

Annie approached with Parker and Hughes next to her and Roy trailing behind.

"Welcome to Atlanta," the woman said. "I'm Governor Chrissie Jordan. I apologize for taking so long to come out and get you."

The governor! Atlanta was Georgia's capital, but it somehow hadn't occurred to Annie until now that anyone there would outrank the mayor.

"Thank you, ma'am," Hughes said. "We're all grateful."

The doctors noticed Hughes's bleeding and bandaged amputated arm. "Let's get you checked out," one of them said.

"I'm okay," Hughes said.

The doctors gave Hughes some space.

Annie felt dizzy, her head still filled with the roar of the helicopter even though its engine was silent. She could swear she could still hear the horde even though she could not.

"I'm told you say you're immune," the governor said.

Annie nodded. "I'm Annie Starling," she said. "This"—she gestured toward Parker—"is Jonathan Parker. We're both immune. Our friend Hughes here is not. And this man"—she pointed at Roy—"is a serial killer."

The governor snapped her head back. "He's . . ." She exchanged worried glances with her aides, with her soldiers, and with the helicopter pilot.

"I can prove it," Annie said. She produced Lucas's cell phone from her pocket. "He took a video of himself slitting a woman's throat on this phone."

One of the soldiers looked to the governor. She nodded. The soldier approached, and Annie handed the phone to him.

"There's no passcode," Annie said. "And the battery is almost half charged. Just open the camera app and you'll see it."

The governor was clearly aghast and seemed unable to figure out what to make of these ragged, stinking, injured, and blood-spattered people standing before her. She looked like a woman prepared for a business meeting who had opened the conference door and found a pack of wolves inside instead of her colleagues. "You've been traveling with this man?" she said.

"We didn't know when we first met him," Parker said.

The soldier who'd retrieved Lucas's phone waved it toward the governor. She shook her head, then addressed Hughes. "This is true? You've seen it?"

"I'm afraid so, ma'am," Hughes said.

"You traveled with him anyway?" the governor said. "You came all the way here him anyway?"

"We needed his help," Hughes said.

The governor shook her head, like she couldn't quite comprehend what she was hearing. Annie understood. She'd felt the same way herself every time Hughes had said the same thing to her. But she understood now that Hughes was right.

Perhaps in an alternate universe they'd made it to Atlanta without Roy. But in yet another alternate universe, they were dead on a roadside in Iowa. In another they were dead on a roadside in Missouri. In this universe, they'd made it to Atlanta at least in part because Roy had helped them. If the doctors could make a vaccine from her blood, Roy would have saved far more people than he had killed.

"He didn't know that we knew," Annie said, "until we got to the wall."

The governor narrowed her eyes at Annie, then scrutinized Roy. Annie could imagine the gears turning in the woman's head.

"Is it really that bad out there?" the governor finally said.

"Worse," Hughes said. "Worse than you can imagine if you haven't been out there."

The governor turned now to Parker. "You two are really immune?"

Parker nodded. "It's the reason we came here."

Roy looked like he'd rather be just about anywhere else in the world. He had to have known this would happen the moment he presented himself to be rescued. He'd be imprisoned and probably executed. But at least he was alive and safe at the moment.

Annie accepted that she'd be effectively imprisoned as well. Roughly two square miles of central Atlanta had managed to hold back the tide with a broom. It was still America in there, but it was a prison. At best it was a tiny, skyscrapering island. And now that its leaders knew the truth, they'd no doubt put Annie in a prison-within-a-prison just as the rulers of Lander, Wyoming, had. They'd be crazy not to. They had to realize, just as her friends did, that she was the most precious person alive. That's why they'd sent helicopters. And it's why they would not let her go.

Annie wouldn't resist. She wouldn't even complain. They were only going to do what she would do if she were in their place.

The governor produced a cell phone from her pocket, opened it up with a passcode, tapped the screen a couple of times, and placed it next to her ear. She held up a finger and took a few steps away from the others for a moment of privacy.

Annie couldn't believe what she was seeing. "What's she doing?" she said to no one in particular.

"Calling someone?" one of the soldiers said and shrugged.

"Her *phone* works?" Parker said.

"You mean we could have—" Annie said.

"Cell towers are down," the soldier said, shaking his head. "She's making a call over the hospital's Wi-Fi."

Annie felt herself go slack-jawed, but she realized, at the same time, that she should not have been surprised. The United States military had built the proto-Internet to ensure that basic communications could survive a nuclear war.

One of the doctors addressed Annie. "Ma'am," he said. "Would you be willing to let us take a look at you?" The latest in a string of surprises. Would she be *willing*? They were giving her a choice? Was there an alternate universe where a twisted version of herself would say no?

"Of course," she said. "If you think it might help."

The two doctors looked at each other and nodded. "We do."

"You've been working on a vaccine?" she said.

"We have," the second doctor said.

"Any progress?"

"A bit," the first doctor said. "But not enough."

"You think I might help?"

The first doctor nodded. "It's the reason we flew out and got you."

The governor returned, her phone still in her hand but down at her side now. "We can put the three of you up in a two-bedroom apartment downtown," she said to Annie.

In an apartment. Not chained to a bed in the CDC. In an apartment!

But of course. This wasn't Wyoming. Annie wasn't going anywhere. This wasn't a pit stop, and she'd come here on purpose. Where else could she even go?

"And you," the governor said to Roy, "will be going somewhere else."

A police car with its lights flashing pulled into the heliport's parking lot. Two officers emerged from the vehicle and approached, surprisingly at ease under the circumstances.

Roy took a step back. Parker seized his arms from behind and held him in place.

Annie looked at Roy from head to toe as if for the first time. He shouldn't have been there. He was supposed to be dead. Poisoned with Oxy, shot through the head and the balls, or blowtorched and cut into cubes. She wished the infected could have ripped him apart right in front of her. It was the least he deserved. She should have murdered him in the car when she had the chance.

"That him?" one of the officers, eyes on Roy, said to the governor.

"That's him," the governor said.

"Sir," the officer said. "You have the right to remain silent. Anything you say can and will be used against you in a court of law. You have the right to an attorney. If you cannot afford an attorney, one will be provided for you."

They cuffed him and walked him to the squad car. One officer got behind the wheel. The other trundled Roy into the back, using a hand to ensure Roy did not hit his head.

FIFTEEN MONTHS LATER

Morning sun warmed Annie's face and hands as she plucked the season's first peaches and placed them into the crate. The air in the orchard was warm and humid and smelled of earth and ripening fruit. The peaches looked delicious, but she wouldn't break her fast for at least another hour. She sipped instead from a water bottle and could still faintly taste the baking soda and mint she'd used to brush her teeth.

Blade worked beside her. She didn't know his real name. He just went by Blade, and he didn't talk much. He wasn't surly, exactly. Just silent most of the time and taciturn at his liveliest. Annie had the feeling he suspected that no one else in the commune wanted to hear anything he might have to say and that he was doing everybody a favor by keeping whatever it was to himself.

"You on security tonight?" Blade said.

"I am," Annie said.

She enjoyed security detail. She had an eight-hour shift three nights a week, from 11:00 p.m. to 7:00 a.m. And she had the morning shift for farm work, from 7:00 a.m. to 3:00 p.m., seven days a week, which meant she had to sleep from 3:30 in the afternoon to 10:00 or 11:00 at night. It only took her a week to get used to that schedule. All she had to do was place an eye mask over her face to prevent afternoon sunlight from keeping her awake during the day, and night didn't feel much like night since she wore military-grade night-vision goggles throughout her shift. They were much better than the cheap consumer-grade monocles she and her friends had used on their way into Atlanta.

Annie didn't know what Blade thought of his security shifts, but he was good at the job. He also worked graveyard, and his team had so far captured three gangs of bandits while Annie's team had only caught two. She caught the first stealing fruit from the orchard and the second attempting a break-in at the barn. Use of force was authorized in self-defense, and she was more than ready if it ever came to that. There was no jail on the compound, so captured criminals were chained to a maple tree in the expansive front yard of the main house until the Fulton County Sheriff's department could come out and get them. Prisoners typically waited there for two days and were provided fresh well water, two square meals, and a bucket.

The Fulton County Sheriff's Department had jurisdiction out there, but the commune was farther out in Rockdale County. Fulton, with its county seat in Atlanta, was the only one left in the state of Georgia with a functioning law enforcement department. No one thought the Rockdale County seat in Conyers would be repopulated for at least another generation.

Dealing with the infected who wandered on to the property was less complicated than dealing with bandits. Every security squad shot to kill. The numbers of infected were small enough now that noise wasn't much of an issue. Most of the infected seemed to have starved to death, and the army had mopped up the horde outside the city walls a long time ago. Annie supposed there'd be some nonzero number of infected out in the wasteland for at least a couple of years, but they were increasingly rare and decreasingly dangerous. Because the vaccine worked perfectly. Annie had spent three days as one of those *things* after she'd been bit, but a vaccinated person wouldn't experience any symptoms at all.

Her peach crate was almost half full. She was getting faster at this, though worrying about smashing the peaches on the bottom of the crate still slowed her down a bit. A third of the crop would be consumed on the compound, another third delivered to Atlanta, and a final third canned on site. Half the canned peaches would be traded for food from other agricultural communes in Rockdale, and the other half would be sent to the city. Georgians were still functioning on a barter economy. No one knew when they'd start using currency again or even if they'd use US dollars again.

Kyle would enjoy this life, Annie thought. He wouldn't have wanted to remain in Atlanta any more than she did, though his reasons would be drastically different from hers. He'd wanted a simple life in the countryside since the day she met him. She could accept that he was gone now, but her life was much lonelier than it would have been had he survived. The men on the commune made it abundantly clear to her, each in their own way, that she could have any of the bachelors she wanted, but she couldn't connect with them. Most hailed from urban Atlanta, and none had spent even a day in the wasteland. She felt a hundred years older than all of them.

Annie heard a vehicle pull into the gravel parking pad between the barn and the main house. It sounded different from the others. It wasn't one of the Sherriff's vans coming to pick up prisoners. There were no prisoners on site that day. Nor was it one the delivery trucks. Could be civilians or could be somebody from the government. Annie hoped it wasn't the government.

"Be right back," she said to Blade and headed through the rows of peach trees toward the compound. Her heart swelled with joy when she saw Parker emerge from the driver's side door and Hughes from the passenger side. She'd been waiting for them to visit for almost three months now.

They'd have to pitch a tent. There were no spare houses or beds, and everyone on the commune agreed that guests mustn't colonize any of the living rooms.

Annie ran across the lawn separating the orchard from the house and embraced first Parker and then Hughes on the parking pad.

They looked terrific, and they'd both lost weight. Everyone had.

Nobody was starving, but all meals were simple and whole. Processed food no longer existed and might not again for the rest of their lives. Hughes had a plastic prosthetic arm and hand attached to his elbow, and he seemed to be comfortable with it now.

They'd both lose even more weight if they'd stay and work the farm with her—everyone on the orchard was thin and lithe—but Parker and Hughes had insisted they'd remain in the city. Annie wished she had the option.

"You finally came," she said, wiping away a tear. "I've missed you."

"Missed you too," Parker said.

"Atlanta isn't the same without you," Hughes said.

"Annie?" Blade's voice. He'd followed her out of the orchard. "Everything okay?"

She nodded and sniffed. "These are my friends I told you about. Parker and Hughes. Guys, this is Blade. He works the orchard with me."

"Good to meet you, man," Hughes said.

Blade just nodded.

"Let me help get them settled," Annie said to Blade, "and I'll rejoin you in a bit."

Blade nodded and returned to the orchard.

"How long are you staying?" Annie said as they walked toward Parker and Hughes's SUV. "I assume you're staying."

"Just for the night," Parker said.

Only one night? She wished they'd stay permanently, but she knew not to say it.

"You brought a tent and sleeping bags?" she said.

"Two tents," Hughes said. "No need to sleep cooped up next to this guy anymore."

Parker popped the hatch and removed a pair of brand-new two-person tents still in boxes.

"You can join all of us for dinner at the big table next to the barn," Annie said, "as long as you help clean up."

"You get much news out here, Annie?" Parker said, turning to face her. He set the tent boxes down on the gravel.

"Not much," she said. "That's how we like it."

"Something you should know," Parker said.

"Only if it's good," Annie said.

"It's good," Hughes said.

"The government," Parker said, "officially declared that humans are no longer considered extinct in the wild."

She supposed that was good news. A bit bureaucratic, though, and obvious now that the vaccine had been delivered to the largest cities on six continents. Still, it was good news.

"All because of you," Hughes said.

"Because of us," Annie said. "Me. You two. Kyle. Even Roy played a part. Not that he deserves any thanks."

"He was convicted," Parker said. "Jury spent ten minutes deliberating."

Annie knew he'd be convicted. The evidence was so overwhelming that the prosecutors told her she didn't even need to testify, that she could go ahead and leave the city if that's what she wanted.

"They going to execute him?" Annie said.

Hughes shook his head. "Governor abolished the death penalty."

Annie looked off into space.

∼

They enjoyed a dinner around the giant table next to the barn with all twenty-four members of the commune and Parker and Hughes as guests. Everyone had a small helping of barbecued chicken, a baked potato, various freshly picked salad greens, and sliced peaches for dessert.

Afterward, Annie took Parker and Hughes for a walk in the orchard. The air was still warm and humid, but it felt softer and milder now with the subtropical sun low in the sky.

"We'd like you to come back," Hughes said.

Annie hadn't expected this. She thought she'd made herself perfectly clear when pioneer groups announced their plans to resettle the countryside. Somebody had to grow food, and she didn't belong in Atlanta.

"I'm happy here," she said. And she was. As happy as she could be, anyway. She liked the quiet, the starry nights, the feeling of solidarity with her fellow misfits. Some of them wanted to live out an adventurous rural fantasy, but Annie suspected others were there to soothe themselves in a tranquil, bucolic environment. "Are you both happy in Atlanta? Really?"

Annie had hated the crowds, the lack of softness, and the smells. Most of all, she had felt like she was visiting from another world.

"It ain't Seattle before the fall," Hughes said. "But things are getting better and easier, and they're going to keep getting better and easier. You wouldn't even recognize the place anymore. The gates are open all day now, and people are moving back into Buckhead and Midtown."

"It's a lot less crowded," Parker said, "and a lot less terrifying. The electricity works. The water works. Hell, even the Internet works, though there's not much to look at."

"That's what you care about?" Annie said.

"We care about you, Annie," Hughes said. "That's why we're here."

"You know I don't belong there," she said.

"You tell yourself that," Parker said. "But don't believe everything you think. Where would I be if I believed every dumb and crazy thing that popped into my head during the past two years?"

"I'm not dumb and crazy," Annie said.

"No, but I was," Parker said. "I thought the virus turned me into a psychopath."

"It did," Annie said, "but only for a couple of days. You're still you."

"I understand that now," Parker said.

"And I'm still me," Annie said, "but I'm not the same me." She closed her eyes and exhaled slowly. She'd already explained this to them over and over again.

She'd seen things that could not be unseen. Understood things that could not be unlearned. She'd perceived the world as it really was, as if she'd snapped out of a delusional state. She'd tried, but she couldn't get back into that delusional state again. People were animals, and they had teeth just like wolves did. Civilization had a dampening effect, sure, but it was an artifice. It was as temporary and as provisional as a Japanese house with paper walls, and far easier to break than to build. It could be—and had been—destroyed in an instant with human nature remaining beast-like behind.

Human beings had existed in the world for, what, a hundred thousand years? And they'd been civilized for virtually none of those years. For all Annie knew, human beings would continue existing for millions more before being wiped out by an asteroid or a supernova. But would the United States of America continue to exist for millions of years? How would people be living during and after the next Ice Age, after the great pyramids at Giza had been ground into sand and forgotten, and after plate tectonics had submerged New York, San Francisco, and Tokyo? Against the maw of deep time, the relatively ordered and gentle world Annie had grown up in had endured for about as long as a lightning flash.

She wasn't going to explain that all over again. Parker and Hughes had heard it enough times already. "It changed me, okay?"

"It changed all of us, Annie. You think anyone is the same person they used to be?"

"It changed all of us differently," she said. "Most of these people"—she swept her arm across the orchard and toward the barn—"lived their whole lives in Atlanta until now. They don't want to live there anymore either."

"These are your people now?" Parker said.

Annie sighed. "They haven't seen what I've seen."

"We have," Parker said. "We're your people."

"You can talk to us," Hughes said. "You can live with us."

"Okay," Annie said. "Let's talk then. I want you to stay. There's another house nearby we could rehab. It doesn't even need very much work. I wasn't going to say that, but I didn't think you were going to ask me to move back to Atlanta, so I'm saying it."

Parker and Hughes looked at each other.

"You two aren't my people," Annie said. "You're my *family*. And I love you forever."

Hughes hugged her then, a bit awkwardly since he had only one fully functioning arm, but Annie didn't mind.

"I love you too," Hughes said. "But I don't know if this place is for me."

"Come here," Parker said and embraced her too. They held each other for a long time. Parker let go first.

"What about you?" she said to Parker. "Will you stay?"

He looked around. "What would I do here?"

"Pick peaches. Patrol the perimeter. Build things. You used to build cabinets, right?"

Parker nodded.

"We could use you," she said.

"I don't know, Annie," Parker said.

"Will you think about it?" she said.

He nodded. "I'll think about it."

She believed he would think about it, but she wasn't sure she believed he would stay.

They headed out of the orchard and back toward the main house in silence, Parker and Hughes on each side of her. She wanted to lean against them both as they walked, but something stopped her. She didn't want them to know how lonely she felt. There was no denying it to herself, though. She knew that the deepest part of her would always be alone, that no one—not even Parker or Hughes—would ever truly understand what it was like to be Annie Starling. She had saved the world, yes, and she was glad to have done it, but part of her would forever be in the wasteland, lost and alone and looking for something to eat.

ABOUT THE AUTHOR

Michael J. Totten is a novelist, a book and magazine editor, and a former journalist who has reported from the Middle East, Eastern Europe, Latin America, and the former Soviet Union.

His first book, *The Road to Fatima Gate*, won the Washington Institute Book Prize in 2011.

He lives with his wife in Oregon's Willamette Valley.